CONFLICT LEMONS

Though some of the places in these stories exist geographically, it is not the author's intention to document any specific person, location, or incident. All names are fictitious, with the exception of those included by permission of the entities. These stories are works of fiction and any resemblance to any actual person, location, or event is completely coincidental

CONFLICT LEMONS

By

Alfonso A. Guilin

Edited by Larry and Norma Holt

Cover by Larry N. Holt

Graphic design and typesetting by SketchPad Publications

Published by CreateSpace™

Dedication

Hopefully this story will provoke an honest
and productive discussion of our country's
current immigration policy.

Al Guilin
Summer 2015

Acknowlegements

...My thanks to Trina Nagele for her willingness to review and make suggestions to improve this story.

***

...Also my special appreciation to the Limoneira Company founded in 1893 and is a world wide supplier of lemons and avocados. In recent years the company is growing and developing a market for a new variegated pink lemon featured on the cover.

***

...And also, I must acknowledge that food would not reach our tables without the dedication and efforts of the people, who grow, harvest and deliver the food to our tables. The bounty that is produced is indeed plentiful.

…And finally, for those who dream:

"Vision without action is just a dream.
Action without vision just passes the time.
Vision with action can change the world."

Nelson Mandela

Summer 2015

Al Gricelin

Chapter 1

Larry Franco and Ginny Gallo were walking to the parking lot. They had just taken their final algebra test at the local community college, Ventura College. They had both applied and were accepted at Cal Poly at the Pomona campus. They were holding hands and laughing as they headed for Larry's car. They had agreed to get a hamburger; then spend a couple of hours at the beach. Life was good for the young couple. They were good students, got good grades and they both had summer jobs starting the following Monday. Larry and Ginny had become good friends since the fourth grade. Their families lived on the same block and they too were good friends. The children of the two families walked in and out of each others' home and no one paid attention to who was coming or going.

The young couple took no notice of the man and woman dressed in black suits that were parked in front of Larry's car in the lower parking lot. When they saw the young students, they got out of the car. The man pulled out a badge, showed it to Larry and said, "Lorenzo Franco, I'm agent Tom Flynn and this is agent Florence Ruiz. We're with the U.S. Border Patrol, and we're arresting you for being in this country illegally."

The students were shocked and bewildered and for several seconds, they looked at the agents, then at each other. Instinctively they grabbed each other by the hand. Finally, Ginny said, "What do you mean you're arresting him for being here illegally, are you kidding?"

In a stern voice the male agent said, "Young lady, this is none of your business. We have a warrant for Mr. Franco's arrest. I suggest you do not interfere. I'm asking you to step aside…and I repeat, do not interfere!"

As Ginny stepped aside, the female agent quickly placed handcuffs on Larry and said, "Mr. Franco, please get into the back seat of our car."

Finally, Larry blurted out, "I don't understand; why are you doing this? Where are you taking me? What about my car? What about Ginny? How will she get home?" There was a fearful panic in his voice. As he was about to get into the rear seat of the government car he said, "Ginny, take my keys, they're in my pocket. Take my car home and tell dad what happened."

The female officer said, "Miss, please don't do that. Let me get the keys." She spun Larry around, and leaning him against the car she searched his pockets and removed a set of keys. "Here you are Miss, listen to your friend, take the car and don't interfere." She handed the keys to Ginny.

Ginny took the keys in her trembling hands and looked at them with tears in her eyes. Finally she looked at the woman officer and asked, "Where are you taking him? His father is going to ask me. What shall I tell him?"

The officer answered, "We're taking him to the Ventura County jail on Victoria Avenue where he'll be processed. He then likely will be transferred to our detention facility in Adelanto out in the desert, until his case is processed and is decided."

Ginny stood and looked at Larry through the rear door window. She saw the fear and confusion in his face, and it tore her heart. As she watched the car disappear, the tears flowed. It took several minutes just standing there until she opened the car door and hurriedly drove home. She parked in front of her house, ran in, and shouted, "Mom, Mom, they arrested Larry...They took him to jail."

Ann Gallo was eating a slice of toast when she heard her daughter run into the house. She was stunned by the panic in Ginny's voice and was having trouble understanding what she heard. She put down the toast. "Calm down Ginny; now tell me, what happened to Larry?"

"Mom, we had just finished taking our math final and we were going to get something to eat and then go to the beach when these cops arrested him. They said he was in the country illegally and they were taking him to the county jail." Although her voice was clear, it still trembled as she spoke.

Not completely understanding, Ann put down the toast and said, "Come on, let's go to Licha's to tell her; maybe she knows what the hell is going on."

Alicia Franco was in her front yard watering her cherished roses. She saw the two women coming over, and she smiled at her two friends. "Good morning girls. How'd you do on the test? Her smile faded when she saw the tears on Ginny's face and the frown on Ann's. "What happened? What's the matter?" she cried.

"Oh Alice, they arrested Larry. They said he was in the country illegally...they took him to jail and then they said they were going to send him somewhere else. I don't understand." Ginny began to cry again as her mother put an arm around her.

"There must be some mistake. Come inside, we need to call Tom. Maybe he'll know something, or at least what we can do." She called her husband and then served coffee to her two friends. There was little to talk about as they waited.

They all looked out the window as Tom Franco's car drove into the driveway. The very tall man removed his pharmacy coat as he walked up the sidewalk; he opened the door and said, "Now, will someone tell me what the hell is going on!"

All three adults looked at Ginny. She said, "I'm not too sure what happened. We had just finished our math final and were about to take Larry's car to go get a hamburger when these two cops grabbed Larry and told him they were arresting him for being in this country illegally. They said they were taking him to the county jail and then somewhere out to the desert for some kind of determination." She started to cry, "Honestly, Mr. Franco, that's what happened. They were going to leave me out there by myself until Larry talked them into giving me the keys to his car to get home. All this happened just a couple of hours ago."

Tom asked, "What kind of cops did you say they were?"

"They were dressed in regular clothes. It was a man and woman and they said they were from the U.S. Border Patrol. They were not very nice. They scared me. I didn't know what to do, so I came directly home." The young girl wiped tears from her cheeks.

Tom went to the refrigerator, grabbed a bottle of cold water and said, "Licha, call Rhonda, tell her what happened as best you can. Tell her I'm on my way to the county jail; tell her to meet me there. There's got to be a damn mistake…there must be some screw up somewhere. Tell her to drop whatever she's doing, I'll meet her there."

Ginny said, "Mr. Franco, can I go with you?"

The tall man looked at Ginny who was trembling and said, "I think you need to stay here and calm yourself. One thing you can do is, think of exactly what happened. Write it down as best you can. If this is going to be a legal hassle, we're going to need all the information we can get."

Tom Franco walked rapidly up to a side building at the county government center where the country jail was located. The fifteen minute drive to the facility had calmed him down. He entered through the automatic doors to the main building and found his attorney Rhonda Davis waiting for him. She quickly took him by the arm and led him to a corner table where they sat down. He sat for only a few seconds and then suddenly stood up and said. "What do you mean he's not here? Where the hell have they taken my son?" His voice was angry and he started to wave his arms, "I want to see whoever is in charge here. They can't just arrest my son and not at least let his parents know."

Rhonda pulled his arm down and forced him back into his chair. "Lower your voice. Calm down. I just checked with Captain Julie Simpson. She's on the way to meet us. Perhaps she can tell us what's going on. In the meantime tell me what you know."

Tom ran his hands through his hair, "That's just it. I don't know what the hell happened except what his girlfriend Ginny told us. That they had just taken a math final at the college and were in the parking lot when two cops arrested him and said they were bringing him here. That's it. It's crazy. They can't do that; can they?"

Before the attorney could answer, a young deputy sheriff approached them and said, "Miss Davis, Captain Simpson will see you in her office. If you and your client will just sign our visitor register, and then please follow me." They signed the register and followed the young man through several locked doors and into a small office.

A tiny woman dressed in uniform stood and welcomed them. "Good afternoon. I'm Captain Simpson, how can I help you?"

Tom Franco was agitated and started to speak, but his attorney grabbed him by the arm and asked him to sit. She said, "Thank you Captain

Simpson for seeing us. We came to see about Mr. Franco's son who was arrested by the Border Patrol, but we first would like to see him. There must be some error. In the meantime, we would like to make arrangements to have him released to his parents until we can get to the bottom of this."

Captain Simpson continued to listen while she picked up the phone and said, "Bring me the booking file on Lorenzo Franco." Then she looked at the couple in front of her and said, "Excuse me, please continue."

"Captain, it's our understanding that the Border Patrol arrested Mr. Franco's son for being in this country illegally and that he was brought here. We'd like to see him and of course we'd like to clear up this misunderstanding. As you might guess, this whole incident has caused great turmoil in the family. And no telling what trauma it's caused Larry."

A young deputy sheriff came in and without saying a word, handed a file to the captain. She quickly glanced at the two page document. She looked up and said, "First, I must tell you. We have no jurisdiction over what the Border Patrol or other federal agencies do in enforcing their responsibilities. Actually, the only relationship we have with them is that we provide occasional holding facilities for their detainees. Usually, we house them for a day or two until they make arrangements for a transfer to a federal facility." The captain paused for a long time and continued, "Apparently, that's what's happened to Mr. Franco. He was transferred with several other detainees to the Border Patrol holding facilities in Adelanto."

Tom Franco unable to contain himself said in a loud voice, "What the hell do you mean he's gone? Good Lord, he was just picked up a few hours go. How can he be out in the desert already? What kind of a place are you people running here?"

Rhonda grabbed Tom's arm and interrupted him, "Captain Simpson, as you can imagine we're astonished at what you're telling us. You must admit it's hard to understand that my client is no longer here."

The woman jailer shrugged her shoulders and said, "Apparently what happened is that the Border Patrol had several detainees here already who were being transferred to facilities in the desert. I guess at that moment Mr. Franco was processed and they just filled the last seat in their transfer van with him. As I said, we have no responsibilities or authority over what they do. We just provide a complementary service to our fellow agencies."

Tom Franco's face turned red and his eyes widened with anger. "I'm sorry Miss, I just don't understand. You have a young man just out of school that's never done a wrong thing in his life, and you just ship him off like a piece of meat. Whatever happened to at least a telephone call? Jesus Christ! What happened to common sense?"

"Mr. Franco, I can understand your disappointment, but you must understand that we have no real jurisdiction in these matters. Basically we just provide a bed for others."

"You're damn right I don't understand. You just sit there and tell me you have no responsibilities, but you had him in your custody, and while he was under your roof he belonged to you. Or else what the hell good are you?" Tom Franco was noted in his small town for his friendly, even tempered personality. He owned an independent drug store and was a well respected pharmacist, but in the confines of the county jail office and in the presence of the woman in charge and his son gone, he was seething.

Chapter 2

T OM STOPPED AT A DRIVE-THRU Starbuck's coffee shop and bought two cups. A few minutes later he picked up his attorney Rhonda at her home in Fillmore. "Good morning," she said as she strapped on her seat belt. "Thanks for the coffee; great idea."

They drove east on Highway 126, then I-5 and then onto the 14 freeway as they headed into the desert. The hills leading into the Mojave Desert looked dry and barren. The south side of the freeway was even more desolate due to a recent fire. They drove in silence, each in their own thoughts— drinking coffee. Finally, Tom said, "You know, I've never heard of an immigration prison out here in the middle of nowhere."

Rhonda said, "To be honest, I haven't either. I did do a little research, and this is actually a private operation run by an independent contractor for the Immigration Service. I was unaware that our government operated this way, but I hear it's rather common. Basically it's a prison operated for profit."

Rhonda pondered the barren landscape, took a sip of her coffee and asked, "Tom, tell me about Larry."

Tom moved to the right lane, activated the cruise control at the speed limit and waited to collect his thoughts. "Bobby was my younger brother. He was one of those fellows that everyone admired. He had talent, great looks, smart and was a great athlete. He was good at every sport he tried. Everything came easy to him. He was loved and liked by everyone...especially the girls. He had a way with girls that we all envied. He got a full ride scholarship to the University of Arizona to play basketball. He was good. On top of that, he kept up his grades. We were all proud of him. In the meantime, I had just been married for a year and became the pharmacist in town. Things were fine...life was fine. Then one night I got a phone call from a police officer near Tucson, he said there had been an accident and that my brother and his wife had died. I was stunned. Then the officer told me that the baby had survived. That he had been strapped in a safety seat. He was bruised a bit, but very much alive. I went from being stunned to being shocked. I was speechless. Then the officer told me that they had found my name and information in Bobby's wallet and wanted to know when we could collect the baby.

Tom drove several miles quietly and then continued, "Ten hours later, Licha and I arrived at the police station of Marana, a little town between Phoenix and Tucson. Bobby was indeed dead and we made arrangements to have his body shipped home. Then this nice police officer took us to his home where his wife was taking care of the baby. It was then that we first met Bobby's son...our son now. They told us the last thing his mother said before she died was, *Por Dios cuida a m'hijito, Lorenzo.*" We stayed one day in Phoenix to buy a few things and to get acquainted with the baby. By the time we crossed the Colorado River, we crossed as a family. Larry became our son. He was our son. He is our son. He will always be our son...a precious gift from my baby brother." Tom wiped some tears from his eyes as he passed a slow truck.

Rhonda asked, "Do you know anything about the mother? What about her family? Where do they come from? In fact, do you know where Larry was born?

"To be honest we were so devastated with the accident, Bobby's death and then finding the baby that we left all that behind us. When we arrived home, we were a family and that was it." Tom paused for a while and continued, "It never occurred to us to delve into the matter. As for the mother or her family we found nothing, but we really never seriously looked. And no one ever contacted us about the accident or the baby."

"So you really have no idea where Larry was born?" She looked out the window for a second, "Have you two legally adopted Larry?"

"We talked about it, but then we would have to tell him he wasn't our son. That was too hard even to contemplate. So we put it off, and then as time went by, it became even harder to think about it. Then we thought when he was an adult, we would tell him. And then when Licha couldn't have children, we thought this was God's answer to our prayers. So we just thanked God and did nothing else."

"I understand, and in a real sense you two are the parents, and he is your son…but tell me Tom, do any other people know this. I've known you guys for years and it never occurred to me that Larry was not your biological son."

"We never told anyone. Yet my mother must have known. When we returned from Arizona, we had the funeral for Bobby, and that was a hectic time. It was such a shock to us and to all our friends. People were coming and going. Even the press got involved because he was the local sports hero. I hate to say it, but it became almost a circus. In all that turmoil, Larry got lost. No one paid attention to him or his presence. People saw Larry and Licha and they saw a son and a mother. And the reality was that in that first day in Arizona, and the next couple of days, the bond was fixed forever. Not only for Licha, but also for me; it was then futile to even think of a legal adoption since it was in fact a real birth. A birth made possible by a tragic death. So we did nothing since, in our own minds, there was nothing to do." Then Tom was quiet for a few minutes and continued, "I guess we always knew we would have to tell him the truth, but time slipped by and we never did…"

"You said your mom must have known. If she confided in anyone, who might that be?"

"I don't know. She never asked or mentioned it to us. She in fact accepted Larry as her grandson…which of course he was. The only person…might be my cousin Berta. During the last year before Mom died, I hired my cousin Berta to take care of Mom. She basically lived with Mom for the last twelve months until she died. My cousin was a blessing to mother and to us because she took care of her during a very difficult time." He continued, "I have no idea what they talked about. It was enough for me that she was there and made Mom's last few days bearable."

They traveled the last hour in silence and in their own thoughts. Then Rhonda said, "We should be nearing the detention center." They turned off the main road and were immediately faced with a large chain link fence and a guard station. A uniform sentry opened a small window and asked, "Good morning, what can we do for you?"

Tom answered, "Good morning. My name is Tomas Franco and we've come to see my son."

The guard looked at a clipboard and said, "I'm sorry Mr. Franco, but visiting time is only on the weekends and you have to make an appointment." He handed Tom a three by five card, "Here's the information and procedure to make the appointment."

Tom became livid, "What do you mean we can't see Lorenzo! We've come all the way from Santa Paula and by God we're going to see him!"

Rhonda then leaned over and spoke to the guard, "Sir, my name is Rhonda Davis. I'm an attorney, and I represent Mr. Lorenzo Franco. If you check with your supervisor, I believe he'll want to talk to us."

The guard closed the sliding window to his post and picked up a phone. He spoke briefly and then looked up twice toward the car and seemed to be describing them. He then opened the window, "You may continue. Please go to the visitor center and park in the area designated for parking and go to the door marked *visitors*, push the speaker button, announce your name and follow their instructions."

Before they got out of the car, Rhonda said, "Tom, I know this will be difficult for you, but you have to control your temper. You have to let me do the talking. Just remember, we're dealing with a jail and these fellows are just following orders. It does no good to get pissed at them...it just makes matters worse."

"I'm sorry Rhonda, but I'm as nervous as a cat. I'll try."

"Now listen Tom, you'll have to do better than try, just follow my lead." They rang the bell and then heard three loud clicks before the door opened. They entered into another room that was also locked and a faceless voice came over a speaker which said, "Please sign the book on the counter with your name, address, phone number and the reason for your visit."

They waited for twenty minutes and Tom began to pace back and forth in the small room. He picked up an old magazine; looked at it and put it down. He looked around the room and noticed two cameras on opposite corners. He finally looked at Rhonda, took a deep breath and sat next to her. He said, "I had no idea a place like this existed out here in the middle of nowhere."

Rhonda half smiled and said, "It is rather isolated, isn't it."

Finally a stout, young lady came out and said, "Miss Davis, my name is Linda Rapp, what we can do for you?"

She motioned to Tom not to move, stood and said, "Miss Rapp, I represent Mr. Lorenzo Franco and this is his father Mr. Tomas Franco and we'd like to visit my client."

"Miss Davis, this is very irregular, visitors are not permitted except for designated times and dates. You can make an appointment online. I believe you were given that information at the gate."

"I understand your procedures, but I called the Immigration Office and they indicated that as legal counsel I was permitted a visit. Furthermore, I was told if we came today at approximately this hour the visit would be facilitated. Especially since when Mr. Franco was apprehended, he was NOT permitted or given the opportunity to make a required call and to confer with counsel. I'm sure if you check with your supervisor they will concur. Furthermore, Mr. Franco is a legal citizen born in the United States and he has all the rights that pertain to a lawful citizen." She delivered her last sentence in a careful, deliberate, unemotional voice.

Rapp looked carefully at Rhonda and said, "Please excuse me." She turned and walked out of the little room. About 10 minutes later she returned and said, "Please forgive me Miss Davis, but since we just received Mr. Franco last night, not all the processing had been completed. Arrangements are being made right now for you to meet with Mr. Franco. It shouldn't be but a few minutes." She looked right at Davis, avoiding Tom and continued, "Regulations as related to me by my supervisor say that the visit is only for counsel. Family visitors must adhere to protocol as prescribed on the card given to you at the gate."

Tomas Franco jumped to his feet, his face red with rage. Just then a male guard opened the door. Rhonda immediately stepped in from of him and said, "Miss Rapp, we appreciate your cooperation, but at the same time, please be aware that I intend to write a complaint to the INS. I assume that our presence and action is being recorded as we speak." Then she turned and faced the corner camera and said, "For the record I am Rhonda Davis, attorney for Mr. Lorenzo Franco, a detainee in this facility. I hereby state that Mr. Franco was detained in Ventura County without probable cause and transferred to this facility without proper notification or ability to confer with counsel as provided by law. Also be it noted that a formal complaint will be filed with the appropriate jurisdiction seeking appropriate redress including monetary compensation for this action."

Then Rhonda turned to both guards and said, "Do you understand what I just said?" The man and woman nodded.

Then she turned to Tom and whispered quietly, "Tom, now listen carefully. Let me go see Larry. I will take note and pay close attention to how he is and what he has to say. So don't give these people anything that will provoke a reaction. Especially don't give them an excuse to use force. Do you understand me?" She grabbed him with both arms and repeated, "Do you understand me?"

Tom was unable to speak. He face was flushed and his eyes were fluttering. He said nothing, but he did nod his head. He sat down in a corner, picked up an old magazine and then he looked up and stared at the camera as it stared back at him. He mentally tried to recreate their trip to Marana. He remembered that they were so shocked with the death of his brother and the discovery of the baby that they gave no thoughts to Larry's mother. No one mentioned her, no one asked any questions; they just received the little boy and sat in a motel all night in a daze. By the following day they were home, they had a son, and it was as if the past had been wiped clean. It now appeared obvious that part of the answer to their present situation was located in Arizona. He began to write some notes and questions on some three by five cards he always carried in his pocket. He also knew that he and Licha would be spending some time in the near future in Arizona.

The return trip back to Santa Paula was quiet. Tom listened to Rhonda as she related her visit with his son. "Larry's fine considering what's he's been through. Curiously, he seemed more concerned about Licha and you. He doesn't want to worry you guys. In order to keep him busy and to keep a record, I gave him a tablet and a pen and I asked him to write down everything he did, what was said to him and who said it. He also wanted me to touch base with Ginny. I promised I would call her."

Not knowing what to say he blurted, "Why the fuck do they call it a detention facility when it's a goddamn prison! I can't believe our government sticks a prison out here in the middle of nowhere. I mean it's got to be a bitch for family members and even attorneys to visit with their clients. What a way for our government to operate."

Rhonda looked at the barren landscape and said, "One problem is that this is not a federal prison or detention facilities or whatever you want to call the damn thing. It's actually a for profit operation run by the Signal Corporation who operates several of these private prisons on a contract basis. They make their money by getting so much per day for housing and feeding and by operating close to the vest on expenses. They make a bundle of money. It's one of those things that the public is unaware of...except for people jailed and for their family members who probably don't even know where Adelanto is located."

"You mean some bloody corporation is actually operating this damn place out here to make money?" He exclaimed.

"Yep, and you're right, it's a bloody corporation. And they're slick. They come out to an isolated place like Adelanto and suddenly they're the biggest employer and taxpayer in the area and within a short time they have everyone eating out of their hand. And no one gives a shit about the poor bastards sitting in their cells."

"I guess I don't understand how can they do this?" Tom asked.

Ronda said, "It's easy; most of these people are not criminals in that sense of the word. Mostly they're Hispanics who came here to work. On top of that, most employers seek and need them to do the work we won't do. The rest of us just close our eyes because we want cheap food on our tables. We also don't get much of a family out cry because most of their families are in another country and probably not even aware that their son is in prison just because he came to pick our lemons."

"Shit, to be honest, it never occurred to me. I mean. I never heard of this place. I had no idea it even existed." He paused; then asked, "Now what? What do we do now?"

"I have an appointment with Judge Mike Foster this afternoon and I'm almost sure we can have Larry released in your custody in a day or two. Just be handy if I need to get a hold of you."

"What about you Tom, what are you going to do? It seems you have a delicate chore of what to do and what to tell Larry.

"Well first Licha and I have to get it together. Then I think we need to have a little talk with Father Jim. After that I think we need to take a little trip to Arizona to find out about Larry's mother. She may be the key to our situation. I hope that God forgives us that we took her son and forgot all about her."

Chapter 3

THE DRIVE ACROSS THE DESERT had an eerie feeling. When Larry came home, Tom and Licha sat down with him and simply told him what had led them to become a family. Larry received the news with no apparent emotion. Yet his posture and calmness indicated a deep reaction. It was then that Tom suggested that they all go to Arizona to see if they could pick up a trace of Larry's maternal life.

Larry's only reaction was to ask, "Dad, would it be okay if Ginny went with us. Somehow I'd feel better if she were along."

Tom and Licha looked at each other and Tom said, "It would be fine, but we would want her parents to agree. If they think it's okay, it's okay with us."

There was a cathartic affect to the long trip through the barren, desolate landscape. Somehow the grim tale of Larry's biological parent's death and his discovery by Tom and Licha was somewhat positive. There was curiosity in Larry's questions. He was aware of his father Bobby. All his life he'd heard stories and saw photos of this remarkable person who apparently everyone admired and loved. Ginny mostly sat in the back with him holding his hand. He also remembered having read somewhere that two or three serious emotional incidents could cause terrible affects on a person. And in the last few days he had been arrested, imprisoned for three days and then told that his parents were not his parents and furthermore that his real parents were dead. It was indeed unreal. Yet there was that curiosity and wonderment. He also was aware of the trauma Tom and Licha were experiencing. He speculated about the eventual outcome. It was almost too much. Somehow holding hands with Ginny eased the tension. Finally he asked, "Dad, what's the plan once we get to Marana?"

"I made a call to the police station and the present chief told me that Chief Don Baxter is now retired, but he and his wife still live in town. I called him and he said he remembered the incident. He said he would go to the office to see what records were still around. He seemed confident that somewhere there was a file that could be useful. He also said that he was retired and was willing to help if he could. We agreed to meet tomorrow at the station at nine in the morning and he said there was a motel right across the street from the station so we can walk right over."

The Marana Motel was a small family-owned operation and next door they also ran a coffee shop. Tom rented two rooms—one for the girls and one for the boys. The two men stayed up late into the night. Tom related almost 20 years of unspoken conversation that had been locked up in his heart. There was kind of a cleansing feeling to be able to finally share the truth with his son.

Larry on the other hand seemed fascinated about his new life. His previous knowledge of Robert or Bobby Franco was sketchy at best, and now he wanted to know every detail about the young man he never knew. Tom continued to tell him stories until he realized that Larry had gone to sleep. Next morning Larry woke up very early, dressed quietly, and walked around the small farming town. He bought a cup of coffee at the café and walked from one end of the town to the other. He sat at a park and watched people go by on their way to work and finished his coffee. When he returned to the room, Tom was already dressed. "Come on Dad, let's go have some breakfast."

"Okay, just let me knock on the door and let your Mom know where we'll be."

"Don't worry Dad, I already checked with them. Knowing them, it'll be awhile before they're ready."

Tom smiled to himself as he heard Larry refer to him as Dad. Had nothing changed? Yet he was very much aware that everything had changed. And nothing would ever be the same. The only unknown of the change was what they were to discover, if anything, over the next few days. That unknown made him cautious and yet hopeful.

Licha and Ginny joined them at the café and the mother said, "Coffee is all I need. I'm too nervous to eat."

Ginny nodded to the waitress and ordered a glass of orange juice. She did take a piece of toast from Larry's plate, spread some orange marmalade on it and ate it.

Licha appeared nervous and said, "Nineteen years ago we were in this town, we were young and all in a state of shock. It was really a double shock. Not only was Bobby dead, but we had a baby on our hands and we weren't too sure what to do. Our first instinct was to get home; a place where we were safe and could make rational decisions. In that entire flurry however, we forgot the mother. She was dead, but she still deserved our attention. I continuously ask God for forgiveness, for that failure. We didn't even know her name…"

Larry reached over and put his arms around his mother. She looked at him with tears in her eyes. He whispered, "It'll be all right, Mom."

There was reluctance in the group as Tom paid for the breakfast. They went to their respective rooms for one last opportunity to compose themselves. While in the room Larry said, "Dad, these last few days have seemed like I've lived a lifetime and a nightmare. I don't know what the bigger shock was: being arrested and tossed in jail or being told that you and Mom were not my real parents. To be honest, it still seems like a dream…a dream without an end."

"Larry, I'll never forgive myself for not telling you sooner, but since the first day we met you in this little town, it never occurred to me that you were not my son. I may have lost a brother, but I gained a son. And that will never change."

Larry hugged his father and kissed him on the cheek, "Dad, I couldn't have asked for a better mom and dad. I guess we should go across the street to see about my birth mother."

Larry went to the adjoining room, knocked on the door and said, "Ladies, let's go."

The four walked across the quiet street. There was a tension and strained smiles on their faces as they thought of the many questions that needed to be answered, but had no way of knowing how or who would ask them. And what about the answers? Would there be clarity to the answers? They opened the door to the police station reluctantly and yet with much expectation. Tom approached the counter and said to the uniformed receptionist, "My name is Tomas Franco and this is my family. We have an appointment with Mr. Don Baxter."

"Ah Mr. Franco, Don is expecting you. He's in our conference room. Please follow me. Can I get you some coffee?" She led them to a small interrogation room with a table and a few chairs.

"Thank you, no; we just had some coffee across the street." Tom smiled at the woman.

"Don, Mr. Franco and his family are here; let me know if you need anything." The woman closed the door and left.

Don Baxter stood up to greet the family. He was tall and lanky and dressed in shorts and sandals. He had a T-shirt that said *Old Men Rule* across the front. He had a ready smile and said, "Mr. Franco, it's good to see you. It's been a long time. Almost 20 years." He looked at Licha and continued, "Mrs. Franco, please excuse my informality, but I haven't worn a uniform for six years and as my wife says, this is my uniform now." He then turned to Larry and looked at him very carefully as a cop might be sizing up a suspect. Finally he said, "You must be Lorenzo. I have to tell you what a thrill it is for me to see you again. Even though you just stayed at our house for one night, you left a great impression on me and my wife. In fact, she would like to see you again. I hope you don't mind."

Although Larry was tense and anxious, his outward appearance was normal and friendly, "Mr. Baxter, it's a pleasure to meet you." He paused, "And in a way, to thank you for your help to me and to my mom and dad." The next pause was long and he took several long breaths as he tried to control his emotions. "Most of all, we appreciate your help in trying to determine who my mother was." Larry's voice began to crack and he turned to Tom who put is arms around him.

Baxter smiled at them and said, "Let's sit and see we what we can find out. I took the liberty to make copies of all that we knew of the accident and your parents. You can have them for your records and to continue in your search for additional answers." He handed them a file folder and opened the one he had and said, "You'll find the information about your mother on the first two pages. Her name was Yolanda McLean. She was 19 years old and she was from Jerome, a little mining town between Prescott and Flagstaff. Her grandparents were Jose and Cipriana Mendez also from Jerome. A few days after the accident, they came and claimed her body and they told me they were taking her home for a Mass and burial.

Larry asked, "Where's Jerome?"

"Jerome was kind of a ghost town of old people. Maybe 500 or so live there now. However, several years ago some Hippies found it and began to revive it. So now it's kind of a tourist town with old miner families and this new crowd. Most of the miners were originally from around here and Mexico and the Hippies are from all over. I wouldn't be surprised if that's where the name McLean comes from. Jerome is just a couple of hours away, it's small so it wouldn't be too much of a problem to explore and find out about the McLean's and the Mendez family. I took a quick look in the phone book and there are several Mendez families still living there. There's also the San Yldefonso Catholic Church which would be a good place to visit. Those places are a good source of valuable information. I checked with a Lupe Vasquez who volunteers there at the church and has access to all the records. I mentioned you might be visiting. She said she was looking forward to helping out. She sounded like a neat old lady."

"If Bobby was attending the University in Tucson, I wonder how he met Yolanda?" asked Licha.

Tom smiled and said, "Knowing Bobby, and his ways with girls, they just flocked to him. No telling where they met."

Licha asked, "Is there a place to stay in Jerome? If we were to leave here soon, we could be there in a couple of hours."

The retired police officer chuckled and said, "They have an old hotel right in the middle of town. It's just down the street from the church. In fact, the hotel is within walking distance of the church and the cemetery is nearby." He paused for a second, smiled, and then said, "I should warn you that some folks say the hotel is haunted."

Ginny exclaimed, "What do you mean it's haunted?"

"Well Josie and I have stayed in the hotel a couple of times and we've never been spooked. It's an old wooden, two story building and there's lots of creaking and groaning mostly because of the way it's built and its age. In fact, the whole darn town is built the same way. So I wouldn't worry."

"We appreciate all you've done Mr. Baxter. Do you think it's worthwhile for us to visit the place?" Tom asked.

"I do, but first I would call Lupe Vasquez at the church to make sure she's going to be there. Frankly, whatever information you were going to find there you already have in that file. And then, if you're planning to return to California, going back on the scenic route is different and nice. Let's call her up. I have her number." Baxter called and had a quick conversation with the lady and hung up. Then he said, "Lupe said she'd meet you at the church at 10 in the morning. In the meantime, she said she would dig up any information she could find."

Just as they were checking out of the motel, Josie Baxter walked over from the police station. She went straight to Larry, hugged him and said, "Young man you are a blessing to your family. It was my pleasure to meet you long ago and to see you now, a grown man."

Not knowing what to say, Larry gave her a hug and then went to her husband and gave him a hug and said, "Thank you Mr. Baxter for everything."

The landscape out of Phoenix changed as the highway climbed up the foothills. The hills were barren, but at least the flatness was erased by the gradual climb. The small town gave several glimpses of its structures as the road wound up and around the hills. Finally they turned off the highway and entered the small town. It was still early in the afternoon, but it was much cooler and tranquil compared with the bustle of the city. The Jerome Hotel and Spa was easy to find. The spa sign was odd in contrast to the old buildings in the area. Tom went in to inquire about rooms. The lobby was empty and he rang a counter bell. A young girl emerged from a back office and said, "Good morning sir, welcome to the Jerome Hotel and Spa. What can I do for you?"

"We need two rooms with twin beds if you have them." Tom noticed that the young lady wore a name tag that identified her as *Cipri Mendez*.

She handed Tom a registration card which he quickly completed and returned. The girl then looked at him for a long time and said, "Welcome Mr. Franco to Jerome. If you need any help or information just let me know." She gave him two keys and then said, "We have a happy hour and snacks from 6 to 7, it's a nice time to relax and meet some of our other guests. Your rooms are just down the hall."

As they settled into their rooms, it was still early in the afternoon. Larry said, "Dad, Ginny and I are going to walk around town; just to get a feel for this place. Maybe get an ice cream. There doesn't seem to be much to look at, so we won't be long. And for sure, we'll be back for the happy hour. We don't want to miss that."

"Good idea. In the meantime, I think I'll just take a nap. Then maybe I can talk your mother into wandering about and looking around."

Ginny and Larry walked toward what was the center of the little town and were drawn to the church. The San Yldefonso Catholic church was large and looked quite elaborate compared with the rest of the town. The young couple walked into the church and walked around the building. The sanctuary was well kept and looked like a church that might have belonged in a metropolitan area. Yet it was here in the middle of nowhere. It was a conundrum that was not lost to them. They continued their walk and finally found a small mom and pop grocery store where they bought an ice cream. They sat in the front of the store and ate. "Did you notice how the lady looked us over, it almost seemed like she was expecting us to rob the place."

Ginny answered, "I did notice. I thought you might have said something to her, but you're right, she was checking us out." Ginny ate her ice cream, looked at her friend and asked, "Larry, how are you doing? You must be going through hell; what with the prison thing and then the shock of finding out about your parents."

"You know, the shock of my parents was more of a surprise. They're like someone I lost; someone I never knew, but at the same time I still have my real parents. Mom and dad are my real parents. I know they're concerned about all this, but how can I be angry with them after all they've done for me…but you know what really pisses me off is being picked up by the Border Patrol! And then being whisked away and tossed into that prison. I have to tell you, I was scared shitless. I heard the two who picked me up at the college say that someone had complained about me; that I was a 'wetback' and had no business going to school and that I should be deported. For those two days in prison I thought about it. Then I came to the conclusion that it had to be someone who knows me, maybe even one of my friends."

Ginny asked, "but Larry, how is that possible?"

"Think about it Ginny. Hell, even I didn't know about my real parents, who they were and where I was born for that matter. So it had to be someone who knows my parents and knows about me. How else can you explain it?"

"I suppose you're right; it makes no sense otherwise," she said.

"You know what else pissed me off is that a good number of those in the prison were about my age and they too looked like they were scared shitless. And they were treated like dirt…just a number…a profit center. The few that I spoke to were young and had come across the border looking for a job and were unlucky to be caught. They also told me that they'd do it again as soon as they could. It was the job they're looking for. They just want to wash dishes. Think about it, they take their chances of winding up in that hell hole just to wash our damn dishes. That can't be right!"

"What can we do? Until this happened to you, I had no idea that this kind of thing happened or that prisons like the one in Adelanto even existed." She finished her ice cream and tossed the wrapper in the trash can.

"Well, once this part of the saga is over, I'm going to become more informed about this immigration thing. There must be something we can do. At least we can inform ourselves and our friends." A couple of hours later he said, "I suppose we should get back, I can't wait to see what happens at happy hour at the Jerome Hotel and Spa."

They were surprised that there were several people already gathered in the lobby and an adjacent patio. Cipri Mendez was setting out snacks near a lemonade fountain. She moved around gracefully as she chatted with the guests. She smiled at the young couple, "You must be Larry Franco. I hope you enjoyed your ice cream. You should try our lemonade; it's fresh. We make it ourselves." She continued to move about the guests.

The parents showed up. They had changed clothes and looked relaxed. "Hi Dad, did you get your nap?"

"I did. I didn't realize how tired I was. I needed the rest. How was your walk; see anything interesting?"

"We just walked around. We went into the church and that was interesting. It's a real big church. You could put the whole town in one service. I guess it was built when the place was booming. It's an impressive place." He paused and said, "Did you see the name tag on the girl? We walked all the way across town, several blocks and ate an ice cream. The lady at the store gave us a good looking over. Then when we got back to the hotel, the girl asked us if we enjoyed the ice cream? I wonder how she knew we ate an ice cream."

Tom ate some chips and said, "I noticed the name tag when we registered. Perhaps after most of the guests leave, we can just ask her if she
knows Jose and Cipriana Mendez or Lupe Vasquez."

The guests drifted off and the receptionist began to clean up. The four were
the only ones left and Tom finally got her attention and asked, "I noticed your
name tag. By any chance do you know Jose or Cipriana Mendez?"

Cipri stopped wiping a table and said, "I never knew Jose, but I know
Cipriana, she's my *abuelita*. I'm named after her. Why do you ask?"

Tom paused for several seconds as if pondering the next question,
"Tomorrow we have a meeting with Lupe Vasquez at the church, do you
know her?"

The young girl smiled, "Everyone knows Lupe; she's married to one of my
cousins. In fact, almost everyone in this town is related to each other."

Larry hastened and cautiously asked, "Have you ever heard of Yolanda
McLean?" Larry grabbed Ginny's hand and looked carefully at the girl
who quit wiping the table.

"Of course I've heard of her. I didn't know her; she died before I was
born, but my *abuelita* talks about her frequently and has on old photo-
graph of Yolanda...with her little baby..." She looked carefully at Larry
and continued, "Just last week she mentioned Yolanda because it was her
birthday and she lit a candle for her."

Things were moving too fast as Larry was trying to make sense of the mystery of this little town. His mind was racing as he looked at Cipri and then at his
parents. Licha smiled at him and mouthed the words, "Ask her."

Larry was known for being quick on his feet and never short of words,
but now he stumbled as he said, "Cipri, we have an appointment with
Lupe Vasquez tomorrow in the morning, what are the chances we could
visit with your *abuelita* after the meeting."

Slowly she spoke and said, "Do you mind if I call my dad and ask him
to come over to meet you. He's her grandson and the one responsible
for her. He's home and we just live a few blocks away. Dad's the game
warden for this area. He's lived here all his life and I would feel better if
he was aware of your visit. Please let me call him."

Tom answered, "Of course. We would very much like to meet him. I
think it's important that we have a frank discussion with him before we
go any further." Larry nodded in agreement.

Within ten minutes, a man dressed in a game warden uniform entered the hotel and first looked at Tom and said, "Good evening, my name is Johnny Mendez." Then he saw Larry and appeared stunned, "Good Lord; you're Lorenzo aren't you? You're the spitting image of my cousin Yolanda! I don't know what to say."

Tom was as surprised as everyone in the room and said, "Perhaps it would be a good idea if we start from the beginning. Some 18 years ago we received a call from Don Baxter, a police officer, telling us that my brother Bobby Franco and his wife had been killed in an auto accident. He also told me that baby had been tossed around, but was okay and that his wife was taking care the little boy. Needless to say, we were shocked over both of those statements. An hour later my wife Licha and I were on the road. That was one of the longest trips I've ever taken in my life. We prayed there must have been some mistake, but indeed Bobby was dead, as was Yolanda. We knew nothing of Yolanda. Mr. Baxter said since we were next of kin, we needed to decide what to do with the baby. Without thinking it completely through, that baby became our son, two days later we were back home and we were a family."

For the first time Licha spoke up and added; "And we still are a family."

Tom continued, "A few days ago Larry's birthplace became an issue and so we decided to retrace the events of many years ago which led us to a meeting with Mr. Baxter earlier today. He suggested that perhaps we could find additional information in Jerome. So here we are."

Johnny Mendez stood up and got himself a glass of lemonade; he ran his hand through his hair. "Wow!" He looked at everyone and then at Larry for a long time. "Wow, I don't know what to say. Let me add what little I know, but before I do, I assume that before this story concludes my grandmother will be involved. Let me say that my grandmother is 92 years old. She's in remarkably good health, but one thing that has haunted her is the tragic death of Yolanda and the mystery of the baby. So I suggest we lay all our cards on the table now, and tomorrow with Lupe at the church, so that if and when we approach grandmother, we have all our ducks in a row and have a good idea of all the facts. Raising her hopes and then crushing them would be too much I'm afraid. Have we got a deal?"

All those in the room nodded in agreement. "I met Robert Franco several times at the University. In fact, I was the one that introduced them to each other. Those two were a combustible mixture. Once they met they were inseparable and that led to her pregnancy. It was a shock to the family, but they were thrilled and they were going to get married. Yet they were both going to school, they had no money; so they waited. In the meantime, Yolie had to quit school and came home to complete her term. Bobby was here every weekend. Then one night the baby came." Johnny came over and rubbed his hands over Larry's head. The baby came quick. Our cousin Lidia, an emergency nurse was in town and she delivered the baby in Yolie's bedroom right here in Jerome. It took Bobby a couple of hours to get here from school and you should have heard the celebration that night. He was thrilled; as was Yolie. We were all thrilled. We partied all night. Later that week Bobby and Yolie took the baby to Nogales to visit her mother who was living there at the time. It was on the way back that they had the accident. Apparently, a deer ran across the road, Bobby tried to avoid it and ran off the road and they were both killed. We didn't know about the accident until two days later. By then we learned Bobby's brother had come and claimed the body and the baby was given to them. For several days there was real grief and mourning for Yolie and for the baby. I know that grandmother prayed for the baby and then sometimes later came to the conclusion that it was meant to be and it was decided to let God do His will."

Licha asked, "So Larry was born here, in Jerome?"

"Yes of course; just a few blocks from here—in the house where we live. Where grandmother now lives in the room where Joaquin was born."

"Wait a minute, who's Joaquin?" asked Licha.

"Well if we follow the story to its conclusion, Lorenzo and Joaquin are one and the same. My grandfather's name was Joaquin Lorenzo Mendez. Yolie named her son Joaquin Lorenzo after him."

Licha asked, "Where was his birth recorded?"

"Hmm, I'm not too sure, but I know where his baptism was recorded because I was his *padrino*, so I'm sure that record is at the church. The baptism was just a couple of days after he was born, and a day later they went to Nogales to visit her mom."

Licha honed in on the legality, "It's important that we locate the official recording of the birth, because some people have questioned his citizenship. We also need to get some affidavits from some of the people who were here during the birth to swear to its occurrence. Perhaps there's an attorney that can do that for us to make it official."

"There's Phil Rogers, he's retired, but he still has his fingers in the law. He would do it if we asked him," said Johnny."

"*Abuelita* has those three old Polaroid photos on her dresser; I think someone wrote the dates and place on the back. I've seen them several times," said Cipri.

"What do you think Johnny? Do you think there's enough evidence so that we can see your grandmother?" Tom was now pacing as he spoke. He was trying to understand all that was happening.

"Well with all that and then the fact that Lorenzo looks just like his mother should be enough, but I think we should all go to the meeting with Lupe tomorrow at the church to see what she can add. Then if there's no doubt, we'll see our *abuelita*. Personally, I'm convinced, but I want to make damn sure. Two disappointments might be too much for her."

Tom clapped his hands and said, "Good, we'll see you all tomorrow at 10 in the morning to see what light Lupe Vasquez can shed on this mystery."

The four met for breakfast, but only Ginny ate. Tom, Licha and Larry just had coffee. They were too nervous to eat. Cipri came by and refilled their cups and said, "I wish I could go with you to the church. I just have to know what happens." She turned to walk away, but then stopped and continued, "I spent all last night trying to figure out that if you're Joaquin what would that make us; third cousins? What do you all think?"

Licha smiled at the young girl and said, "I have an ancestry computer program and when I get home I'll work up the family tree; especially with this new branch."

Larry asked Cipri, "Tell me about your…our great grandmother. What kind of person is she?"

"Well she's over 90 years old. They moved here when the copper mine was booming. Great grandfather was a foreman in the stamping mill. He worked here all his adult life. My namesake's life was and continues to be the church. She did everything, but mostly provided the flowers. Every

Sunday and holiday she had fresh flowers on the altar. She has a large garden behind the house mostly just for the church. The church is her life, especially since grandpa and Yolie died. She's active, walks to church every day and she's funny. I just love her."

Jerome in mid morning was delightful. It was quiet with only some doves cooing in the trees as they all walked to the Church. They walked into the church briefly and stood quietly each in their own thoughts. Then they walked next door to an old wood plank house; a sign on the front door read, **San Yldefonso Church Office.** Lupe Vasquez was waiting for them and led them to the back of the house to a small kitchen. There was a round chrome table with several folding chairs. Johnny was already there drinking coffee and talking to the very attractive lady in her sixties. She was laughing when she turned to welcome the Francos. "Good morning, what a blessing it is to see you. It seems like I've known you forever. Please sit down. I made a fresh pot of coffee. Can I get anyone a cup?"

"Thank you, but we just had one." Answered Tom, as he shook the lady's hand. "Also, we very much appreciate your help in this matter. I hope we haven't caused you any inconvenience."

With a ready smile she said, "Good heavens, no! It's my pleasure. And what a thrill it is for me to be able to help my good friend Cipriana who is a pillar of this church. Now on to this business; Johnny has told me about your quest and I think I can shed some light on it. She opened a file and read, "Joaquin Lorenzo McLean Franco was born here in Jerome, Arizona on July 7, 1996. Two days later he was baptized by Father Joel Olivas, who happened to be visiting our parish." She looked at Larry and said, "You were named after your great grandfather Lorenzo Joaquin."

Licha had her hands clasped on the table, "Thank you Lupe for the information, but what proof do you have that he was born here?"

Lupe raised her voice almost in jubilations and exclaimed, "The best proof...I was there! I helped with the birth. Our cousin Lidia, Cipriana and I helped with the birth. Later in the day Doc Martin came by, examined Yolie and the baby and said, they looked fine and left." I believe the doctor registered the birth at the court house. He wasn't much of a doctor, but he was meticulous in his paper work. So I would check with them. Of course, I have the church records and I'll give you copies of them."

Larry took the papers and began to read them and Lupe continued, "Oh Joaquin, you look so much like Yolie, she was a pretty *güerita* and she was so much in love with Roberto.

We were all devastated at the accident."

Johnny stood and said, "I have to leave, but I'll be going by the courthouse. I know the folks there. If there's a record, I'll get a copy. In the meantime, I'll make arrangements for you to come to our house for lunch to meet a most important lady. I'll make arrangements with the Judge to come over and we can get statements from all of us as to the birth. It might cost us a couple of bucks for the judge and his secretary."

Tom added quickly, "That would be great. And the cost is no problem."

Then Johnny took Larry's hand and said, "You have a rich heritage starting with all your names, Joaquin, Lorenzo and Larry and you have your family. I know *abuelita* will be thrilled to see you again, but you need to realize that she's 90 years old, so you need to be sensitive. She loves Cipri so I want her to be with you when you meet. If I know her, she'll want to take you to her small bedroom to be alone with you. Don't worry, it's her way and I can assure you it will be a memorable meeting…for you and especially for her."

Larry looked at his new found relative and said, "Don't worry. This whole thing started out like a nightmare, but it now looks like an adventure. It's kind of mysterious, but an adventure nevertheless. I'm looking forward to meeting my great grandmother."

They returned to the hotel to gather and to relax prior to the meeting at the Mendez home. For some reason, Licha changed her blouse. She examined herself in the mirror for some time. Tom asked, "Why did you change shirts?"

"I don't know, I thought we needed to make a good impression on Mrs. Mendez. I mean, I want her to know we've done a good job raising Larry. I guess I want her approval."

"Don't worry; we've done a good job. She'll approve." Then Tom looked into the mirror and said, "Perhaps we should have made an effort to touch base with her family. In retrospect, that would have been the right thing to do."

At noon they all gathered in the lobby and Cipri said, "Don't worry; my Nana is a neat person. She'll love you, but she'll want to do things her way." They all walked six blocks to the Mendez home. The house looked like the rest of the homes except it was twice as large as those surrounding it. They noticed that a buffet table was set and the house smelled of delicious food cooking.

Linda Mendez was busy pouring iced tea into a large class dispenser, she turned and with a great smile said, "Welcome, welcome to our home. I'm Linda and we've been waiting for you for a lifetime it seems. Please sit and I'll go get my grandma-in-law. She's been combing her hair for an hour and I know she's changed her shirt at least twice!"

Cipriana Mendez was a small lady with long, grey hair fastened in the back with a large barrette. Attached to the barrette were several small feathers. She walked with a handmade wood cane, and with a radiant face, went to everyone and shook hands. Lastly she stood in front of Larry for several moments. Finally she said, "*Ay Dios mio, gracias por m'hijito y por mi Yolanda.* She looked at Tom and continued, "Thank God for visiting an old lady. Please sit down. She took Larry by the hand and said, "Excuse us for a minute." She walked down the hall slowly leading Larry. Cipri followed them.

Larry walked slowly slightly behind the woman and entered her bedroom. The room was semi dark and lit only by an open window and two votive candles in front of a small shrine of Our Lady of Guadalupe. There was an orderly clutter to the room. She sat in a stuffed chair and pointed with her cane to a chair for Larry to sit. Cipri sat on the bed. Cipriana opened the drawer of a small chest next to the chair and removed a candle wrapped in tissue paper. She removed the tissue carefully, then smoothed it out and folded it carefully into a small square. She said, "About 18 years ago we went to the shrine of Mary Magdalena in Sonora, Mexico and prayed to the Virgin and promised I would light it when I saw you again. The Virgin Mary has never failed me. I want you to light it Joaquin, light it for me and for you and for your mommy and for your daddy."

Larry took the candle, and with a long match, lit the candle and placed it with the two others. The three candle flames flickered and danced and gave the room a sparkle and brightened it. The old woman said a prayer quietly. Larry could make out a word or two. She then took out a small jewelry box and removed a silver chain with a rustic looking cross. "The copper that my Jose processed also yielded some silver. He accumulated the metal and had this chain made by one of the men, but he handmade this cross by himself. He gave it to your mother. She wore it all the time. She wore it when she gave birth to you and when she died. I've been saving it for you. Come here and kneel in front of me. I want to give this to you...a gift from your mommy." She reached over and looped the silver cross over his head. "Wear it for my Yolita y Roberto *que en paz descansen* and wear it for me."

They returned to the dining room and had lunch as if it was just another day in a small town with friends. After lunch there was more talk about family. Finally Larry said, "This has been an extraordinary time for me, but since we're on the subject of family, can someone tell me where the McLean name comes into the picture."

They all turned to Cipriana who was drinking tea. She carefully put down the cup on its saucer. She took a napkin and blotted her lips and looked around at everyone. "Ilan McLean, now that's a name from the past. In the early fifties the copper mine began to experience some production difficulties. So the copper owners brought a miner from Ireland to see what could be done to extend the life of the mine. Every one called him *El Güero.* He was tall, skinny and had red hair and the bluest eyes you've ever seen. My daughter, Rebecca, worked in the office at the time. She was just twenty and had never been out of town or seen a pair of blue eyes. Before anyone knew it she became pregnant and Yolanda was born. About the same time it was determined that there was not much could be done about the mine and soon thereafter, he was transferred to Africa. Later we heard that he was killed in a miner's strike somewhere there. He promised he would return, but we never heard from him. In the meantime, Rebecca met a man who owned a grocery store in Nogales, Mexico. She lived there until she died. She never had any more children. She was the one that Yolie, Roberto and you were visiting when they had their accident."

Chapter 4

FTER TWO MORE DAYS in the small ghost town, the family returned home. They stopped in Prescott and then had lunch at
the Grand Canyon. On the way back, all four of them took
the opportunity to read the two files. The file from Marana was a techni-
cal police report, but the files from the Jerome church and from several
notarized affidavits, were full of personal observations. On a long stretch
though the desert, Licha said, "Goodness Larry, we've made a huge discovery about your life. And part of that discovery is all the names you
have…Lorenzo, Larry and Joaquin." She paused and continued, "It seems
wise to select the name you want to legally use. For example, for your
social security number, drivers license and so on."

Ginny said, "I like all the names, but for official business, I suggest: **J.
Lorenzo Franco.**

And we could still call you Larry."

The young man repeated the name several times and asked, "What do
you think Mom?"

"I like it. It sounds very sophisticated and it incorporates and honors
all your names; yes I like it very much it; has a nice ring to it."

"Okay, I like it too. What do we have to do?" asked Larry.

"Well, first thing we need to do is go to the Social Security office in
Ventura and get a new SSI card. Then we should go to the DMV and get
a new driver's license. And finally we should see Rhonda, our attorney,
and get her advice to make sure we have all the bases covered."

It took several weeks to get all the documentation done. First Larry
received his new driver's license and then his Social Security card. It was

his same number, but with the J in front of his name. At the same time, Rhonda Davis addressed a three page letter to the Border Patrol with a detailed explanation of what had happened and of the new circumstances. Included were several signed affidavits regarding his birth. In the meantime, Larry was encouraged to continue his connections with his family in Jerome. He called them frequently. Mostly he spoke to his cousin Cipri who related the family's circumstances. Cipriana was hard of hearing and Larry felt awkward yelling into the phone.

The first week in September Larry and Ginny were in Ventura shopping for some clothes for their trip to Pomona for the fall quarter. When they returned to the car, a police officer was writing a ticket for an expired parking meter. He looked at the two and addressed Larry, "Is this your automobile?"

Larry said, "Yes, but we had enough time, something must be wrong with the meter."

The officer, ignored the comment, "May I see your driver's license and car registration please." The officer took the documents to his car and was obviously entering the information into the mobile computer. He returned, and said, "Mr. Franco, I note you have a warrant for your arrest. I suggest you not make a fuss. Please put your hands behind your back."

"Oh God, not again! Officer, this is all a big mistake. This has all been taken care of…"

"Sir, I see you have a warrant for your arrest. You then have to take care of this with the proper authority. In the meantime, I have to remind you that you have the right to remain silent and anything you say may be held against you."

"Where will you be taking me officer?" He asked.

"To the county jail on Victoria Avenue."

"Officer, if I may call my attorney Rhonda Davis she can explain and avoid lots of problems and headaches."

"When you get to the jail you'll be afforded a call to your attorney."

Larry looked sadly at Ginny and said, "Call Dad and see if he can meet us at the jail and tell him to get Rhonda there as soon as possible…Oh shit, I just can't believe it!"

This time Tom, Licha, Ginny and Rhonda Davis were waiting when the officer drove up to the back door of the station. The jail captain was also present.

The arresting officer noted all four had their arms crossed and a grim face. He hesitated to get out of the car. When he got out, the captain said in a strained voice, "Officer Lopez, please remove the handcuffs from Mr. Franco." He then addressed Larry, "Mr. Franco, I personally want to extend our apologies for this unfortunate incident. Apparently our computers have not been updated. I can assure you that at our next shift, all officers will be advised of this new information."

Larry had a chagrined look on his face, "In a way I can't blame officer Lopez, but I would hope that in the future he would check more carefully. To be honest, what worries the shit out of me is that next week I'll be at Cal Poly in Pomona, and I wonder what kind of information they have on me there. Could this happen to me there? Or what happens if I were to get on a plane?"

The captain looked down at her feet, "I suppose it's possible, but I will have the Sheriff write you a letter that you can show if you have any problem."

"That's not good enough. For God sakes, I'm a citizen like you are. I shouldn't have to carry a document in my pocket so I can show it to every cop who doesn't like the way I look. I mean, what kind of crap is that?"

Mr. Franco, I know it's an inconvenience..."

"An **inconvenience**! Last time I wound up in Adelanto in some 'prison for rent' because you guys screwed up here. I'm fortunate that I have my friend Ginny, my dad and my attorney, but what happens to some poor bastard that's not that fortunate or can't speak the language. In fact, I saw many young men just like me in that prison. I wonder how many were thrown in that hole...and are still there."

The jail officer said, "I don't know what else I can say..."

Finally Rhonda stepped in and said, "Perhaps it's better that we all say nothing more before things get out of hand. I think Larry, if it's okay with you, I will start legal proceeding for pain and suffering. Sometimes it's not until an agency has to shell out some money that they clean up their act. What do you think?"

In disgust he said, "Please be my guest. Do whatever it takes so I won't have to live this nightmare again." Larry turned into his parent's arms and said, "Mom, Dad, I want to go home."

Chapter 5

"Alice, Duce here. A group of us girls from an Interfaith Group are looking into this immigration mess. There's so much conflicting and emotional problems with it that we're confused. We decided we'd study the issue and thought you'd be interested in it. Especially after what happened to Larry."

Jeri Larkin was an old college acquaintance. However, in college they were not particularly good friends. They ran in different circles and had different interests. While Alice followed a very conventional life style in school, Jeri was always in the forefront of some movement; supporting black students, civil rights and anti war campaigns. Several times she was arrested, but that only seemed to inspire her even more. When she returned to Santa Paula High School as the history teacher, she was married and then subsequently divorced. She had two children in the local middle school. While she had calmed down from her college days, she still was an activist on issues of the poor and disadvantaged; as she called them. They had recently renewed their friendship. While not intimate buddies, they had come together through various programs in their local church. Alice cringed when she thought of Jeri's nick name in school...*Duce*. It was a nickname given to her by her brothers. She was born with only her thumb and index finger on her left hand. The defect was not noticeable because it didn't seem to hinder any of her activities. In fact, the lacking digits seem to inspire her to excel in sports and even to playing a guitar. And the missing fingers did nothing to dampen her social activism. Even though she was missing three fingers, she was still a remarkable and pretty woman. The nick name didn't seem to bother

her. In fact, she used it herself with her good friends. Alice noticed that recently, she was using the name when she was around Alice; as she did when she answered the phone.

Alice Franco had been aware of the immigration issue, but only in an intellectual, but somewhat peripheral level. It was a contradiction in thought and it was not an issue she fretted about. However, since the incidents with Larry, she became more aware of the wide implications this had on their community and the country for that matter. Even more interesting was that many of her friends and family were similarly unaware or just didn't care or worry about the issue. As one of her friends put it, "As long as there's lettuce in the store and my lawn gets cut," it was of little concern and consequence to them. However, listening to Larry's experience in the desert prison facilities and subsequent detentions brought the issue to the forefront in a dramatic fashion. So the issue became not only personal, but a moral issue, so she quickly answered, "Jeri, it's good to hear from you. How have you been? Listen, I too have been pondering this immigration mess. I would like to get better acquainted with the issue. What did you have in mind?"

"It's not completely clear in my mind either, but I've spoken to a dozen or so friends and invited them to my house tomorrow night. I've asked the local Methodist minister to give us a quick overview of the issues. She's new in town, but she has been involved in this for years. Then after listening to her, we can decide what, if anything, we want to do."

"Count me in. What time's the meeting? Can I bring anything?"

"Just bring yourself at 7 in the evening. Also, I mentioned your experience with Larry and she was very interested. I wouldn't be surprised if she asked you to tell us about that incident."

Alice answered slowly and said, "Well okay, but I don't want to get into any personal accounts. Frankly, the whole damn thing was a nightmare and is still painful."

"Excellent…I mean, not excellent that Larry got picked up, but great in that we can hear directly from someone we know in true detail not as an intellectual tale."

Bonnie Cho, the Methodist minister, was a tiny Asian woman. She spoke English with a slight British accent which gave her an even more mysterious aura. She also spoke with what seemed a slight hint of humor as she related sad tales about people and her work. "You may think that I don't take this subject seriously, but really, the only way I can discuss the subject is by having a sense of humor about it. Otherwise, I would be in perpetual tears and unable to do anything. And in the final analysis, this will eventually require action and we can't' do that if we're in tears all the time. In a perverse way, we will have to enjoy this treacherous journey if we really want to help; having a sense of humor helps."

The small woman opened her purse, removed a tissue and blew her nose, and then carefully refolded the tissue and put it back in her purse, "You know, I studied for the church because it occurred to me that Jesus had a sense of humor; kind of a jokester, if you will."

Alice cringed and asked, "What do you mean Jesus was a jokester?"

The minister smiled, "I don't mean to be blasphemous, but look at all the challenges he put in front of us. For example, the subject we're here to discuss. Everyone from all political parties, liberals and conservatives, religious and atheists gripe about immigrants, but we all want what these productive and cheap workers will provide for us. We don't want to see them or hear about them, we just want them to cut the lawn and then leave, or better, disappear." You have to admit that's the height of hypocrisy and I can just see Jesus smiling at that contradiction. Especially since the solution is so simple."

"What do you mean simple?" asked Jeri.

Again Cho smiled and said, "Simple. We know that the majority of the illegal immigrants come here to work. It's the poverty that they're escaping from in their own country; they want a job, money, and a better opportunity for themselves and their families. So the job is the key! And the key to the job is the owner, the president or the CEO of a company! I would enact a law that said the owner or the CEO of a company who directly or indirectly hires an unauthorized worker is fined, say $1,000 for the first worker apprehended; for the second one the fine would be $10,000 for each additional apprehension plus six months in jail for the CEO or the owner. Simple, problem solved."

"But that's unfair. The outcry would be deafening," said Alice.

"It very well may be unfair, and no doubt there would be an outcry when your friend who has her lawn cut by an illegal Mexican spends a night in the pokey. **Remember the focus is on the job!** You can build the highest border fence and hire thousands of border patrol, but I can assure you that hunger and greed will win every time. *No fence has ever stopped desperation and never will!* The big problem is that our focus is always on the undocumented person and that's the biggest error we commit. Either we focus on the job, **and more specifically, on the one person who gives the job,** or we will continue tilting windmills."

One of the ladies asked, "But if we have no one who wants to do this work, what happens then?"

"Excellent question; and the answer is that we let people come in legally. We've done that many times. We've done it with permanent immigration or with people who come here legally on temporary visas. Then we keep track of these people. Also any bright CEO will then quickly agree to use one of these systems to keep his sorry ass out of jail."

"You seem to put the entire onus on CEOs. Most of the ones I know are nice people and are trying to do the right thing, why should we put all the responsibilities on them? Isn't the immigration issue a government function?" asked Alice.

"Of course, but government is not going to act, there's too much regional and geographical differences at play for politicians to act, but more importantly, remember how I started the discussion…the emphasis is on the job…on the person. Who ultimately gives that person a job is the CEO." Again the Methodist minister smiled, as if she was sharing a joke.

What about the mom and pop store that has only one employee, what happens to them?" asked Jeri.

Smiling, she answered, "They'll get caught just once and I can pretty well assure you of that. And once they see their friends and competitors punished, people will fall in line. Let me repeat, the focus is on the job, and more specifically, the person ultimately responsible for giving the job. It's the job! The job! The job!"

"How was your meeting with the gals? Anything that might be interesting?" asked Tom as he got a beer out of the refrigerator.

Licha smiled and said, "Actually, it was interesting. Duce invited the Methodist minister who spoke on how to solve the problem immigration situation."

Tom took a drink from the bottle and asked, "And how would she do that?"

"Simple, she would fine every CEO, business owner, restaurant owner or housewife who hires an illegal alien $1000 for the first offence, $10,000 for the second one and six months in jail."

Tom almost choked on the beer, "What kind of a solution is that, for god's sake."

"Again, the lady said it was simple. Up to this point all efforts to control immigration is to focus on the poor person crossing our borders. She argues that desperate and hungry people will cross any obstacle to get a job. In fact, people will die, and have died, crossing the desert or climbing a fence to get a job. We know that for a fact. We read about it every day in the news. If no one will give them a job then the main attraction is no longer there. That's where the CEOs of the world come in. Because they ultimately set employment policy and I'm sure they don't want to go to jail. It's as simple as that."

"That's crazy," said Tom.

"It may very well be, but no more crazy than the policy we've been following up until now; especially with the results that we've been getting, which stink. At least we can agree on that. Think about it from the numbers standpoint. To solve the problem we have to go after an estimated 10 to 12 million folks who are breaking the law. If the focus is on the folks who provide the jobs, then we're talking about ten percent or 1 million. It seems to me that it would be easier to concentrate on one person rather than ten."

"Hell, but big business, the chamber of commerce, manufacturing and small business will oppose any such legislation." He added.

"Cho noted that in fact and in a way she's counting on it. Simply because the folks you just mentioned are not well liked by the public in general. Recent polls indicate that they're even less liked than congress itself."

"Well, Licha you're right, but these folks you just mentioned have lots of money and they can hire every PR guy in the country and they will."

"Rev. Cho is sneaky. She thinks the way to accomplish this is to introduce a long comprehensive employment bill, one that will have lots of pork and then on page 1003, there will be just a few very obscure lines that will have that language hidden in the pork. Furthermore, she said it will be called the Worker Protection Act or WPA.

Tom laughed uncomfortably and said, "Tell me how this thing is going to happen? Is this just a pipe dream or is there some kind of impetus behind it?"

"As I understand it, there are some folks now putting together such a bill."

"That's crazy Licha; they could never sneak that by all the watchdogs in Washington. Hell the attorneys and lobbyists would be all over that in a second."

"You would think so, but Cho says that's done every day in Washington. And remember the pork; the lobbyist and lawyers are addicted to pork. And just think of the litigation and the billable hours this will generate?"

"And you say this gal is a preacher; she sounds devious as hell," he laughed as he took another drink of beer.

Chapter 6

LICHA WAS IN FRONT OF THE HOUSE watering her favorite roses when Larry drove up. Larry hadn't shaved for several days and looked tired. He smiled faintly and said, "Hi Mom, how are the roses doing?"

She dropped the hose and gave her son a hug, "Larry, what are you doing here? Is school out on vacation or something?"

"Can we go inside Mom? I need a Coke or something."

Licha removed a Coke can and gave it to him. She poured herself a cup of tea and sat at the counter and waited. It was obvious her son was troubled. Yet he looked healthy other than he had a disheveled look. She waited until he had consumed most of the drink. "What's going on Larry?"

Larry was close to tears and said, "A couple of days ago the Dean of Students called me in and wanted to know why there was a warrant out for my arrest and what kind of crime I had committed that warranted my prison incarceration. She furthermore told me that I had lied on my admission application by not telling them of my criminal record." The young man finished the soft drink and crushed the can between his hands and tossed it into the trash can.

"Oh Lord, not again…did you explain to her what had happened?"

"I tried Mom, but she wouldn't listen. She was more bothered by me not admitting my prison stay. She was even more concerned that I would not admit to the crime I had committed. She mentioned several times how she was responsible for the safety of all the other students. Then she called in the Security Officer and he too grilled me about my time in prison. He asked me about my parole status. Mom, the guy was a pain in the ass. He wouldn't listen to what I had to say. They kept questioning me for almost two hours and finally I got fed up, told them they could go to hell, and that they could shove their school up their ass! The Dean told me all this would go on my record. And I told her what she could do with the record. Then the Campus cop escorted me out of the office and told me I was lucky not to be arrested."

"Oh Larry, it must have been horrible. One thing we need to do is call Rhonda and tell her about what happened. She's filing a claim and she can add this to it...I don't know what to tell you, honey, but one of these days you'll think about it and laugh."

"It is kind of funny, when you think about it isn't it," but the young man wasn't laughing.

That evening they went out to their favorite Mexican restaurant. Larry had calmed down. He had related this story to Rhonda Davis, the attorney who said she would amend her complaint accordingly. She also said she would call the school Dean and try to clear that up. Finally Tom asked, "Larry, what will you do now?"

"Dad, I don't think I want to go back to that school, even if they were to beg me. I don't think I can forget the doubt...the almost hate...in their eyes. Maybe I should just take some time off and consider the other schools that accepted me." Larry took a bite of his chili relleno and continued, "but on the drive down I thought about the people in Jerome. I wonder what you guys think about me going to visit them for a while till this blows over. Maybe I could even get a job. It would give me a chance to get to know them a little better...It's kind of my world; a world I know nothing about. Frankly, I'm so damn confused that I really don't know what to do. It's just an idea."

The parents looked at each other and finally Tom said, "Now that sounds like a good idea. I mean after all, you have a connection with those people. You should get to know them better, but I think you should call your Uncle Johnny and discuss it with him. Make sure it's not going to be an imposition on them."

Larry smiled and then frowned and then said, "Oh shit, I left in such a hurry I didn't even let Ginny know I was leaving. She'll be ticked off at me."

Licha said, "Well son, it looks like you have at least two calls to make." She leaned over and hugged and kissed him.

For the first time Tom and Alicia were alone. Larry had made arrangements to spend at least two or three months in Jerome. In fact, his uncle Johnny arranged for a part time job in the copper mine where his great grandfather had worked. Although the mine was closed, the company still maintained its ownership and mostly provided security for the old plant. The old-time watchman decided to take a couple months off and Johnny wrangled the job for Larry. The pay was minimal, but it was a job. The family house had an empty room upstairs that was sparse, but adequate. By the time Larry arrived a few days later, his cousin Cipri had cleaned and prepared the room for him. The duties were simple at the abandoned mine. A couple times during the day he was to walk around the main premise, check the locks and make sure that children did not play close to the area. The most interesting thing was that the security center was the old corporate office building. In this office was located a mini library with many books and files of the mine's history. And there was a lot of time to just leaf through these records where Larry could relive the life of his great grandfather, Jose Joaquin or JJ as he was known. These bits and pieces of information, and with discussion with his great grandmother Cipriana, added to the knowledge of this part of his family. His uncle Johnny, and his cousin Cipri, added the contemporary faction of the family. More importantly, all this discovery lessened his anger of his seemingly never ending problem with immigration in California and a law enforcement computer system that had latched on to him and would not let go.

Chapter 7

THE GATHERING BEGAN WITH MUCH SOFT CHATTING mixed with some apprehension. The group had grown. It was still mostly women with four or five men present as well. The group quieted down as the Rev. Bonnie Cho walked to the front of the room with a cup of tea in her hand. "First, let me welcome you to our gathering. I wish I could tell you that this will be an enjoyable evening. On the contrary, I can almost guarantee that some of you will be very uncomfortable. You will doubt and you just might say what the hell are these people talking about and walk out. If you do, I will not blame you."

There was some uneasy stirring as the people settled down. A new couple arrived late and some chairs were moved to accommodate them. Cho took a drink from her tea then sat the cup down and smiling said, "We're here to talk about our country's immigration situation, but before we get specific, let me ask you a question. Since I'm kind of new to this town, tell me the name of one of the most important men in the community. Someone with wealth, position, respect, family connections, business and land owners, in short, the person you would call Mr. Santa Paula."

There was some stirring as a few people were whispering names to each other and several names were called out. Finally, Tom Franco from the back of the room said, "That's an easy question; in my book it would be Maxwell Martin."

There was a buzz among the people and in general there was a unanimous agreement. Bonnie said, "Tell me about Mr. Martin, if you will."

The comments flowed easily: "His family was instrumental in founding our town; They're probably the largest land owner and farmer in the area; they founded and mostly own the local water company; he's politically connected in Sacramento and Washington; he's on the boards of several corporations and banks; he's a big supporter of the community, the schools, the scouts, the hospital and various other organizations."

"Mr. Martin is a real gentleman, a great asset to our community and well respected by most folks around here." said Tom. "There's no way anyone would wish him ill much less convict him of a crime that would send him to jail. I mean, if Mr. Martin goes to jail, what does that mean for all of us here?"

Cho smiled mysteriously and said, "Under the law being discussed now, the president, CEO, owner of a company or organization or housewife who is caught with an illegal alien would be fined $1,000 for the first offense, $10,000 for the second offence and serve 6 months in jail. And then a similar fine and jail time for each subsequent occurrence. Nothing complicated about that; it's straight forward and simple."

From the back of the room a lady raised her hand and asked, "Rev. Cho, are you aware that Mr. Martin and his family are big supporters of the Methodist church? If I'm not mistaken, his family donated the land and provided most of the money to build the church complex that currently exists."

Another voice added, "And you can say the same thing about the hospital, the Boys Club and almost every other organization in town."

"Wow, this fellow Martin sounds like he walks on water...pretty remarkable guy. Well let me introduce you to a person who knows him pretty well and perhaps we can get a different impression of this person." She walked to the kitchen and hugged an older woman and led her by the hand to the front of the small group. "Friends, it's my pleasure and honor to introduce you to Mrs. Maxwell Martin!"

Melina Martin was a tall, slender woman with long, well combed hair tied in a bun that made her look even taller. She also stood very erect; towering over the small preacher. She carefully removed her gloves and then looked elegantly at the group in front of her. "How nice it is to see you all. It's unfortunate that we only come together when we're facing such troubling times and trying decisions in our lives, but together we gather in hope. I don't know how I would have managed when the body of our son Maxie was brought home from Vietnam. It was a heartache that still lingers to this date. And I know several other mothers who have similar voids in their hearts and family." Then she paused for a long time, and continued, "And I also know mothers whose sons were here in this country without documentation, but they still went to that faraway land to die just like my son for a country that considered them *illegal aliens* and unworthy! Some of the mothers I know still live in doubt even after their ultimate contribution. I asked myself, how is that still possible? So when this young lady asked me what I thought about legislation that could put my dear husband in jail in order to give us a humane legislation on immigration, I told her I would visit Max every visiting day and bring him all the books he hasn't had time to read; like a dutiful wife would do."

There was some rustling in the group and finally one of the men asked, "Mrs. Martin how does Mr. Martin feel about this legislation and about the possibility of doing time?"

"His first reaction was to tell me that he hires people to run his various operations and he seldom gets involved in the day-to-day operations. Then I asked if he knew that he might have illegals in his employ and he said he didn't know. Then after a second thought, he said that there was a pretty good chance that somewhere in his various operations there might be one or two. In fact, he said, the odds were pretty good that there were. He quickly added that he's never thought about it, and no one ever asked him about it."

Tom raised his hand from the back and asked, "Mrs. Martin, did you by any chance ask your husband how his friends and colleagues would react to such a law?'

"Ah, I asked him that very question." She smoothed a sleeve of her blouse and said, "I can't repeat his exact words in mixed company, but he said his friends would have a GD conniption fit." There were chuckles on how Mrs. Martin avoided using her husband's profanity while still conveying the idea of exactly what he meant. She continued, "I should also tell you that I mentioned to him that I was coming to this meeting and what the agenda was. With some resignation he said, the immigration problem was such a mess that perhaps something drastic along these lines might be the answer. He did suggest that this law should apply to everyone; house wives, government entities, schools, churches and especially politicians. He also pleaded that along-side this penalty, there be a practical program that would allow temporary workers to be admitted lawfully. Perhaps similar to the program utilized during the second war for farm workers."

Rev. Cho looked at the crowd and asked, "Anymore questions or comments?"

Mrs. Martin sheepishly raised her hand, "Max did ask me to ask you. If he finds a long time employee who is illegal should he dismiss him? And then he asked if he needs workers, and only illegal are available, what should he do? And finally he asked that he be given an answer to these questions from this group before he was willing to expose himself to jail time and to the ridicule of his friends."

There was a long quiet in the room; finally Tom answered, "Mrs. Martin, thank you for coming and thanks to Mr. Martin for his willingness to support what some might consider drastic action, but in the meantime, I think Mr. Martin should continue his present policy. He for sure should not dismiss anyone or let his crops spoil for the lack of workers."

Mrs. Martin deliberately looked at everyone in the room and they all concurred with what Tom said, "Thank you, I'll pass that on to Max and give you all our blessing in your efforts to give us a sensible immigration law. One more thing, I know some of you will think it's odd for me, the wife of one of the largest land owners in this area, to be encouraging putting him in jail, but I think of one of my Jewish friends that reminded me of one of their old sayings. *To overlook an evil is more evil than the evil itself.* Just something to keep in mind as you all continue your discussion."

Rev. Cho picked up her tea and looked at her audience and said, "I met Mrs. Martin the first day I reported to this ministry. Immediately, I introduced this subject to her and without much prompting she agreed something needed to be done—even if Mr. Martin had to spend time in jail. Actually, she said she too would be willing to do time, to get a sensible, comprehensive immigration law passed."

Licha raised her hand and said, "Reverend, as it is now, the focus is on illegal aliens that we don't know, have never seen and will probably never see, so in a way, it's easy to send them to jail, but if the focus is changed to the jobs or employers, these people we know and are here sitting in this room. They're friends, neighbors and even relatives. Suddenly it becomes a personal problem."

"You're absolutely correct Licha, but remember, for the last several decades the emphasis has been on the person crossing the border illegally, and that's been a dismal failure. No, the focus needs to change and that focus is the job. Remember it's the Job. Now, just for fun, let us all repeat in unison: Jobs! Jobs! Jobs!" The meeting ended like a rally with people clapping as they joined the jobs chant.

Chapter 8

There were not many young people in Jerome except for an occasional tourist passing by. Larry and Cipri were thrown together by this fact, and on top of that, they became good friends. Cipri and her family and friends were filling blank pages in Larry's life. Cipriana sat with him almost every evening and told him stories. He also accompanied her to church every Sunday and for Wednesday evening Mass during the week. The short walk to the church with family and friends became part of the lesson program. Not only was it informative, but it was funny. The old lady had a wicked sense of humor. Occasionally she would lean over during Mass and whisper something to Larry and they would both start to giggle. Cipri would frown at him or even poke him in the ribs when they got too loud. "You two are terrible," said Cipri as they walked to the store to get an ice cream. "What was she telling you that set you guys off?"

"I can't tell you, but it was something about the priest."

"Oh, good heavens, no telling what she told you. Next time we go to Mass, I'm going to sit between you so we don't get excommunicated." They ate their ice cream as they walked back. Cipri said, "Are you familiar with the local Indian tribes around here?"

"No, not really; why do you ask?"

"Well you now know that you have a good chunk of Irish blood in you, but rumor has it that we also have some Yaqui or Apache blood in us. Anyway, I have a good friend that lives on the Res and they're having one of their pow-wows this weekend; I thought we might go. It's not far and it's kind of fun."

"Sure, it sounds like fun."

The ride to the outpost was just 40 minutes up in the hills. Cipri drove her dad's pickup slowly up the hill and was continuously looking at the surrounding vistas. "I just love it up here during this time of the year. Some people say it's barren and non productive, but in a way, it's just the reason that I love it. There's a beauty in the simplicity of the landscape, don't you think?"

Larry looked at his third cousin and then at the landscape she was referring to. Compared with his home town, it looked barren indeed, but the overall brownness of this part of Arizona did have a stark beauty to it. He tried to look at it through her eyes and that made it even more attractive. She turned off the highway on to a dirt road and then on to a large dirt parking lot. The place was full of cars, pickups and horse trailers. The gathering was overwhelming with the delicious smell of all sorts of food being cooked. They walked around easily. Cipri was well known and many people came up to hug her and say hello. She in turn introduced them to her cousin. They came to a small tent where a young woman dressed in a colorful leather shirt was selling jewelry. "Cipri, my God, how great to see you. It's been ages. How have you been?"

Cipri gave the young woman a hug and said "Luna, I've missed you. Sorry I haven't had time to make it up here." She took Larry's hand and said, "Luna this is my long lost cousin I told you about. He's staying with us to learn about who he is. So of course I brought him to you.' She looked at Larry and said, "Larry meet Luna Martinez; Luna meet my cousin Larry Franco."

"So this is the guy. Wow, it's so nice to finally meet you Larry. Tell you what, let's go visit my aunt, she sells some fabulous *mansanillo* tea and we can chat for awhile. And you can tell me about yourself."

Luna had a long talk with the young couple and finally said, "Well Larry, it sure sounds like you've had a couple of personal blows in your life recently, but let me tell you, you have great strength and resilience running through your blood. I'm proud to tell you that you have energy from my people. Yolanda, your mother and I traced this rich mixture to our people who live in these hills. You have the richness of your Irish grandfather who traveled all over the world. So within you is the endurance and energy of many different ancestors. This hybrid energy will help you overcome this obstacle…and…more importantly, to sustain and prevail in the trials that are to come." This last part she spoke quietly and with a hint of sadness. She finished the tea she was drinking. Then she continued, "Now Larry, let's go back to my shop. I want to show you a ring that you'll need and will help you in this journey."

As Cipri drove home, Larry twirled the silver ring on his finger. The ring was plain in its simplicity. It had a small, round, green stone with a prominent dark speck about the 5 o'clock position. Luna had told them that the speck, or the flaw or irritant, as she put it, was a good sign. Because this defect was surrounded and overwhelmed by the goodness of the green jade, the stone of the Good Spirits. "Remember this when you face the trials that you'll face in life," she had said. Larry looked up as they entered the little town and said, "I wonder what 'trials to come' Luna was talking about?"

"No telling. Even though Luna's only a few years older than I am; she's already considered a spiritual person by her people. People come from all over to see and consult with her. They say she can look into people's future. She's also an artist; she probably made the ring she sold you. And don't let the pretty *Indian Maiden* look fool you. She has a PhD in psychology from the U of A. I feel very comfortable talking to her. If you ever need someone to open up to, she's the one."

Chapter 9

LICHA MET WITH BONNIE CHO at her office in the Methodist Church. Cho had just completed a memorial service for one of her parishoners. She smiled as she saw Licha. She removed her alb. Under the alb she wore a pair of designer jeans and a plain white blouse. The simplicity of her attire translated to a classic look on the slender woman. She said, "These albs save me much time when I have to dress in a hurry and this garment hides many embarrassing situations. Thanks for coming here to meet, it's so handy for me, but I also know that it's an inconvenience for you."

"It's no problem and no inconvenience. In fact, compared with what some people have to go through to cross the border, this is a piece of cake. Bonnie, I've been thinking that unless we put a face on this immigration issue it will not sell. Most of the people I know don't even know there is an *immigration issue!* So unless there's a face they can relate to, or an issue that affects them directly, it'll go in one ear and out the other."

Cho answered, "Licha, I agree with you. What do you have in mind?"

"Well I've been thinking about our family. Frankly we were like the folks I just described; we had no idea, or just didn't care, about this business. Yet when our son got embroiled in it, we've been living a nightmare. I know it's been a blow to him personally. Yet we're fortunate to have the friends and resources to fight, and eventually we'll be okay, but now I think of those mothers who have no money or connections with their sons closeted out in the middle of nowhere. It just breaks my heart."

"I agree Licha, what do you have in mind?"

"Well I haven't really discussed it with anyone, but as you know, our son Larry got picked up by the Border Patrol and put in prison. The whole thing was a tragic misunderstanding, but his name was entered into the government's computer system and it seems like he'll be there forever. His name keeps popping up and we have to untangle him. He's so messed up that he left school and is now working in an abandoned copper mine as a security guard with nothing to guard. His young life and ours have been jolted. I again have to tell you I haven't talked to Larry or Tom for that matter, but I wonder if Larry and his troubles could be the poster boy for this campaign?"

The Methodist Minister was thoughtful for a long time and she said, "Licha, you're absolutely correct that this fight cannot be about ideas; it has to be about people…human faces, mothers and children…flesh and blood, to be brutal about it. And your idea about your son is brilliant, but I can assure you it will become nasty. Can you take the blows, and more importantly, how will this impact Larry? Opponents have lots of money; they are very committed, and will have no compunction about destroying you and your family or anyone else who gets in their way."

Licha took a deep breath and shuddered; "It scares me to death. It scares me even more to know that there are hundreds or thousands of people who are in prison because all they wanted was a job; a simple job. Good Lord, how can we live with that…how can I, live with that?"

Cho took a deep breath and said, "First, let's go across the street and get a cup of tea. I find a cup of tea and a brief prayer helps greatly. Perhaps we can get a better insight on this dilemma. As they sat, the minister asked, "Licha, tell me about the issue of Larry's birth, I overheard a couple of ladies discussing it the other day."

Licha outlined the death of Larry's parents and the subsequent events that led to the arrest by the Border Patrol. "We're not Larry's birth parents, but he's our son. In a few months he will be our legally adopted son."

"Hmm, I'm sure all this will come out and will be fodder for the opponents, are you ready for that?"

"They wouldn't stoop so low to use that tragic incident against us, would they?"

"My dear, I'm afraid they would and will. To be honest, if I had similar information on them I would use it. This will be a game of hardball; it won't be for the faint hearted."

"Oh!"

Licha cooked some chicken soup, one of Tom's favorite dishes. They ate quietly. With Larry gone, the conversation during dinner was usually sparse. This time Tom listened carefully to the idea that Licha was proposing, he said, "I pretty much agree with your notion that having a personal story with a name and face is more effective, but why does it have to be Larry?" The poor kid already has weathered several blows. Think about it, first the immigration fiasco and then finding out that we're not his real parents. Now you're considering throwing him to the wolves. I mean that's asking a lot from our son."

I agree it's a terrible thing to ask of anyone, especially of a young man, and especially our son." Licha stood and put her bowl in the dishwasher. "Of course we would not do it unilaterally. Bonnie said she would not be a party to this unless it was thoroughly explained to Larry. And, that after an appropriate period of time, he willingly agrees and will not be forced. Secondly, she said he would have to agree to go through some intense training to anticipate the problems he would face and the way to act and respond to personal attacks; especially, how to react to the press. This, in fact, would be a full scale public relation effort and would have to be managed accordingly."

Tom looked up at his wife and said, "Honey, we need to think about this. What would you think about taking a few days off? We can head east, think about this, and if we just happen to go near a ghost town in Arizona, we can chat with our son."

Later that evening Tom answered a call from Rhonda Davis, their friend and attorney. "Tom, sorry for the evening call, but the boys from immigration called me late this afternoon and said they just wanted to run a couple of ideas by me. I told them I would see how you guys would react."

"Good to hear from you Rhonda; tell me what do our *friends* have in mind?"

"Well just remember, this is just a conversation at this point, but essentially, for this not to become a big, prolonged, legal entanglement, they suggested a few things. One, they would issue a written apology. Two, they would guarantee that Larry's record on this matter would be removed from their system and any other law enforcement data programs. And three, they would acknowledge that this misunderstanding, as they call it, has interrupted Larry's education so they will reimburse him financially."

Tom listened carefully and then said, "Tell me Rhonda, what do you think? And, I don't understand what they mean financially."

"If I understood them correctly, and reading between the lines, they're talking about $100,000. To them this would be equal to complete his education and about the savings to them in the form of legal fees they would not have to incur. From my viewpoint Tom, I think these guys have moved a lot to get to this point. I'm sure we can wrangle a little here and there, but we have to remember that the government has deep resources to fight this forever and the last thing you want to do is drag this out because they win every time."

Tom answered, "Rhonda, thanks for the information and your efforts. In fact, we're going to Arizona tomorrow morning and we'll talk to Larry; because in the end, it will be his decision. Are you sure this is the general outline of a settlement we can mention to him?"

"Yes, but make sure you stress that at this point we're just beginning this legal dance and we can make a few adjustments, but not many I think. It might be a good idea to call me; I might have some more information in a few days."

"Great, we'll talk in a couple of days," said Tom.

The long trip across the desert seemed shorter. Both Tom and Licha kept thinking and rethinking the conversation they were going to have with Larry. The young man was going to face some very difficult decisions. Yet as parents they were going to be a remote audience at best, but hopefully supportive of whatever Larry decided. The prospective unfairness and the seriousness of what he might face was not lost on them. Especially as Licha had related to her husband what Rev. Cho had shared with her and the media thicket they would be involved in if Larry agreed to get active.

It was late when they arrived at the Jerome Hotel and Spa. There were only a few people sitting in the lobby. Tom walked up to the hotel registration desk and said, "Good evening Cipri, I wonder if you have a room for a couple of nights?"

"Good Lord! Mr. Franco! You scared me to death! Is anything the matter? Does Larry know you're here?" The young lady turned pale.

Tom smiled and said, "Everything is fine, Cipri. We just had a few days off and decided to take a little trip and before we realized it, here we are."

"You mean Larry doesn't know you're here?"

"I don't think so, especially since we didn't know where we were going, but I wonder if you can call him and let him know we're here."

"I can't call him now, but I know where he is. Every Wednesday he and grandma go to Mass. In fact, they should just be getting to the church about now. Mass starts at 7 o'clock." Cipri watched Larry's parents holding hands. Suddenly she remembered and wondered what Luna had seen when she met Larry.

Tom looked at his watch and said, "Thanks, Cipri, just check us in and we'll walk over and surprise him.

Shock, it will be a shock for Larry thought Cipri. Since things were quiet in the lobby she called Luna Martinez just to talk. "Luna, I was just thinking of you, things are quiet here; I was wondering what you were doing?"

"Right now I'm waiting for a couple who I've been talking to for a couple of months. What's up with you? And what's up with your friend Larry?"

"Oh, things are nice here, a little quiet, but nice and peaceful." She paused for a second, "At least they have been quiet..."

"...So what do you think the parents want with Larry?"

In shock Cipri said, "Luna, how did you know that Larry's parents were here? Good Lord, they just walked in, they said they were just out for an outing and wound up here. How did you know?"

Luna chuckled and said, "Now Cipri don't be reading too much on a good guess. Let me give you a hint, I don't have any special insight except I've trained myself to listen carefully to people, their circumstances and their actions."

Cipri smiled to herself and said, "Well his parents just walked in. They said they went out for a ride and wound up here. They want to talk to

Larry, so I told them he was in church right about now and they walked over to join them."

"Sounds rather natural for parents to want to see their son, doesn't it?" Luna paused for several seconds and continued, "Listen Cipri, my guess is that Larry will want to chat with you so just listen, listen carefully. Depending on what you hear, you can suggest that he might want to talk to me. Just to get another viewpoint on whatever the dilemma is."

Cipri looked at the phone she was talking on as if she could see Luna, "Luna, do you think Larry or his parents are in any kind of trouble?"

"I have no idea, but it does sound rather odd for two parents to show up unexpectedly. You said they had no idea they were coming here, and Larry apparently is unaware of them. It just sounds kind of strange, don't you think so?"

"I know Larry has been rather jumpy recently. I know he misses his parents and he feels guilty about his girlfriend who calls him almost every day. Yet I think he enjoys being here. He and grandma have become good friends. Every night they sit and talk. She tells him stories about our side of the family and recently I noticed that he's writing some of it down."

Luna listened and said, "What about you Cipri, how do you feel about your cousin?"

"I don't understand, what do you mean, how do I feel about him? She noticed that suddenly her face flushed and she felt defensive.

"I don't' mean anything by my question. It's just that Larry's been around for awhile and he's bound to have an impact on his new family, and the family on him for that matter. In any event, just remember, if he just wants to talk, tell him I'm a good listener."

The evening Mass had already started when they walked in. There were only about 20 people present. They noticed that Larry and Cipriana were sitting in the front. They saw that their heads were close together; apparently they were talking as an older woman was reading the Scriptures from the ambo. They sat quietly towards the back of the church. During communion they both walked up and as they returned to their seat they faced Larry and Cipriana and smiled. Larry's face lit up in a shocked, astonished smile.

"Mom, Dad, what in the world are you guys doing here? Why didn't you let me know you were coming?" Larry was genuinely happy to see his parents. He hugged both of them. Then hugged his mother again and gave her a kiss on each cheek. Both mother and son had tears in their eyes.

"Oh baby, we miss you." Licha looked up to her son. He was now taller it seemed; a different person; a grown man. Even his voice seemed different, yet he was her son. "Your Daddy and I decided to go for a ride and before we knew it we were here!"

Cipriana watched the reunion and her face had a mixed expression; one of happiness and at the same time the dread of the eventual separation of her recently found grandchild. She whispered to Larry, "Invite your parents over to the house; we can have some coffee and a better place to visit." They walked back to the house just two blocks away.

By the time they got to the Mendez home, Linda had already brewed a pot of coffee and set out some *pan dulce*. Cipri had called from the hotel and she knew that grandmother would be bringing home guests. "Licha, Tom, what a nice surprise! We're so glad to see you. I have to tell you, recently I've noticed *someone* kind of moping around." She ran her hand over Larry's hair and messed it up. The young man smiled at his aunt.

Cipri walked in after her shift at 10 o'clock. Larry was sitting by himself at the kitchen table writing in a small record book. He had the pen in his mouth when she walked in. She went to the refrigerator and poured a glass of milk. She took a bite of the sweet bread and said, "I have to tell you it was quite a shock to see your parents walk in. They said they were just driving and wound up here. Wow, talk about going out of their way!"

"I must admit they startled me too. For a second I didn't recognize them. It wasn't until grandma poked me in the ribs that I noticed them. We came over and just talked. Apparently they were taking a few days off and here they are...so they said. The only problem is, I know my parents. Especially my dad; he's very organized and thoughtful. He's not the type to just go off on a whim. Anyways, we're having breakfast at the hotel in the morning. They said they had a couple of ideas they wanted to discuss. In fact, I was waiting for you. I was hoping you could be with me when we talk."

Cipri thoughtfully looked at Larry and said, "Of course, if you don't think I'll be in the way."

After Cipri went to bed, Larry continued to sit at the table nibbling on the sweet bread. He contemplated what his parents had told him. They were not too specific because, as they said, they were not too sure themselves what they were proposing. He did remember, however, that they mentioned any participation on immigration would be nasty and not for the fainthearted. He wondered what that meant.

His brief encounters with immigration officials assured him that any interface in this arena would be very controversial, and any discussion would be in the gutter. He wondered how could he become the focus? What would that mean for his own life? Yet the more he thought of how he was treated in that short period of time, the more he saw the need for some action. Additionally, recently he had spoken to other people who had been entangled in immigration issues. Deep down he knew it was a system with significant faults and needed to be remedied. But why did he have to get involved? What was in it for him? These questions whirled in his mind and did not become any clearer when he went to bed, or when he woke up early in the morning.

Cipri was already up helping with breakfast. Cipriana was also up and was dipping some *pan dulce* in her coffee. "*Ay m'hijito*, it's good to see you up early. I understand you're going to meet your parents. How nice it was for them to come all this way to see you." She again dipped her bread in the coffee and continued, "Please tell them to come visit me again before they leave. There are a couple of things I'd like to talk to them about."

"I really don't know what plans they have, but I'll tell them of course." He then looked at Cipri and said, "Ready? I told them I'd see them at 10 before I had to check in at the mine."

"Are you sure you want me to go with you. They may just want to talk to you about a family matter?"

Larry smiled at his cousin as they walked to the hotel, "Well, you're part of my family. And I'd very much like to have you with me; if it's okay with you. You don't have to worry. Mom and Dad are really nice people. They're cool."

"I understand they're nice people, but I just don't want to make it awkward. Oh, by the way, I spoke to Luna last night and she said if you ever wanted to talk to her, she's available."

He took his cousin's hand as they walked, "Hmm, that's good to know. Actually it's a good idea. I may need to bounce some ideas around with someone who can look at things with no preconceived ideas."

As they walked into the hotel, Licha and Tom were sitting in a corner eating breakfast. They both smiled when they saw the two young people. "You're just in time for breakfast." said Tom.

"Thanks Dad. I already had some cereal, but I will have some hot tea."

Cipri quickly said, "I'll go to the kitchen and get it. The regular I suppose?"

Licha noticed the smile Larry gave to his cousin. Communications without words; she smiled at herself and wondered about this relationship. "I never realized how peaceful it is up here. For the first time in a while, I slept really well,' said Licha.

Larry chuckled, "Well Mom, I'm glad you slept well, but I have to confess, I was up late. Just sat there and stared at the wall. Then I slept poorly…mostly I dreamed about young boys and girls who get caught up in the immigration whirlwinds."

Cipri brought out two cups of tea, gave one to Larry, and sat next to him. Larry looked at her and smiled, but said nothing. "Cipri and I have talked about immigration issues and I asked her to listen to what you have in mind. She also has a friend who lives on the reservation that I'd like to talk to before anything is decided." He looked at his parents and said, "First tell me about this Methodist minister Cho."

His mother answered, "Rev. Bonnie Cho was born in China, but immigrated to Hawaii as a baby and then to the mainland. She attended Cal Berkeley and was in the import business before becoming an Ordained Methodist Minister. She was recently assigned to our small town, but apparently is still involved in the church's overall Immigration Ministry. She seems like a very methodical person and believes in serious preparation in anything she tackles."

Larry looked at his father who said, "Son, I really don't know her well, but I agree with your Mom's evaluation of her."

"Well what does she have in mind?"

Licha moved her breakfast plate to one side and said, "The last decade or so has been a mess for immigration. Lots of people talk about reform. Some folks talk about opening the border to anyone, and others talk about kicking the 10 or 12 million that are estimated to be here illegally, out of the country. In the meantime, the ones who are already here find themselves in an awkward position to be sure. Then there's the issue of how to deal with those who want to immigrate to this country. It is a complicated and thorny issue; no doubt about it."

"I don't think I understand the issues completely, but where would I come into the picture? I mean, what can I contribute to the discussion?" asked Larry as he removed the tea bag from his cup and took a drink. He then put the tea bag in Cipri's cup. She smiled at him, dunked it a couple of times and she too took a drink from her cup.

"Cho says it's a basic public relations principle. That an issue becomes real when people can identify with a person; someone who looks like them or in their family or group. The idea of *immigration* as a concept by itself is a tough sell, but a face with a name and with the right kind of story makes the sell easier. As she told us a box of soap is a hard sell, but the same box in the hands of a smiling, pretty girl sells the product better." As Licha said this, she smiled at her son and realized that perhaps she really didn't know her son. Did he always drink tea, for example? Had he changed?

"Mom, what about school? It's always been my thought that I would return to school to finish. I don't want to get so involved that this would screw up chances of graduating."

"Larry, in the final analysis, graduating is the most important goal in the short term. And this is one of the issues that need to be discussed with Cho," said his father.

"Dad, you sound somewhat reluctant about all this?"

Tom was about to finish off some toast and hesitated, "Actually, I am reluctant. I think the main goal is to finish school. In my mind, school trumps everything; this is the one thing that will impact your life in the long run. However, I grant you that immigration issues are of great importance to the country and especially to those who get caught in the net of the unknown and uncertain. I don't know much about public relation issues, but it makes sense that a face will make the project more palatable." Tom put some marmalade on his toast and continued, "but in the end, this is really your decision. I would only ask that you consider it carefully. Talk to as many people as you can and then whatever you decide, we'll be on your side."

Licha noticed that the two young people moved closer as Tom spoke; as if there were some understanding between the two. They picked up their tea cups and took a sip at the same time and looked into each others eyes for a split second. "Honey, we're leaving tomorrow, early. Just think about it. Talk to people around here and then let us know whatever you decide. However, if you agree to participate, we need you to talk to Rev. Cho and some of her people who will tell you in realistic terms how deep and turbulent these waters might be."

They noticed that Cipri nudged Larry and he said, "Great. I'll give it a good thought. And by the way, just so you know, I haven't forgotten school. In my mind it's also on top of my list. Actually, I've looked into enrolling at the University of Arizona as on option. Nothing serious at the moment, but since my father went there, I thought it might be a consideration." He paused momentarily, "Just a thought...Oh and by the way, my grandmother asked me to invite you over to the house, she said she wants to chat with you before you left."

Chapter 10

L una Martinez was rinsing some dishes as she saw Cipri and Larry drive up to her house. Her small house was nestled in a grove of mesquite trees which almost hid the log house. There were actually two small houses on the property. The second one she used for a combination office and prayer room. It had a small table and one chair. The rest of the walls and floor were covered with colorful blankets, pillows and baskets. One wall was decorated with a wreath of dried ears of white corn. In the middle of the room was a large, round rock with a smooth depression in the middle. The depression was black from ashes of past fires. There was also a hint of incense being burned on the rock. On the wall, opposite the wall with the corn wreath, was a crucifix with the tortured body of Jesus. The Jesus had been carved from the root of a tree using the root structure to recreate the body hanging on a cross. The body of Jesus emerged from the root as a distinctive, tortured, painful body that gave a hint of hope with its upraised roots, arms which seemed to be reaching for the heavens. The three sat on the floor as Luna tucked her legs underneath herself. She said nothing, but had a slight smile on her face.

Cipri felt uncomfortable with the silence and broke it, "Some preacher lady in California wants to use Larry as a poster boy to fight for a better immigration law. It's a campaign that will be, or could be, nasty even according to the preacher. So what should he do?"

Luna said nothing, but repositioned her legs and looked at Larry and then at the crucifix on the wall behind the young couple. After a long time Larry finally said, "Mom and dad were here and apparently there's a pastor at a church in Santa Paula who wants me to participate in a campaign to change the immigration law. She thinks that by using me and my recent experience with the border patrol that it could be an effective way to change the law."

After a long pause Luna said, "What do you think of the idea of someone *using* you?" She stressed the word by extending the pronunciation. Somehow drawing out the word made it sound ominous and in addition, she said it with a slight smile which did not convey mirth.

Cipri felt a shudder go through her as she reached over and gently grabbed his hand. Luna noticed the attraction of the young couple and the uncertainty of what they were trying to determine or decide. The young man was facing a difficult decision and on top of that there was an obvious relationship developing between the two young people.

Finally Luna asked, "What do your parents think?"

Larry answered quickly, "Dad wants me to finish college first, but I think Mom feels that immigration is an important matter that needs attention…even if I have to devote some time to it."

"What does your heart tell you, Larry?"

He paused, "I'm confused. I know finishing school is important and I want to do that. I agree with dad, but the few days I spent in the Adelanto prison were a nightmare. I remember several young men about my age that had been in there for months with no hope. When I mentioned the unfairness of my situation, it didn't seem to matter to them. And the reality was that compared with their situation, mine was of little significance. I never thought of justice as something tangible, but when justice is suddenly taken away from you, it's like a kick in the teeth. Then it's no longer just an amorphous concept—it's real."

Luna said, "Larry, when you think of justice, do you think of it as a principle that applies to you only?"

"I did. I've studied some injustices in history, in the world and even in our country, but it was always a remote academic notion, but suddenly I saw injustice face to face and I didn't like it. I didn't like it as it applied to me and now, I don't like it as it applies to others either, but now what? Should I just bitch and complain like most people or should I act?"

Again Cipri reached for Larry's hand, she said nothing for a long time, but just held his hand. Then slowly she said, "Martin Luther King fought for justice and look what happened to him." Luna slightly nodded her head and looked at Larry with a faint smile.

"Good Lord, is that a possibility?" he asked.

Cipri answered, "This world is full of nuts; someone is always willing to shoot you just for the hell of it! If they think they have something at stake, they can shoot you or hang you and feel righteous about it."

Luna finally said, "Let me ask you both a question. This immigration problem has been discussed for years. Historically, immigration has always been a contentious issue. Even world wide it continues to be a problem. Recently congress, the president, unions, employers and churches have all indicated it's a problem. However, there's a huge difference in the solution each side would use for a resolution. So I would ask a question; if all of these high powered politicians, executives and preachers can't come to a solution, what can a young man do?"

"Oh Luna, that's my point; not only can one sole person do little, they could be hurt and on top of that, no one would give a shit if it happens." Cipri was adamant in her statement and her voice was close to cracking.

"I've thought of the huge obstacle to make sense of this quagmire, and it may be impossible to remedy, but what if we don't try? What does that say about us if we don't even try…not even try." He repeated slowly.

Luna looked at the two young people sitting in front of her. They were both struggling with the same issue, but from opposite ends. One from the notion that there was no point in trying and the other from trying even if there was little chance of success! Additionally, they were both inexperienced youth; especially when it came to tackling the vexing immigration dilemma facing the United States and many other countries around the world. Not only that, but history was replete with people migrating from place to place causing chaos and conflict as it happened. The results were never pretty or satisfying from any viewpoint. At best, animosities were subdued by time and political force. Uneasy peace existed throughout the world just like the present dilemma faced by this young couple.

Luna looked over the young couple's heads at the crucifix and said, "You know, I'm looking at Christ who was hung on a cross because he insisted on trying to right the wrongs of his times."

"You mean someone could be killed; look what happened to Him!" exclaimed Cipri.

"It's been known to happen. There are nuts in this world as you just said, whether we like it or not. Someone is always willing to pull the trigger. People have been killed for less. All we have to do is read the local paper to see what idiots can do. On the other hand, this country was founded on people seeking liberty and who were willing to endure hardships and, in some cases, even death, to live free." Luna unfolded her legs and re-crossed them again. "but the real question is, what are we willing to do for justice, or put it another way, what are we willing to do to correct an injustice? Or in other words when we see injustice do we just shut our eyes?"

"What does that have to do with Larry? Why doesn't someone else do it?" Cipri was close to tears and her voice cracking as she spoke.

Luna said, "My people tell a story about when the white men came. First there was plenty of room for everyone. So the settlers were welcomed; if not somewhat tolerated. Then they claimed the land. Then they killed the buffalo. Then they moved the Indians to reservations. When the Indians rebelled they were hunted and killed. So at one time, natives roamed their land in freedom and now they roam the land soaked in their own blood, but is now owned by someone else. The same thing happened this century when the German's began their ethnic cleansing program. Some groups of people didn't object until it was their turn to be in Hitler's crosshair and by then it was too late. So in a sense this issue has nothing to do with anyone specifically, but yet it affects us all. So, it has to do with all of us; whether we want to or not, like it or not."

Larry took Cipri's hand and said nothing. Then quietly Luna opened a small leather bag and removed some dry sage and placed it on the rock. She lit it with a match and fanned it with some feathers until the smoke began to permeate the small room. She stood in front of the young couple; put her hands on each of their heads, and murmured a prayer and then left the room. Larry and Cipri stayed for about 20 minutes and watched the smoke waft throughout the room. They drove back to Jerome quietly with only the lingering hint of the sage that had enveloped them completely. Equally lingering was the question of justice…or injustice; action or inaction?

Chapter 11

BONNIE CHO WAS DOODLING ON HER DESK pad as she waited for Lucinda to answer her phone. Lucinda Llamas was the Executive Director of Human Rights, Inc. A small, but powerful and well financed group of liberals, whose mission in life was to erase boundaries and borders of which she was the founder and organizer. "Lucy, Bonnie here, what's new in the big city?"

"Ah Bonnie, good morning; glad you called. What news do you have for me about the kid who might be our poster boy?" Lucinda was a tall, slim woman who favored wearing long, colorful, clingy dresses which made her look even taller. She walked around her office as she spoke on the cordless phone. As she spoke, she arranged books, closed drawers and cleaned some lipstick from her teeth. She moved with nervous energy as she talked. "Tell me, what's the kid like?"

"Actually, I'm going to meet him in a couple of hours. For the last several months he's been living in Arizona trying to get himself together; as I hear it. I've spoken his mom and she thinks he might be the one, but she wants us to talk to him and see for ourselves. She tells me, however, that the dad is not as enthusiastic. He wants him to finish school first, but he's got the right kind of a story if he agrees. I hope to see which way he's leaning and then give you a call to see if we go to the next step."

"Great, but Bonnie doesn't scare the shit out of him like you did with the others. Instead, tell him about all the romance and fun he will be exposed to!" Bonnie could hear a couple of chuckles before she hung up.

She didn't want to meet Larry at her church and he readily agreed to meet at the local Foster Freeze in the middle of the afternoon. The place was essentially empty after the lunch crowd. She ordered a small sundae and he ordered a cone and they found an empty corner. They sat across from each other and ate their ice cream. "Well Larry, it's nice to finally meet you. Your parents have told me a little about you and your problems with the boys from immigration. Tell me about your recent stay in Arizona. What were you doing there?"

"Well in an odd sort of a way, this immigration fiasco has helped me discover a new me. That is, a new family. I mean an additional family I never knew. I mean it was a terrible shock to be picked up by the Border Patrol, but it was, perhaps, even a bigger shock to learn that my parents were not my birth parents. It's kind of confusing, but my dad is not my real dad, he is my uncle. My real mom and dad died in an auto accident in Arizona just a couple of days after I was born. My mom's family is from Jerome, Arizona and to get away from all the BS from immigration, I went to visit these folks in that little town. My uncle there got me a job and more importantly, I got to meet and live with my new family for a few months."

Cho asked, "What did your parents tell you about our project to reform the immigration law?"

"Just that; that there was a project to begin a campaign to make a change and that the project needed a face to make the issues meaningful and real to voters. And that perhaps my story and my face, as they said, might help."

"That's pretty much the crux of the problem and what the campaign is all about, but did they tell you that this would not be easy. That our opponents have lots of money and are not afraid to play hard ball. These boys can get nasty, personal and incredibly vile. This is not for the faint hearted. On top of this, we would have to spend a good amount of time preparing this person to be an able spokesman for our side. And perhaps, just as importantly, to be able to withstand all the negative abuse that will be heaped on this individual."

"What kind of things do you think they'll come up with?"

"Well in a sense, you've been through two shocks recently. Being picked up by the Border Patrol and being told your parents are not your birth parents. Studies have shown that three shocks can be enough to cause real emotional damage in a person. You already have two, but I can assure you that you'll have several more if you agree to this adventure. In fact, I can guarantee you that there will be more. I'm sure they'll question your legal status and when they find out, they'll drag your dead parents and your mom and dad into the fray. And it'll be nasty, of that I can assure you." Rev. Cho mentioned all these things in a straight forward manner as if it were just another normal, casual conversation.

Larry listened carefully; he blinked his eyes several times as he tried to comprehend what Cho was telling him. Also ringing in his mind were Cipri's admonitions when he left her and her family when he got on the Greyhound bus to come home. On the long trip home; there was nothing to do, but look at the desolate landscape and contemplate the challenge he was being asked to take on. As Highway 15 dropped into the San Bernardino basin, it was then that he decided he would take on the challenge. In a sense there was relief in making the decision, but not overlooking the apprehension that still lingered in his belly. Finally he looked carefully at Cho and studied her face. He saw the Asian minister, but more than that, he saw a face of commitment. He wondered briefly if he had commitment. Finally, after finishing his ice cream cone, he said, "I'm not too sure I know exactly what I'm getting into, but I'm willing to give it a try."

"Great, but let's make a deal. I want to introduce you to Lucinda Llamas who will be directing this campaign. I want you to meet her and talk to her frankly. Once you get to know her, and if you're still willing to jump into deep water, then we'll really be on our way."

"Great, I look forward to meeting her."

Lucinda wore a long dress that looked almost like sleep wear. She walked around her office as she waited for her meeting with Larry Franco. She reread the five page informational biography on the young man and she was intrigued. She had directed her staff to research him in great detail. If she and her organization were going to invest much time, energy and expense on the young man, she wanted to insure that it was a good investment. Additionally, the immigration campaign was important to the organization and to her personally. She looked at several photographs in the file in an effort to get a feeling on him. She noticed that in all five photos he was smiling or had a slight grin. The grin was especially intriguing because it gave a hint of devilishness. Also, he was a handsome young man who would look good on camera. So on paper he appeared to be an excellent candidate for the work to be done. Now she needed to verify this in person. To see what kind of fiber this young person was made of.

Her secretary announced him, "Larry, welcome; we finally meet. Thanks for coming to see us." Larry sat in one of the chairs, but Lucinda continued to stand, half leaning and half sitting on a table behind her desk. She was looking down on Larry. He seemed embarrassed to look up at her, so he focused on her knees.

Reluctantly he raised his eyes to see her, he smiled and said, "Thanks for your interest in me. Frankly, I'm not too sure what you have in mind. This whole thing as it was explained to me recently, has been rather confusing for me and my family."

Lucinda smiled and said, "I understand. Immigration policies in this country have always been tenuous and controversial and they continue to be so even today. However, regardless of what one thinks of the situation, the fact is that hundreds, no, thousands of men and women sneak across the border to work. And no matter what many think, the fact is, they are hired and are working for us. We can act innocent and act as if this were not happening, but the fact is it happens. Our organization's effort is simple; we want to recognize that fact, be aware of who these people are and treat them like human beings. Now while we have an estimated 10 to 12 million people here living and working under the radar, there are many who seem to be satisfied with this underground economy. However, I think you'll agree that this type of system leads to all sorts of problems and abuses. All we want to do is recognize we need people to work and then permit them to enter the US and work out in the open like any other human being. This underground employment system is good for no one except those who want to abuse and take advantage of these people who only want to work."

Larry looked at the woman as she walked around her office, "All this sounds so rational and logical. Why do people oppose it, and why would they attack me if I were to get involved?"

"Listen Larry, the first thing we need to understand is that these folks are not rational or logical. They fear anything foreign, but they like cheap labor and one thing they understand is that illegals or *wetbacks* are cheap labor and they want them around as long as they stay out of sight and don't make waves."

The young man was hesitant and said, "I'm not too sure I understand all the implications of what you're telling me. However, I do understand that I was put through a wringer. And I also understand that what I went through was insignificant compared with what others go through who get caught in this mess. So if I can be of some help to modify the system, I'd like to help."

"Great. I can assure you two things; before this is over you'll wind up hating us and especially me. Secondly, you'll walk taller when you walk down the streets of our cities." The director went to the young man and shook his hand and gave him a hug. She handed him a loose leaf notebook, "First let's start with some reading material. We've tried to boil down the essential elements of this campaign in these position papers. Please read them carefully. Also mark them up, ask questions, but get the concepts down. More importantly, believe in them, because if you don't believe in what you're doing, the whole effort will be futile." She paused then smiled at him and said, "Especially when things get tough; you'll wonder why the hell you got involved with us."

Instead of going home, Larry stopped at a coffee shop, bought some tea and sat in a corner and opened the notebook. The binder had four sections. The first had a list of names, addresses and phone numbers of the organization's team. Each name also had one or two sentences about what they did. The second section had several position papers and arguments supporting the organization's position. The third section had a list of opponents and several articles supporting their oppositions. It also identified individuals nationally and locally who would be likely opponents. It also had a fourth section that had blank pages. The first page of this section had this simple note: *Records are paramount. Write down brief notes of any conversations, agreements, observations, dates and places regarding these efforts. Be mindful, these notes are your own, but could become public.* Larry read and reread this statement and after thinking about it wrote in the journal a brief description of the meeting with Llamas.

Two days later, early in the morning, Larry came to the office for his first meeting. There were three other people in the room. They did not introduce themselves. One was an older man who was already sweating—even though the room was cool. The other two were much younger women and were very attractive. The apparent leader was a tall woman; she wore jeans and a tight T-shirt which accentuated her well developed breasts. She looked at Larry with distain and said, "Alright buddy, why are you looking at my tits. My breasts are not for you to stare at or to even dream about, do you understand me?"

Surprised, Larry's eyes blinked several times. He had a slight grin on his face, yet he said nothing. "Okay friend, the first thing we're going to do is wipe that shit-eating grin off your face. You think this is funny? Do you think we're just here for your entertainment?" The woman continued in that vein for several minutes. Her comments became more degrading and crass. Yet Larry's sole reaction was to blink his eyes. Finally she said, "I understand you don't even know who your parents are; that makes you some kind of a bastard doesn't it?"

Larry blinked more rapidly and then finally said, "You know…I didn't catch your name, mine is Larry Franco and it's my pleasure to meet all of you." Although his voice and comportment sounded and looked normal there was enough strain to be noticeable. He also noticed that his undershirt was soaked and was stuck to his skin and he assumed that his face was flush. The verbal tirade continued all morning. The comments from the ladies became even more pointed, personal and vulgar. It wasn't that Larry hadn't heard these comments and obscenities before, it was that he had never heard them from women, especially from these very attractive and well rehearsed ladies. Finally he asked, "What are the chances of getting a glass of water?"

Finally the leader smiled, "Okay, I think we can all use a break. Larry, let me introduce myself, I'm Alix Raya with the Foundation out of DC. I'd like to say I'm sorry for our methods, but I think you'll understand that we don't have much time and this is a game of hardball. It's not for the fainthearted, that's for damn sure."

Larry still had the faint smile on his face, "I'm glad to meet you…I think. Also, I think I understand your methods although they're kind of tough. I must admit you flustered me."

"Usually by now people expect an apology for our methods, but you won't get one from me. My chore is to make you so tough that you'll be able to walk on fire bare foot. And let me tell you, before this is over you'll be wondering why in the hell you got involved with us. And the only reward for you, and for all of us, is justice. That is justice for people that come here who just want to work." She paused for a second, referred to a binder on the table, "Now tell me about your girl friends, Virginia Gallo and Cipri Mendez?"

Again Larry was startled, "What do you mean *my* girlfriends?" He paused for a few seconds, "I've known Ginny since grade school and we're good friends. And Cipri is my cousin, who lives in Arizona. What do they have to do with all of this?"

Alix smiled and said, "Most likely they'll have nothing to do with the campaign. On the other hand, if I'm asking about them, you can be damn sure the boys on the other side will be asking too—especially if our campaign is successful and they get desperate. I can assure you they'll come out one way or another. Now tell me about Cipri?"

"There's not much to tell. She's my cousin in a way, a distant cousin. She lives in Arizona and I just met her and her family a few months ago. I also lived with them for a while."

"That's not what we hear. We're told you two became an item and became more than just good friends."

"I'm not too sure what you heard, but she's my cousin and I guess we became good friends…it never occurred to me that she could be my girl friend. As I said, she's my cousin."

"Well let me tell you, cousin or no cousin, she's on our radar screen. You can bet if I know about her others will find out about her as well." For the first time Alix smiled, "And by the way, where I come from, third cousins are fair game…keeping it in the family as they say."

Larry was flustered as he contemplated what Alix was insinuating. It was such an odd thought that it had not registered in his mind. Yet when the idea was brought up by Alix, it somehow seemed plausible and he wondered about it. He said nothing and continued to smile as a warm feeling developed in him. Then he said, "I don't know why anyone would want to drag the girls into this, but if they do, shouldn't we at least warn them of the possibility?"

"Good idea, we'll let you do that. If they have any questions let me know and I'll talk to them if needed."

Chapter 12

For two days Larry pondered the comments that Alix had made. He was perplexed. The idea that he might have feelings for his cousin disturbed him and yet he warmed up to the idea the more he thought of it. What actually made him uncomfortable was, since his return, he had reconnected with Ginny. In a sense he liked both girls and it was an awkward feeling. Somehow Luna Martinez's name came to mind and it occurred to him that he would like to discuss this dilemma with her if the opportunity ever arose.

The meetings with Alix and other staff members continued for several days. The days were unreal in a sense. First there were relentless attacks from the three people. When one got tired and needed a break the other took over, but there was no break for Larry. Yet when they broke for lunch or for the day they chatted and drank a few beers. These later sessions were welcomed, but they were also confusing. One moment he hated them and the next minute they were discussing the latest movie or baseball game and tossing empty beer cans into the trashcan.

"So what have you heard from your long, lost cousin? You know you need to invite her for a visit. In a sense it might be a good idea if we met her and gave her a brief overview of what's going on." Alix opened another beer and took a deep drink.

"Good lord, you guys would scare the shit out of her and she might never speak to me again." The two beers made Larry speak more freely as he chuckled.

In a more serious tone Alix said, "Would it make a difference in your life if she never spoke to you again Larry?"

"Of course, after all, she is my cousin. And I like her very much. It's okay to like your cousin isn't it?"

"Of course, but seriously Larry, it would be a good idea if you could get her to come out here for a visit. It would be interesting for her I'm sure, but also to be fair with her she needs to know what could happen. You don't want some damn idiot to catch her flatfooted somewhere where she could be embarrassed or humiliated. Then you can be sure she would never talk to you again. Think about it."

Somehow the beer and Alix's tone made him look at her more closely and he saw that she was serious, "I guess you're right. Let me talk to my parents. Maybe we can invite her for a visit…"

"I think that's a wonderful idea, honey. Why don't we wait until your dad comes home this evening and we can call Johnny and see what he thinks. We also need to consider your great grandmother. If things get really weird, we at least should make them aware of it. I would hate to have her dragged into this issue."

That evening Larry called his family in Arizona and spoke to Cipri who answered the phone. After he explained briefly what the call was about he said, "Dad wants to talk to Uncle Johnny."

After just a few minutes, Tom hung up. He turned to Licha and Larry and said, "Johnny seemed a little concerned, but apparently he's aware of the importance of immigration that he supports the efforts, but he wants to know as much as he can so he and the family don't get bushwhacked. He said he'd make arrangements for Cipri to come for a visit in a few days. He'll let us know. By the way Larry, he gave me this phone number for a Luna Martinez, Cipri said you might need it. I suppose you know what it means."

"Thanks Dad." Larry looked at the number for a long time. That evening he called Luna, "Hi Luna, this is Larry Franco calling. How are things on the Res?"

"Hi Larry. Just got off the phone with Cipri and she said you might be calling. She told me she was going to visit you all in California in the next couple of days. She mentioned something about the immigration program you're involved in. She wasn't too sure what it was all about. Frankly, she sounded confused."

"Hell, I'm not surprised; I'm confused. I've been thinking about this immigration situation from the day I was picked up by the Border Patrol. Then mom got involved with a reform group and then somehow the play came down to me. They tell me it could be dicey and they've been putting me through some intensive conditioning program so we don't get caught with our pants down. Then it was decided that if they, the opposition, gets down and dirty they might take some verbal potshots at my family and friends, so we need to bring them up to speed so they can anticipate any possible backlash. I'm sorry that other folks might be dragged in, but as I understand it, this is the reality of life."

Luna laughed, "Well Larry, this is what happens with family; you get dragged in whether you want to or not. I'm not too sure what this is all about, but if Cipri and her family can get dragged in, it's a good thing that they at least should be forewarned." She paused, "But what about you Larry. How are you coping? This has got to be a new venture for you; especially after your recent episode with the Border Patrol and the discovery of your new family."

Larry laughed and said, "You know I didn't know what a dull, un-eventful life I led before all this. I mean, my biggest concern used to be what shirt I was going to wear to school or where Ginny and I would eat or what movie to watch. Now I worry that what I do in California could possibly hurt my great grandmother who, until a few months ago, I didn't even know existed!"

"Welcome to the real world Larry." Luna was writing a few notes as she spoke, "At least you have the luxury of thinking and planning your moves rather than just having to react to the unexpected. But let me caution you, suddenly you'll be faced with the unexpected, so plan for that as well. Now let me ask you a personal question; how do you feel about Cipri? As you know, she's a good friend of mine and I would hate to have her get hurt."

Larry paused, "You're the second person that has asked me a similar question. I just met my cousin. She's a nice girl and I like her. What's more, this person implied that there was more going on than she just being my cousin."

"I don't know who hinted at something going on, but let me tell you, anyone who sees you two together would come to a similar conclusion.

Let me ask you a question, if you met Cipri in school for the first time and she was not a relative, would you be interested in her?"

"Of course, she's a neat person. She's smart, she's funny and she's pretty; of course I'd be interested in her." Larry lowered his voice as he uttered the last comment as if he didn't want anyone else to hear him.

"Well just remember she's your third cousin and where I come from that's not an impediment for not having a relationship. On the other hand, if you have no interest in her, I would caution you to be careful and not lead her on. Because, if I know her at all, she too might get attached unknowingly…and perhaps she may very well have already formed an attachment, if you know what I mean."

Larry hung up the phone, but he continued to look at the instrument as if it might continue to communicate with him. Finally he called his mother, "Mom, will Cipri stay in the guest room?"

Lucinda was leafing through a file when Alix walked into her office, she glanced up and smiled at her friend, "Alix, how's it going gal; any news to report? How's our boy doing? You haven't ground him down to a pulp have you? We need to have something left of him so we can put him out in the field." The questions were asked in rapid fire without waiting for an answer.

Alix sat without being asked. She grabbed a candy from a dish and unwrapped it methodically and put it in her mouth and, with the candy in her mouth, she said, "Actually, I'm impressed with the kid; he's tough. It's hard to tell when we're getting under his skin. His only reaction when he's getting pissed is that he gets a slight smile, but he's good. In a couple of more weeks we can throw him to the wolves and he'll be okay, he'll handle himself well."

"What about his girl friend, the one from Arizona?"

"I just met her last evening. She seems like a nice girl. She doesn't know it, but she's in love with the kid. Everyone else seems to know it, but her. Shit, I don't blame her, the kid's good looking."

"What about Larry, how does he feel about her?"

As I said, he's harder to read, but if I were a betting girl, I would say he too has feelings for her. All he has to do is open his eyes and he too will see it."

"She won't complicate matters will she?" The tall woman went over to the file and rustled through it and pulled out a paper. "What about all his problems with the immigration folks, is all that taken care of?"

"Not quite, but according to one of my friends in the department, they have a verbal agreement. It's in the process of being documented and getting final approval from the boys in DC. Basically, as I understand it, it's a letter of apology plus a financial amount for his future educational expenses. He will then agree to halt any legal action and not seek additional compensation from the department. It's a typical deal they agree to when they screw up."

"When will it be concluded? And does it say anything about him not taking part in the kind of effort we want him to undertake?

Alix took a pen from the desk and wrote a note to herself. "I don't think so, but I'll check to make sure. We can't have something like that screw things up at this time. We've already spent too much time and as I said, the kid is good. We got a good one and we need to hang on to him. What about his girl friend, could she screw things up?"

"Since she's here from Arizona, touch base with her. We need to make sure we talk to her and check her out. She could be an important piece of the puzzle. Can you make sure you talk to her?"

"Okay." Alix wrote a note to herself and put the paper into her shirt pocket. "I'll check her out in more detail."

Lucinda walked around her desk and asked, "Alix, suppose we were on the other side and Larry was the poster boy. How would you attack him; what are his vulnerable points?"

"Actually, I've thought of that quite a bit. She looked at some 3 by 5 card and said, "If I were the other guy, I would first tackle him on the immigration arrest. Although, INS is making an apology, they'll be reluctant to reveal the deal they made with him, especially about the money. The rumor mill will go crazy over that. Secondly, his mysterious birth and death of his parents and the relationship with his father/uncle is murky enough to entice the conspiracy junkies. Then thirdly, the kid has a relationship with his pretty girl cousin that he hasn't yet acknowledged, and if someone were to drag her in, or his new-found family, he would get pissed for sure."

"Hmmm, I agree with you. So our efforts will be to prevent that information from getting out, but knowing damn well it will get out. Then we need to make sure that Larry is aware and prepared for that eventuality. Also, since the girl is going to be out here, let's get her feet wet so if she does get attacked, she's prepared."

"I agree with you. It just happens that Larry has agreed to meet with her in the next couple of days. So I'll set up a brief orientation for her so she can get an idea of what's going on without giving her a heart attack." Alix took another candy and ate it.

Chapter 13

Larry and Cipri walked into Alix's office. Larry said, "Alix, this is my cousin, Cipri Mendez from Jerome, Arizona. She and her parents are here for a visit."

"Cipri, it's nice to meet you. Thanks for coming to our office; it gives us a chance to chat and to let you know what we do here. Please sit down." Alix noticed that the young couple sat on a large couch, yet they sat next to each other, almost touching. She smiled and continued, "We're a small organization that feels that our immigration policies over the last three or four decades are disasters. We have, people tell us, some 10 to 12 million people in the country that are here illegally. Over time some have brought or created families and most are living underground. Yet we all grudgingly acknowledge them and in fact we need those of work age. The work they do in most cases is menial, but important. For example, we all like to eat and as you can tell by our girth as a nation we all eat too well. These workers are instrumental, if not necessary, to our farm output. Similar things can be said of other similar industries. So we need them, we hire them, we eat the product of their efforts and yet we don't want them here. It makes little sense; it's a contradiction of immense proportions. Our group wants to remedy that by having some common sense reform that would permit the work being done legally and morally. Basically our idea is simple. The key to it is jobs. And the key to the jobs are the owner, CEOs and individuals who hire people. The principal focus of our efforts is to pass a law that would make it illegal to hire any undocumented person; a law with teeth. And the teeth would be a $1000 fine and six months in jail for anyone who hires a person. There are other details, but none is our thrust. Now we know this would cause chaos, but at the same time we would permit employers to contract people from abroad so they can perform the work needed legally. We know this is a radical solution to the problem, but once you focus on the essence of the problem…the job; then the answer is easy. To effectively control it one has to focus on the individual who controls the job…and that person is the CEO, the owner or the housewife who gives the job."

Cipri stirred and said, "There's a young man who works in our kitchen who I know is illegal, but the owner of the hotel lives in Phoenix and hardly ever comes to Jerome; he lets the local manager do all the hiring. How can you put him in jail if he has nothing to do with the actual hiring?"

The CEO is the ultimate person responsible, they set the policies and only when he's on the hot seat will the policy change. It's human nature, it's survival, it's self preservation, it's cover your own ass, it's that simple."

Cipri looked at Alix and then at Larry. "Wow, it sounds simple, but my guess is the CEOs of the world are the most powerful folks around and they're not going to go to jail without a fight, but that's just my thinking. So what does all this have to do with Larry and me?"

"That's simple, Cipri. Any campaign of this magnitude is tough when it's just a concept or an idea. It's even worse when most of the voters have never given this issue a second thought. However, if we give the campaign a face, a credible story or something they can hang their hat on, an emotional attachment if you will, then we have something people can relate to."

"There will be opposition I suppose. Won't they try to mar or destroy that face?"

"Probably, that's what I would do if I were directing the opposition group. And that's what we've been doing here; preparing Larry to be able to withstand and to counteract such an effort. And we'd like to provide some training for you if you get involved."

Cipri looked at Larry and then at Alix, her eyes narrowed and focused on Larry, "Is this what you've been doing? Is this what my parents were trying to tell me on the way here? Was your stay in Jerome so dull and uninteresting that you jumped into a middle of a firestorm as soon as you left?"

Larry took her hand, smiled and said, "Cipri, all my life I've been like most people and didn't give a shit about immigration. In fact, it never entered my mind one way or another. So when I was caught up, it was a shock to me—personally. Then I spent those few days in prison and I saw people, flesh and blood, just like me who were there, forgotten just because they wanted a job and a better life. While in your little town and meeting all my new family, it occurred to me that my life was connected to many other people. In a sense, I realized that I was also connected to those poor bastards in prison. So can I help them? Hell I don't know, but I do know that I should at least try. Frankly, I get the feeling that it will be a monumentally futile effort, but I just can't close my eyes. Yet I'm sorry that my new family, and especially you, could be dragged into it."

Cipri was thoughtful and unconsciously took several deep breaths. "I know I tend to be a skeptic; some people would even call me shallow. I guess that's my nature, but I want you both to know, especially you Larry, that running through my blood, and yours as well, is the toughness of people who lived and prevailed in a harsh land—a land that winnowed the weak and selected those who lived to pass on the *'tenacity gene'* to us. Frankly, my first reaction is to go home to my little world, but I also see the importance of lending a hand to those who struggle. I'm putting you both on notice. If I think you're just using me, or bullshitting me, you'll find out I'm not a soft, little girl from the hills." As she said this she was looking directly at Alix until she acknowledged her comments.

For the next several days Larry and Cipri were subjected to various scenarios that might come up. Not only did they both respond to the subject matter, but it was obvious that the two young people were responding to each other and for each other. It was apparent to Alix and the rest of the team, even though it was probably not obvious to the young couple. Or at least they were unwilling to acknowledge it just yet.

Chapter 14

"GOD DAM IT MAX, what do you mean you're not going to help us oppose this legislation. Don't you understand they want to put your sorry ass in jail?"

Maxwell Martin carefully lifted the martini glass to his lips and tasted his favorite spirit-gin. Drinking cold martinis after a round of golf was his reward after his usual frustrating time on the links. He was intent on enjoying his drink even though he had been badgered all afternoon by his good friends. The four men had been friends for years and had settled many issues on the greens as well as later in the bar of the country club. The usual social lubricant that made difficulties ease and resolvable was gin. He was intent at least to enjoy his first drink. He paused and then took a second sip and then looked at his companions. He smiled, raised his glass to them and said, "Well boys, I really didn't have any choice when Mel explained the situation to me. And you guys know her, when the good woman makes up our mind, it's made up."

"Oh come on, Melina must know we could all be behind bars. Hell, even she could do time if this were to go through." Jim Riley took a drink of his beer and continued, "Listen, I read that there are 10 to 12 million illegals in the country. Most of them are working for someone—someone like us. Shit, the jails would be full. Hell, the whole country, including most of the politicians, would be behind bars."

"I think that's just the point; if so many good citizens are involved, and if we had a legitimate way of getting the workers we need legally, then everyone would cooperate," Max said. The martini tasted even better by the third taste. He ate the olive.

"You mean if we don't hire illegals, but we can get the work done with workers who are permitted to be in the country legally, we would all cooperate?" asked his friend.

"That's essentially the trade off. We no longer hire those not here legally, but then we're provided a method of obtaining guest workers legitimately. It has to be both, otherwise it won't work, and I sure as hell wouldn't be part of the effort."

"What of the unions, they're against a guest worker program, hell they killed the last one in the mid 60s."

"That's true, but as I hear it, they're also being realistic. The unions have found out they have little chance of organizing an illegal workforce. However, if these new people are permitted to come in and the unions can convince them to join; so be it. In a sense, the unions have a better shot at them than they have at present." Max finished his drink, smiled and motioned to the bartender for another round.

"That might mean we'd have a unionized workforce for God's sake!"

"Possibly, but if we play our cards right, it can be avoided. They would be just like any other workforce. And frankly, the unions have not had much success recently, so we'd just have to take our chances with them. Frankly, if I could have a steady, legal, reliable workforce, unions would be the least of my problems."

"What if the eventual legislation has the jail part, but no legal workers, what would happen then?"

Max laughed, "First we'd lose many of our crops, lawns wouldn't be cut and dishes wouldn't be washed. The public outcry would be so loud that things would be rectified quickly. However, I've been assured that the new legislation would only pass if a little, if not most, of what the respective factions want and need were included in a comprehensive compromise. Finally, if food supplies diminish, prices increase and if there's a chance people could go hungry, then it's felt a solution would be found in a hurry."

"Good Lord, that sounds complicated, does anyone think the boys and girls in Washington are capable of a compromise? Recent actions would give us little hope."

Max took another sip of his new drink, "That's the fly in the ointment; we just need to get the boys in Washington off their dead asses. And we can do that...because in the final analysis we control the money for their election campaigns. So let's use that leverage."

Melina was putting flowers in a vase when Max walked in, "Hello honey, how was your game?"

Max walked over behind his wife, kissed her on the neck and reached around and grabbed both breasts. She smiled and said, "Did you have more than one martini?"

"I confess, I had two and I think I'll have another one. Can I get you one?"

Melina Maxwell giggled, she knew her husband well; "Oh my, so early in the afternoon...I think I will join you dear..."

Chapter 15

LARRY AND CIPRI were early for their afternoon session. They sat outside on a street bench and for awhile just watched cars drive by. "Grandma called this morning and she said she missed us, she especially said she missed you. She also said she wants us to return as soon as we can. I told her what you were doing and she said she would pray for a successful venture."

"Actually I miss her too. In fact, I miss the little town of Jerome. I like the quiet and the peace and the tranquility. Even though I know that Alix is just doing her job, I get the sense that she enjoys putting us through the paces. She seems to be focusing on you in the last couple of sessions. How are you doing with all the attention?" Larry said as he reached over and tentatively touched her hand. She in turn took his hand and squeezed it.

"Don't worry about me Larry, as I told them, I can take care of myself. You're fortunate you've never seen me really pissed off; it's not a pretty sight."

"What's happened in your life that can get you so stirred up?" he asked.

"Well you know some people, and especially kids, can be mean. Some people don't like Mexicans, and some don't like Indians, and then some people don't like Mexicans who have Indian blood in the mix. Then throw in a little bit of Irish; then you get it from all sides. Hell, some Indians, Mexicans, rednecks, even blacks don't like us *mestizos*. So like I said, we get it from all sides, but you know I'm proud of my heritage; proud of all my ancestors. I believe I get strength from that whole mix. Luna tells me that it's the mixture that provides the resilience to contend with adverse forces. Some folks call it hybridization. I call it kneading and blending. It's very much like cooking. Think about it; a bread, a soup or a cake made of just one ingredient is bland, awful tasting and not nutritional, but a soup with meats, bones, vegetables, salt and peppers can be fantastic, nourishing and life sustaining. That's how I look at my life; as a hearty, healthy soup."

Larry smiled and said, "What can be said of a third cousins mix?"

"Third cousins can make a richer, savory soup!"

Alix looked at her two charges and smiled. They both were quick and didn't get rattled easily; both qualities they would need if the campaign evolved as expected. She was curious how Larry would react to her latest request. She had gone to the local Goodwill Store and purchased several shirts and jeans for Larry. Larry's present wardrobe was not extra ordinary, but it was neat and preppy. She purposely bought some old shirts that had odd patterns and a size larger than what he wore. She mentioned this as she put the large plastic bag at his feet, as their discussion began. He eyed the bag, but said nothing.

At a break that didn't prevent Cipri from saying, "Good Lord, the woman has gone too far. She now wants to dress you! Is all this really necessary?"

Alix laughed as she overheard the comment and said, "'Well *that woman* doesn't want to dress him, but consider this a costume. If you go to a play or a movie you'll see characters dressed in appropriate costumes for the period or time of the action. Frankly, this effort is the same as such a performance. The dress needs to complement the story we want to tell, otherwise it becomes less believable and our efforts get watered down."

Cipri looked at Alix and laughed, "It's a good thing I already buy many of my outfits at Goodwill or you'd be dressing me too."

Alix joined in the laugh, "Actually, we considered you as well, but you're right, we don't have to do much with your wardrobe, and we really don't think the news people will check you out. However, I am sure that sooner or later some enterprising reporter will follow leads and that eventually they'll track you down to Jerome. So we appreciate your participation and preparation here so you won't get blindsided. In fact, you can help us out. When you return home, you can give your family a mini lesson on what you learned here so they won't be caught off guard either."

That night Larry and Cipri went to the movies. Cipri and her family were leaving early in the morning. After the movies they bought a coke at a drive-in. They stayed in the car before they went inside and just talked. "I just want to say I enjoyed the last few days here. I even enjoyed the meetings with Alix. She can be an abrasive bitch, but I suppose that's her job. And she does the bitch bit well."

Larry was quiet for a long time; finally he said, "I want to thank you for being here. All this preparation can be overwhelming, but with you here it's been almost fun. I wish I could go back; especially to see the old woman. I've learned so much from her and I get the sense there's much more to learn. I miss her." Larry paused then continued, "And I'll miss you."

Cipri leaned over and kissed him on the cheek and then slowly she cupped his face in both of her hands and kissed him, long and tenderly. She pulled back several inches as if she were seeing him for the first time and then she kissed him again. "And I'll miss you too."

Larry took a deep breath, "You know, ever since the Border Patrol picked me up, my life has been in a turmoil. First there was the arrest, then the prison, then finding out that my parents are not my birth parents, then finding a complete new family I never knew anything about, and then finding you...my cousin. Frankly, I'm not too sure what's going on. And on top of that, it seems I've become the poster boy for immigration reform. Shit, talk about a hectic several months, but I must confess, some of the things that have happened I like very much."

"Hectic, I agree with you that it's been hectic, but I also wonder if there's some kind of a plan to all this. Luna would burn some sage on her meditation rock and look into the smoke and see a pattern."

Larry then kissed her again, "When you get back, go to see Luna and ask her to put an extra pinch of sage in for me; then call me. In fact, I'd like it very much if you call me every day if you can."

"Count on the pinch and on the calls..."

Chapter 16

MAX WALKED INTO THE MUPU GRILL, the local farmer hangout, and greeted his neighbor, Joe Miller. Miller was a long time friend and fellow farmer. Their parents were also good friends and both families were instrumental in developing various farming operations in the county. Miller reached out and shook hands, "Well Max, how're things going with you and Mel, we haven't seen much of you two lately."

"We've been fine, just a little more hectic than I'd like it. You know Melina, between the museums and the hospital, she's busy and always seems to drag me in, but thank God, we've been fine. What's going on with you guys?"

"We're fine, but we are concerned about all this talk about immigration reform. It's upsetting some of the people working for us and frankly it's kind of upsetting us. I was shocked to learn that you favor this new law that's being proposed."

"Well I agree with you Joe, life has been hectic and there's been plenty of annoyance with the field labor. As you know it's been several years since labor contractors took over most of our field workers. In all honestly, for many years a good percentage of workers were here illegally. No one seemed to be concerned about it and everything was quiet for years. Now the Border Patrol and unions apparently want to put a kink in the present system. The results are that we're having a labor shortage; something we haven't had for ages."

Joe became excited, "That's just it, now they want to put us in jail if we're caught using illegal labor. Hell, I really don't directly employ any workers except for my supervisors and equipment operators. All the field workers work for Guillermo's Farm Labor Service. Hell, I hardly ever see them. He sends me a bill on Monday and I send him a check on Friday. It's been that way for several years now. If there are illegals in my fields, it's Guillermo's problem; not mine."

"I understand your frustration Joe. Shit, I have a similar arrangement with my guy. It's worked well and it just relieves me of one more headache. Labor issues are one thing I don't have to worry about. That is until now." Max paused and studied his friend for a few minutes and it occurred to him that perhaps they were getting old. "The problem is that my labor contractor was my foreman for many years and I encouraged him and helped him get his contractor's license. On top of that, he works almost exclusively for me. Hell, he still lives in one of my houses. The majority of his workers worked for me directly in the past and in a sense they still do, but now it's indirectly through my contractor. The fact is that they're the same workers, the same foreman, the same work and as I said, some of the workers still live in our houses."

"Listen Max, I understand the system and even why we all went to contractors. It's one sure way of avoiding unions and ultimately we found out it's even cheaper in the long run. And as you say, we no longer have a labor headache. In a way, it's no different than the relationship we have with other folks who provide us other services like, pesticide applications or an electrician or plumber for that matter."

"I understand the theory and principle behind the contractors and it was a good idea, but now it may come back to bite us in the ass. Good lord, it was one of my attorneys who came up with the idea as a way to isolate us from the unions and other governmental rules and regulations."

"The problem that faces us is now simple; if we hire a labor contractor, he in turns hires illegal labor, but it's you and me who go to the pokie. What kind of deal is that, it makes no sense..."

"I agree, it makes no sense, unless they provide a mechanism for us to obtain seasonal, labor legally through this new law. If they don't, it won't work."

Max took a drink of his coffee as he studied his friend. Ventura County's mild weather, its proximity to the Los Angeles metropolitan area made it ideal to grow row crops and several tree crops. The down side was that all these crops required lots of hand labor for planting and harvesting. Over time, Max and the farming community developed this successful industry with new, modern farming methods, except for the need of labor. The few efforts of mechanization usually proved to be inefficient or too expensive. So the fallback was always on the backs of farm workers, who were mostly from Mexico. And since the elimination of Public Law 78 that allowed the Bracero Program, a large percentage of the workforce was still from Mexico except they crossed the border and worked in the fields illegally. In the short term Max saw no alternative unless the crops were changed dramatically or labor was admitted legally.

"Listen Max, I understand that it is a bitter pill that we may have to swallow, but I really don't trust the people who are working on this. My concern is that if there's a section that permits jail time, some liberal, radical SOBs will find a way to apply it to us. It's just too dangerous and too much temptation to those who don't like us." Miller smiled sadly as he got up, "Have a good day Max, I look forward to seeing you behind bars one of these days."

Max waved at his friend and wondered about the future, got up and paid for his breakfast.

Chapter 17

W HEN LARRY ENTERED THE BUILDING for his session with Alix and her group, he felt dejected. He had an empty feeling. Cipri and her family had left early in the morning and he felt a void in his chest. Also, he knew that today was to be his last day with Alix. And even though the time with Alix had been tense and unpleasant at times, she too was leaving him. On top of everything else, he knew that if her job was finished, that meant that his time to go to the front lines was coming. He looked forward to this new experience, but still there was some trepidation in his outlook. He thought about his past meeting with Luna and wished he could share some sage smoke to ease his doubts. His mother had washed the clothes that Alix had bought at Goodwill and he wore them for his last meeting. Even though they were somewhat unsightly and had a rumpled look, they felt comfortable in a strange sort of a way. They were loose, soft and comfortable and somehow his personality seemed to reflect his new look. As he walked into Alix's office, he checked his reflection in her office window and took a deep breath. "Good morning, I understand this may be our last meeting. What's your next assignment?"

Alix looked up and studied her new creation. She smiled to herself. She smiled at the idea that he was her creation. She saw a young man who appeared to be comfortable in his old clothes and more importantly, comfortable in his own skin. Even though the shirt was a size too big, she could see or rather feel his inner strength. She walked up to him and straightened his collar, looked at him closely; then she gathered him in her arms and gave him a long, tender hug. "I've always like the Mexican *abrazo,* it communicates more than a simple handshake. Did you know that the handshake was just a way to show the person you were approaching that you had no weapon in your hand? An *abrazo,* opens your arms and body to the person, in a sense, we become one. There's a vulnerability to it that I like."

Larry smiled and said, "I like it too," as he returned the hug and felt her warm body. "So tell me, now what? Do you know what the next phase is? Mom asked me and I'm not too sure what to tell her if anything at this time."

"I really don't know the details, but Lucinda has been working out a series of events over the next few days to get your feet wet as it were. All she wanted to know from me was if I thought you were ready. And I told her you were. She'll be over in a couple of hours to let us know. In the meantime, I thought we'd just review a couple of things. Also now would be the time to ask any questions you might have."

Larry considered for a few moments and said, "Actually, I feel pretty good about all the things we've covered over the last several weeks...except one."

"And what's that?"

"It's about my parents; My mom and dad and my mother and father. You must admit that my birth, the death of my parents and being raised by mom and dad is strange to say the least. I know if I wanted to make an issue about someone with that kind of an odd background it would make for good fodder. I just wonder what will happen if someone takes a shot at my parents? My real concern is my reaction about my real parents, who I never knew. Can I remain silent about someone I never knew, a couple who just a few months ago I never knew even existed? Two strange people who I met only in a faded photo and via a whole new family I never knew even existed?"

Alix chuckled and said, "Well young man, I must admit you do have a strange beginning. It's certainly not the thing we run into on a daily basis. The thing you have to remember is the memory of your parents, a sacred mystery that you have to delve into more to find out about them as you go along in life. For example, just think, you wouldn't have met your cousin Cipri and as you say, a whole new family, if it hadn't been for that tragic accident many years ago. And what can we say about your mom and dad who took you in as truly their own son without asking a question. It wasn't even a question about adoption because in their own mind, you were indeed their real son, apparently without a doubt. That my good friend is true love and that's what will pull you through, even when things get tough…and they will get tough, I can assure you of that!"

Lucinda Llamas walked in, opened a file and looked at Larry, checking out his new look. She walked all around him and studied him. "Great look; one thing I would suggest is that you let your hair grow. I noticed that you always have neat, short hair. You probably go to a barber frequently. I suggest you miss a couple of appointments and get a shaggier look."

Larry began to laugh, "That's great! One thing Dad has always had a thing about is short hair. You'll notice he has short hair, that's always neat and well cared for. He'll have a fit when he sees me. First thing he'll want to do is take me by the hand to visit his barber. If you ran into him you might do me a favor and let him know that the hair and clothes is part of the new look." He laughed and continued, "Shit, he'll have a conniption!"

Lucinda laughed too, "I'll make a point of running into him one of these days and clue him in. I may even suggest that he let his hair grow a little longer too."

"Good luck; that'll be the day. Just try to remember what he says so you can let me know." The thought of his dad with long hair lifted his gloom.

Lucinda's eyes danced at the two young people in front of her. She especially focused on Larry who was to be the key element in the campaign to reform the immigration laws of the country. It was a heavy burden to put on such a young man. That's why she had enlisted Alix Raya, a foremost trainer and perceptive person in this arena. She and Alix had agreed that Alix would put pressure on the young man to try to make him crack. Alix said, "I did my best to put a dent in Larry and he withstood all I could give. His only reaction when he gets tense or pissed off is that he gets a slight, crooked smile on his face and becomes very quiet."

"Good, I'll keep that in mind, but what are his weak points? What will our opponents focus on?"

"Actually, he pointed that out to me and I agree. He has this odd history, being born of a young couple who died a couple days later in a tragic accident and then being adopted and raised by his aunt and uncle. He was not legally adopted until recently. He was born in a private home. Not so strange in itself, but enough for somehow the Border Patrol to pick him up; not only once, but twice. He's been in prison for a few days. And even though the Border Patrol folks have apologized in writing and even made a monetary settlement, he's still been in a prison, right or wrong. With enough smoke and half truths that our opponents will use, it will be enough to create doubt. That's what they will want to do; create doubt and confusion. And to be honest, it will work to a certain extent. That's why we need to be alert to support him. And, of course, he has to have the balls to withstand the blows."

"Does he have the balls?"

"I think he does, especially if we can support him physically and psychologically. And a key to this support will be his distant cousin that he just met. They've become very close, closer than either one of them would dare to admit. So anyone making an issue of Cipri could affect him. We need to do some work with her so she doesn't become a distraction."

"What are you suggesting, Alix?"

"Well, on my way back to Chicago, I'd like to stop over in Phoenix and take a drive to Jerome and visit with Cipri and her family; get to know them. Just to let them know we care for them. So they won't get blindsided. And make them aware they can call us immediately if something goes awry. In fact, there's a medicine woman they told me about that I'd like to also meet." Then Alix laughed, "As I said, I'd like to talk to this Luna Martinez, she sounds like an interesting gal. And in a way I think we're in a similar business."

"Alix, you have a weird sense of humor, but have a good trip. You'll enjoy that part of country this time of the year. Just keep in touch if there's anything of significance we need to know about."

Two days later Alix called Cipri from the Phoenix airport; to tell her she would be in town for a couple of days and wanted her to set up a meeting with Luna Martinez. "I was so fascinated when I overheard you talk about her; I just wanted to meet her. Also, you told me you work at the local hotel, can you get me a room? I should be there later this afternoon."

Cipri was surprised to hear from Alix so soon. In fact, she was astonished; she never expected to hear from the bossy woman again. It was not that she didn't like her; it was just that she had never met a woman with such a strong personality. And she was somehow intimidated by her. Now she was coming for a visit and wanted a place to stay. When she got home from Santa Paula, she sat down with her grandmother and related all that had happened during her visit. Grandmother was very interested and asked many questions; especially as they related to Larry. When Cipri mentioned to her grandmother that the woman was coming for a visit she said, "Of course, she will not stay at the hotel. She'll stay here with us. In fact, she can stay in Larry's room. That should be fair. If it's good enough for my great grandson, it's good enough for her. Besides, I need to get to know her to make sure she's not taking advantage of anyone in my family. So, she'll stay here, you'll see to that." The old woman's voice left no doubt what she wanted done.

Cipri's first reaction to her namesake was to object. She wasn't too sure if she wanted that woman to be in her home, with her family. Yet after some time, she realized what her grandmother was doing and besides, there was no arguing with the old woman. She wanted to know this woman in some depth and the best way was to have her close; even if it was for only a few days. Later in the day she called Luna. "Luna, I have a favor to ask you. This lady, Alix Raya from Chicago, is coming by for a couple of days and she'd like to meet you. She's the person sent out to put Larry through the wringer before they throw him to the wolves."

"Sounds like an interesting gal. I look forward to meeting her. In fact, for the next several afternoons I'll be free, but call me to make sure I'm home." Then she paused for several seconds, "Do you think I should get an additional supply of sage?"

"The way I see it, you better get a bale of the stuff, so we can smoke this big city gal out. She's not here by accident. I mean, not too many people come by just to say hello to me or to see you. They must be concerned about something." As Cipri made these comments to her friend, her mind began to conjure up various scenarios for what she now considered might be the reason for this mystery visit.

Luna heard the doubt in the young woman's voice, "Now Cipri, don't start getting all riled up. It may be that's she's heard of my famous sage rock and wanted to get cleansed. One can get pretty contaminated living in the big city."

"That's for damn sure…Actually, I rather liked her. I wasn't too sure I liked what she was putting Larry through. Sometimes she was brutal. Finally it occurred to me, it was her job to make sure he had the staying power for their campaign. From what I saw, they expect a dirty time, meaning, the anti-immigration folks will tear down anyone that gets in their way. From what I hear, they've got tons of money and play hardball."

Luna listened carefully and said; "Now you're making me curious. I've never heard of such a person, but it sounds like what I do occasionally. Now listen Cipri, this sounds very much like the stories I heard from the old chiefs about the conflicts and wars in our past. The first thing they did with the young warriors was take away their women, limit their food, cleanse them in a hothouse and then they toughened them up physically and spiritually. It was not until the warriors were ready that they sent them into battle. If there's a chance you're going to die, you should have every edge you can have on your opponent. And this was how they put the edge on the young warriors. Not much different than sharpening a knife on a whetstone."

"What do you mean they took away their women? What the hell does that mean?"

"Simply, it meant there can't be any distractions when it comes to going into battle. I'm sure it's the same in this case or in any trial we get into where we need to focus intently on the goal at hand. Same thing here I suppose, they're just trying to get the boy ready to go into battle."

Cipri thought about this for a second and said, "Well, in that case, he can say goodbye to his girlfriend, she didn't impress me too much."

"Which girlfriend are you referring to?"

"Some school chum he's known for years. She seemed like a nice girl, but she wouldn't last a minute in what he's going to be involved in."

"What about his other friends, men or women, how do you think they'll react? Do you think they'll be supporting his efforts or will they be looking at this effort as a discomfort?"

"Any friends worthy of the name 'friend', have to be supportive." Cipri said looking at the phone she was holding as if she could see her friend on the other end of the line. Tiny tears formed in her eyes.

Luna could almost feel the introspection her friend was going through and she smiled to herself. "Listen Cipri, think about our little chat here and I look forward to seeing you and your friend in the next day or so."

The following day, Luna was in her yard moving some rocks when Cipri and Alix drove up. She watched the two women exit the old pickup and walk toward her. It was a curious sight; the young woman walked with her eyes on the ground. Alix, on the other hand, was looking at the far horizon with a slow, circular motion taking in all the surrounding vistas. She examined the land with military precision. She made one quick sweep of the area; then her gaze returned and took in the sight in quarter segments looking carefully. She seemed to be making mental notes. It was not until she checked out the landscape that she focused on Luna who had a hand full of rocks. She gave Luna a similar examination, she then smiled and walked up briskly to Luna extending her hand, "Hi, you must be Luna. I've heard so much about you. I just had to meet you. I'm Alix Raya and we have some mutual friends." The two women were similar in age and appearance except that Alix's city pallor contrasted with Luna's sun kissed skin.

Luna took the extended hand and then added a hug, then put her arm around her and led her into the house almost ignoring Cipri. "It's my pleasure to have you here. I seldom get to see visitors such as yourself. It certainly makes my day. Can I get you anything to drink? I mean, I have a very native drink...Coke Cola...regular or diet."

"The real stuff; we big city girls drink our stuff straight, no messing around." She waited while Luna got the drinks and then said, "Listen Luna, I want to thank you for taking time to see me and I also want to thank you for what you've done for Larry. Apparently, in your brief meeting, you impressed him."

"I can't take too much credit. That young man has his head on straight. With the right kind of support and guidance, I'd go with him anywhere."

She also gave Cipri a drink and said, "Cipri, I mentioned to Mom that you were going to be here and she said she wanted to see you. I think she wants to show you some of her work. Take your Coke and walk down to see her, see what the old gal wants to show you." Cipri seemed relieved, smiled and walked out the door.

Alix noticed this exchange between the two women and watched Cipri walk away. "Now that was smooth. I was wondering how I could get a few minutes with you alone. That is one bright young lady, but she's tends to be suspicious and she's skeptical of me and my relationship with Larry; especially if someone wants to take advantage of her or anyone in her family.

You're right, she's bright, and can be a great friend, but you don't want to piss her off. She has several blood lines running through her veins and all her ancestors have a low boiling point. So it can be a dangerous combination. One bit of advice I can give you is to make sure you get on her good side."

"I'll keep that in mind. I've already experienced some skepticism from her, but we were able to keep it contained. I'd like to talk to you more about her, but my real reason for coming here is to talk about Larry and your insight of him, and of our work…and frankly, I wanted to share some sage with you to look at myself." Alix seemed embarrassed as she made the last comment.

Luna laughed and said, "Well you came to the right place; one thing we have plenty of around here is sage. Come let me show you the sage room and some of my best blends." They walked into Luna's office-sitting room. She opened her Coke and raised her can to her visitor in a toast. She motioned Alix to sit by the large, flat, incense rock. When she sat and raised her eyes, she focused on the crucified Jesus made from an old mesquite tree. Alix was not a religious person, in fact, in many ways she considered herself an atheist or at least an agnostic. Yet the Jesus-root on Luna's wall momentarily unsettled her. Quickly, she closed her eyes and took several deep breaths and when she opened her eyes she was *almost* back to her normal self. She smiled at herself and then at her host who had apparently sat her in that position in order to watch the reaction. Without saying anything, Luna carefully selected a leather pouch and removed two small sage bundles that were tied with dry grass leaves. She lit both ends of the bundles and gently blew on them to make sure they were lit. Within a few minutes the small room was engulfed with the sweet smell of sage. She said nothing and sat across from Alix, closed her eyes and crossed her legs. For a long time she just sat there. It was hard to judge how long they sat, but the sage burned out and the smoke cleared, but the distinct aroma permeated the entire room and the two women. When Luna appeared to return she took a long drink from her Coke can and smiled. She smiled at herself and was amused at the contradiction of the Coke and the ancient ritual she had shared with her new friend. "So tell me about Larry and this work?"

"Well you must know by now that there's a campaign to get immigration reform. I mean the mess at the border and all the people living in the shadows of our society has become a scandal. Yet there seems to be no great urgencies to remedy the situation. Many of the players such as the employers, our government and even our unions, seemed satisfied with the present arrangements. In the meantime we have over ten million people; men, women, and kids living in never-never land. The hope is that we can get some comprehensive law which will satisfy all these groups so we can get on with a just society. It was determined that we couldn't get this done with just words, concepts and TV ads. We need to put real flesh and blood in our efforts and Larry is part of that flesh. We want a program that is realistic and believable. Larry's tragic background, his run-in with the Border Patrol, is a good story to tell. My job was to prepare Larry for this encounter. To make sure that he could represent the reform point of view, and just as importantly, withstand all the crap he'll run into. And we know that when the shit hits the fan, many people get covered as well. That's why his family and friends are important. Not that they are part of the effort, but at least they should be prepared if some nosy reporter sticks a microphone in their face and asks a dumb question...which they will."

"You mean your whole campaign is based solely on Larry?"

"Well not completely, of course; it's really a multiphase effort, but the main effort will be with Larry. And if it's effective, and he does a good job, my hunch is, the final push will be mostly on his shoulders. You should know that the brain behind all this is a gal by the name of Lucinda Llamas. She's considered the guru of this type of campaign. She selected Larry and frankly she picked me to put him through the paces. And in fact, I'm here to touch base with you and his family so we don't get tripped up by a pebble we might have missed."

Luna took a drink from her Coke and said, "Well as you probably guessed, I don't know Larry that well. I do however, know his Jerome family. I can tell you there is a tenacity that runs through their veins. And if a drop of this blood runs through Larry he will do what needs to be done, but I have to warn you or anyone in your group not to cross them because there'll be hell to pay." Luna paused for a second and continued, "As an example, Larry and Cipri just met a few months ago and there's more depth in that relationship than they will admit to, but in my opinion, it's profound and it can be complimentary if managed properly."

"As I told you, that young lady reminds me of myself. And as I said, she's one of the reasons I'm here to make sure she's complimentary to our efforts. We sure as hell don't want her to be against us."

Cipri returned with a smile on her face and two feathers tied to the right side of her hair. Her hair and the feathers bounced as she walked. "Your mom insisted on giving me a new hairdo. She said it was part of my heritage. What do you think?' She twirled as she spoke. Luna and Alix looked with admiration as the young lady danced in front of them.

Chapter 18

L
ARRY LOOKED AT HIMSELF IN THE MIRROR AND SMILED. He almost did not recognize himself. In several weeks his hair was considerably longer and had an almost unkempt look. He was growing a mustache. His clothes, while clean, were too large for his slim, lanky build. Yet, the new look was comfortable in body and in mind. However, he did have a pang of uncertainty. He was going to meet his dad for breakfast and he wanted to dress and meet him in his new persona. Although Tom Franco had not said anything to his son, it was obvious he was uncomfortable with his son's new look. More than anything, he was concerned that Larry had dropped out of school for the semester to concentrate on the immigration reform campaign. They met across the street from the drugstore for breakfast at the Mupu Grill. His father was a regular in the restaurant and was sitting at his usual corner table reading the Santa Paula Times when Larry walked in. He looked up and there was a slight twitch in his eye. "I ordered breakfast for both of us, I hope you don't mind?"

"No, that's fine. The food is always great here." Larry looked at his dad in a different light. It was as if his new look affected how others appeared to him. His father still dressed and looked the same, but he looked older and somewhat more subdued. Larry was well aware of Tom's great interest in education and that he was disappointed that he had dropped out to work on the immigration program. His father was well aware of the debate going on in the country and supported the reforms being discussed. Yet, he was concerned that his son was involved even to the point of forestalling his education. Why, he wondered, couldn't the folks in Washington get their ducks in a row without adversely affecting the lives of young men like his son? In his disappointment, he was learning to take pride that this young man was thinking beyond himself. That he was in a sense, willing to sacrifice part of his young life on issues that most young people didn't even consider. At a similar age, Tom's main interests were girls, sports and a 1957 Chevy. Suddenly he felt shallow and inadequate compared with the young man sitting in front of him.

The following evening he felt even more inadequate, yet with pride, when he saw Larry being interviewed on television. Larry's appearance, although made up to a certain extent, was genuine. He spoke quietly, but with a sincere eloquence, "One afternoon after taking a final exam, I was arrested and that same day I was in a prison far away from my family. Then a few weeks later I was arrested again. Subsequently, the authorities have apologized to me and to my family, but there is no way they can erase the trauma they caused me and my family, but thanks to my parents actions, I was quickly released. In the few days I was in that prison, I saw several young men, just like me, who had been there for weeks and months with no hope. In some cases, no one even knew where they were. Isolated and with no hope, there was a helplessness that crushes the soul. So I'm asking our leaders in Washington to return hope to the many, many people who are languishing in our jails. In the majority of cases their only crime was coming here to pick our oranges or wash our dishes. For that we throw them into an isolated dungeon and forget about them. I'm fortunate, but not special. What we need is immigration reform that will allow people to come to work legitimately. That's not too much to ask, is it?"

"Mr. Franco, don't you think putting business owners in jail is too drastic for just giving a job to a person? The woman reporter smiled at Larry and the camera.

"You're probably correct, but yet we think nothing of putting young men and women in jail for just looking for a job. Isn't that kind of drastic? The problem is that we focus on the weakest link in this chain. At least the owner has power and can influence legislation. The youngsters in prison have no one. Remember, owners do not have to go to prison. The legislation we're proposing will provide an avenue to secure the labor needed legitimately. Then the employment relationship will be above board where everyone can see what's happening." Larry smiled at the camera.

Afterwards, Lucinda put her arm around the young man and said,

"Larry that was an impressive first outing. How did you feel? Were you nervous?"

"Yes, but it was not as bad as I thought it would be. What did you think?"

"Frankly, I think it was impressive as I said, but you must know that we selected a friendly reporter as our first test. The next one will try to tear your head off, but don't worry, as long as you stick to the basics as we discussed, it'll be okay."

Larry shrugged at the idea of being roughed up on television.

"What the hell did they do with my grandson, he looks like a bum," cried Cipriana as she spoke to her family who had gathered to see the interview.

"Oh grandma, don't worry, he's still the same Larry. The old clothes and the long hair is part of his new persona; it's part of the theater. Deep down he's the same uptight Larry we all know. What did you think of what he said? Do you think people are going to find him credible enough that they'll pass this legislation?" Cipri had a smile on her face knowing what Larry had gone through to get him to this stage.

"The kid makes sense, but I worry about those idiots in Washington. Some of those good ol' boys wouldn't know good sense if it bit them in the ass!" The old woman chuckled at her use of profanity.

Alix watched the interview with the family and was interested in their reaction. She said, "I know the lady that interviewed Larry, and she's a good egg and pretty much agrees with what we're doing. So this was an easy pitch; about as friendly as one can get in TV. From now on, it'll be more difficult and some of the interviews that are scheduled later on will be brutal. And...I must alert all you in this room; one of these days someone will stick a microphone in your face and try to trip you up."

"What do you mean?" asked the old woman.

"Well if the campaign goes like we think, the opposition will start to panic and then they'll get down and dirty. They'll try everything to discredit our efforts and the personalities like Larry. I wouldn't be surprised that in a few weeks you'll find people wandering around here asking questions about his family."

"What will they be looking for?" asked Cipri.

"If I know them, they will be looking for things out of the ordinary. For example; Larry's birth and his parent's death. Larry's adoption without ever being recorded; his arrest and his prison time. And the sudden discovery of his new family, all of you, that has enough mysteries that would make a great story. Especially with some elaborations here and there. All they need is to create doubt."

"Why would they come here, to our little town?" asked Cipriana.

"Desperation; they'll become desperate and will reach for anything they can throw at us that will create doubt; anything, and I mean anything. So, I just ask you to be alert. Be aware, and be cautious." Alix let her comments sink in for a minute, "One thing I can guarantee you is that right at this minute, the opposition is looking for any information they can find on Larry. The computers are humming right now."

The following day the two Ciprianas drove to the reservation to meet with Luna. The older one was concerned and wanted to meet with the tribe's medicine woman. She waited until she took her first sip of tea and said, "Listen Luna, I understand you met and spoke with the woman Alix and discussed how she fits in with this immigration business and with Larry." Then she lowered her voice and continued, "I was hoping you could make some of your best smoke so that we can pray for a good outcome."

Luna said nothing as the three women sat around her rock. She carefully removed a small bundle of sage from a leather pouch, she raised it up to the four corners and then to the crucified Root-Christ and lit it. She blew gently on it and then placed it on the rock and let the sweet smell envelop them. For a long time they just sat quietly. Then she began to hum very softly and then with her eyes closed, she spread her arms and then again was silent. After the smoke had dissipated she opened her eyes, smiled, and took a drink from her tea cup, "We all need to be supportive of this effort. We need to be strong. Things will happen that we don't like. There'll be some bad times. There will be nicks and scratches, but in the end these trials will make Larry and all of us stronger. We need to keep our wits about us. Remember panic and anger will be our biggest enemy." Luna said all this in a quiet, deliberate tone and looked directly at Cipri, who finally turned her tear filled eyes first to the smoldering ashes on the rock and then to the root cross on the wall.

"I like Luna, she does wonders with sage," said the old woman as they drove home.

Chapter 19

A LICIA FRANCO GOT UP TO TAKE HER GLASS to the kitchen to get a refill. On her return she offered a sip to her husband, "Well *Tomás*, what did you think of our son?"

He smiled as always when Alicia gave a Spanish intonation to his name. "I liked it. He was calm and straight forward. I like that he didn't become hysterical like some minorities get when they're on camera. I do wish though, that he would wear his regular clothes. He has too much of a shaggy look for my taste. Otherwise, I thought he did very well. What did you think Licha?"

"I was just thinking of our trip long ago to Arizona to find out about Bobby's death and that we came back with that new life in our hands. How ironic that from death comes life; and from that death life continues. Think about how our son gets life from his dead father and mother and from us; that they continue to live and have an effect on our lives through Larry. I hope they're as proud of him as I am. You know, I like his appearance. This is his persona. He looks comfortable in those old clothes and they add character." Then as a mother she continued, "I just hope if he's serious about that mustache, he keeps it nice and trimmed."

"That reminds me, Mr. Martin is coming by the store later on, he asked if he could talk to me. He said it had to do with the work that Larry's doing."

"Oh my goodness, are we having repercussions already? Did he say what he wants?"

"Well he wasn't too specific, but he said he saw Larry's interview and wanted to *touch base* with me. Those were the words he used." Tom thought about growing up on the Martin Ranch. All the summers and weekends he worked on the farm. He also benefited from Mr. Martin's generosity when he began his studies at the university. Without the assistance of the Martins, he would not have become a pharmacist and now own the local drug store.

Maxwell Martin walked into the drugstore. He had not been in the store for decades; it was not a place he frequented. He looked around curious. Yet the store; the displays, were pretty much what he remembered from his visits long ago. He worked his way toward the back where the pharmacy was. He addressed the young lady at the counter, "I'd like to speak to Mr. Franco. I have an appointment with him."

Just at that moment, Tom walked in from the back and said, "Mr. Martin. Good afternoon. Why don't we go back to my office and we can talk there; how about a drink?"

"Sure, a Coke would be nice, if you have one." Maxwell opened the can that Tom gave him and took a long drink. "I saw a young man on television last night talking about immigration. He said his name was Larry Franco, I'm assuming he's your son?"

Tom also took a drink and said, "Yes sir, Larry is our son." Max said nothing and expected Tom to continue. Unsure how to continue, he said, "A few months ago Larry was leaving school after taking some finals and he was arrested by the Border Patrol and before anyone knew about it he was locked up in prison out in the desert. If that wasn't bad enough, a few weeks later, he was picked up again and was about to relive that nightmare. Fortunately, we were able to prevent that one. In the meantime, the sheriff and the border patrol have apologized and even made financial restitution to him. All this caused him to get involved in this issue to try to pass Immigration Reform that would prevent things like what happened to him. Furthermore, the more he looked into it he became aware that the whole immigration policy in our country is a mess. So he's agreed to help out."

"Well I agree with your young man. This immigration issue is the biggest mess I've seen in a long time and needs to be addressed. I suppose you know that one of the features of the law is that the onus would be put on the employers. People like me. They would actually send me to prison for each worker they catch me with."

"...And guys like me. For example, I just found out that the young lady you met at the counter has no papers. She was brought into this country when she was only a couple of weeks old. She was raised here, went to school here, speaks only English and she's attending nursing college. This summer she'll graduate and already has a job at the County Hospital. We desperately need registered nurses. And she'll be great. We need her, but she works for me. I now know she has no papers. What am I to do? I can't fire her. She's worked for me all through high school. She is exactly the kind of people we need in this country. The whole damn thing is a mess!"

Mac chuckled and said, "Well Tom, I came here looking for some sympathy and it looks like we're both in the same pickle. In my case I'm sure I have many employees working for me directly and indirectly who are undocumented. To be honest, I have no idea how many, but I face the same problem you just described. I'm really here because Melina told me to talk to you. You see, she supports this Immigration Reform effort and as you might guess, if she supports it, I support it as well. She wanted me to tell you that if your family or Larry get any kind of problems from my group of people, you're to let us know. I'm not too sure we can control everyone, but we'll try. As you might guess, we too have our share of nuts when it comes to immigration issues."

"You mentioned Mrs. Maxwell, how did she get involved in the issue?"

"I guess through some of her lady friends in the church. She's been concerned about this for many years and she now sees a chance for some reform. I agree with her. Especially since part of the new reform has a provision for guys like me and you to obtain workers legitimately via some type of guest worker program. Actually, without this feature it won't work, no matter how many people get put in jail."

"Mr. Maxwell, thank you for your visit. I'll tell Alice about our chat. Also, Larry will be here for the weekend; what are chances that you two can talk? I think it would be great for Larry to hear from you and how you see things."

"Hmm, I'm usually with some of my friends on Saturdays at the club. I wonder if he could meet us there for lunch. In fact, why don't you bring him and we'll all have lunch. It'll be good to hear from both of you and my golfing buddies need to be aware of this too." Max reached into his pocket and removed a business card, wrote a name and phone number and said, "This is the name and number of my attorney. One of the fellows in his office has helped us on immigration issues in the past. Have your young lady go to see him. Let's see if we can help her. Like you said, one of these days I may need the hands of a skilled nurse, I want to make sure she's well qualified."

Maxwell Martin's group had already completed their round of golf and were sitting on the outside patio overlooking the 18ᵗʰ green. They were drinking martinis and beer and laughing when Tom and Larry arrived. All four men stood up and were introduced. "Tom, Larry, thank you for coming. We're just about to order lunch. Take a quick look at the menu, the waiter will be here in a few seconds. In the meantime, let me introduce you to my friends. Boys this is Tom Franco and his son Larry. Tom's family worked for us for many years. He now owns the pharmacy in town. His son Larry is a student and recently he's become a TV star." Max said the latter in a joking manner. "Seriously, Larry is undertaking an important issue that could affect all of us and I asked him to join us. It's important we try to understand what's at stake in this squabble."

"I'm sorry Mr. Martin, this is more than just a squabble," interrupted Larry. This is really inhumane. What I experienced and from what I saw others go though, this is close to a crime against humanity. To criminalize, to imprison and to dehumanize people just because they want a job is more than just a squabble." Larry's sudden outburst surprised all the men including his father Tom.

Max Martin took a drink of his martini and quietly said, "You're right Larry, what happens to these people who only want to work is tragic. I'm sorry I was flippant, but we just had a good afternoon on the course and the four of us usually take this time to unburden ourselves from our usual daily worries and grind. Kidding and bad jokes are part of that effort. I apologize."

Larry's face turned crimson and he looked at his folded hands for a few seconds, "I'm sorry too gentlemen, but I've been under some pressure recently, trying to get involved in an effort that I don't completely understand except what has happened to me recently." He smiled meekly,

"Frankly, I've never even paid attention to all the issues of immigration until I got caught in it."

"You don't have to apologize Larry. The fact is, most people don't have an idea or don't give a damn about this issue as long as the lettuce they eat is fresh and their lawns are cut cheaply." Max smiled and took another drink from his martini.

Tom looked at his son and said, "You can count me as one of those citizens who never gave immigration a thought. To me it was a problem for other people in other lines of work. My surprise recently was to learn that in my small business I face the same problem. I have an illegal immigrant in my employment. And under the new law being proposed, I could wind up doing time, but I agree that if the new law is comprehensive and well constructed, it could solve this touchy problem. It might not solve my personal issue, but it would help for the majority of people involved."

"Larry, Tom, thanks for coming out to have lunch with us. I can assure you that this fight will drag on for a long time. In the meantime, we have to keep our heads. And most of it will fall on you Larry. I heard your interview the other night and I was impressed. My guess is that it was a friendly interview. Just make sure you keep your cool when you run into the nuts of the world." Max took a long drink and continued, "By the way, I'd like to help. Some of the boys in our association agree with what you're doing, but we can't be overtly out front in our support. So here's a small check to help with some of the incidental expenses that are sure to arise."

Larry just looked at the envelope. Not knowing what to do he handed it to his father.

"Dad, I'm confused. I thought growers liked the illegal workers. I mean, they work cheap, live in hovels and no one gives a shit about them." Larry said this as they drove away from the country club.

Not all farmers are assholes as you're suggesting. In fact, the Martins have always had a great reputation for being good employers. In fact, I'd say most of the farmers I know are good people. Like any group or profession there are assholes—it seems it can't be helped. Most of them want to do the right thing if they can, but recently the immigration process is a mess. So we have an illegal system. Everyone seems to know about it, but no one wants to do anything about it. That is until now. So we'll have to see how this plays out."

"What about the money that Mr. Martin gave me, what should I to do with it?"

"I really don't know son. I suggest you tell Lucinda about it. Don't try to hide anything. I'm not sure, but it looks like one of those things that can come back and bite you in the ass."

Chapter 20

"I SAW YOUR INTERVIEW. You looked different and you even sounded different. Are you alright?" Cipri was looking at her own refection in the mirror in her room as she spoke to Larry on the phone.

"I'm fine, but I did get my first taste of what the next couple of months are going to be like...and it's not going to be fun. In fact, I wish I could be there with you. When I first got to Jerome, I thought it was such a small, boring town. I didn't think I'd last a week. Now in retrospect, I know I was wrong. There's a lot to be said about peace and quiet...and the people there."

Cipri smiled at herself in the mirror, "It sounds like you miss us, or perhaps someone special?"

There was a silence and then Larry answered, "Well to be honest, I miss you. In fact, I wish I could be there with you at this moment. Everything seemed easier when you were doing this with me. Now things seemed disjointed. Hell, I even miss Alix and all her badgering."

"Wow, if you miss Alix, things must be rough! Seriously Larry, your appearance on TV was really good. Even grandmother liked it; although she wasn't too keen with your clothes. Oh by the way, are you letting your hair grow and a mustache as well?"

"Well you know about the clothes that Alix bought me. I first thought it was a dumb idea and wouldn't matter, but honestly, they are more comfortable and make me feel more at ease and in character. It helps to think of this as a performance and the clothes as part of the wardrobe. Dad is more uptight about my outward appearance than I am. What do you think?"

"I like the more comfortable look. I just wish I could be there to be more comfortable with you..."

He paused for a moment and said, "Let me talk to grandmother, I want her to be comfortable with all this."

"*Mijo*, how are you? We just saw you on TV. For a minute I didn't recognize you. How are you doing with all this nonsense? Whatever you're doing, I wish it was over so you can come back to us. There're still many things I want to tell you and I don't have much time left."

Larry was startled by her comments, "What do you mean you don't have much time left? Are you not feeling well?"

The old woman chuckled and said, "What I'm saying is that I'm an old woman and I'm not going to live forever."

"Listen, Grandma, one thing we know about this little job is that it'll end this fall. One way or another, win or lose, you can expect me there a few days later. Because I have many questions that only you can answer. By the way, next time you see Luna, please tell her I'd like to meet with her as well. I've got a couple of questions I'd like to ask her."

"This wouldn't have to do with you and Cipri would it?"

"How did you know?" he asked.

Again she laughed and said, "I may be an old lady, but I'm not blind." The grandmother handed the phone back to Cipri.

"What was that all about? What does she mean she's not blind? Of course she's not blind. Nothing ever gets past her. She has eyes like a hawk." Cipri instinctively knew they were talking about her. She knew she was the favorite of her grandmother. The old lady basically raised her while her parents worked. She related stories about incidents and especially about her past family. She made sure that the young girl knew about her ancestors and that Cipri was aware of all the blood lines that surged through her veins. More importantly, Cipri assumed that she was given all this family information as the depository of family history for future generations. She thought seriously about the responsibility that her grandmother was entrusting to her.

As she heard the stories, she wrote the names and relationships in a small notebook Cipriana had given her. Now she flipped to the page in her mind with Larry's name. She contemplated their ancestors. These relationships confused her, but as far as she could figure, they were third cousins. That was not close; not too close, was it? She asked herself.

Cipriana came back to the room and whispered in her ear, "Ask him if he's talked to his priest about what the church has to say about immigration?"

Cipri wrinkled her brow at the sudden change in conversation. "Nana wants to know if you've talked to your priest about how the Church sees this immigration business."

Larry too was somewhat taken aback at the mention of the church's position. "I have no idea. Hell, I have no idea who my priest is for that matter. And what does that have to do with what I'm doing?"

Cipri chuckled and said, "I too have no idea why she just brought up the subject, but it must have some significance or else she wouldn't have mentioned it. Knowing her, I suggest you find out who's the local priest and have a little chat with him."

Father Sean Flynn was a Jesuit priest who was temporarily assigned to St. Sebastian's parish. He had just spent the last three years at a Mission in the border town of Tijuana. He made an odd impression. He spoke English with a slight Irish accent. Yet his Spanish was perfect. More specifically, his border Spanish was perfect, the result of drinking lots of Tecate beer and smoking Domino cigarettes with his border parishioners. Years of working in the interior of Mexico and on the border gave him a different perspective on the immigration situation. Being an immigrant from Ireland also colored his viewpoint. The priest looked curiously at Larry when he walked in, but said nothing except, "Good morning son, what can I do for you?"

Larry was somewhat intimidated. He had gone to church mostly to complete his first communion and confirmation. Having completed these sacraments, the church was no longer part of his young life. In fact, he could not remember the last time he attended Mass at St. Sebastian's. Priests always scared him and he was uncomfortable as he sat down. "Good morning Father. My name is Larry Franco and I'm involved with an immigration group who wants to urge Congress to take a look at the system we have now. I know the church has always been concerned with immigrants and I was hoping you could give me some information or perhaps recommend a book I could read on the subject."

Suddenly the priest recognized the young man sitting in front of him, "You're the young man on TV! The other day I heard you talking about immigration reform. I saw the interview and I was intrigued with you and what you said about your recent experience with our friends from the *Migra*." The priest got up, shook Larry's hand and gave him an *abrazo*. "Well young man, tell me again what you want to know about the Church, wetbacks and borders."

"Well Father, for some reason I was selected and I agreed to help in trying to bring some logic and fairness to this immigration debate. In the meantime, my grandmother who is a very wise person, suggested I check out how the church has handled this situation throughout time. So here I am." After the hug, the priest lit up a cigarette, smiled and waved at Larry to continue.

"However, until a few months ago, I didn't know I had a grandmother and then I discovered an entire new family. You see my birth parents were both killed in a car accident a couple of days after I was born in Arizona. A day later my uncle, or my dad's brother, picked me up and adopted me so that's how I wound up with a new family. Just recently I met my great grandmother. I had a chance to stay with her and she's been filling me in on her part of the family. She's a big supporter of the church and she suggested I find out the church's position on immigration."

"Well Lorenzo...is it okay if I call you Lorenzo? Larry is a fine name, but Lorenzo has such dignity; if you ever have time check out our San Lorenzo, he was quite a guy. Since the very beginning our church has been on the move. From Abraham to Moses to David and the New Testament, our people have wandered. In more recent times, the church spread from Europe to the new world and the migration continues. One thing we can say is that with every step one group took another group was quick to complain. For example, let me tell you a story. A man in the 1820s once said about certain people; ...*these foreigners have illegal plans to upset the harmonious purpose of our nation. They care only for themselves...they are not grateful for the favors given them.*" Would you, Lorenzo, like to guess who it was that uttered these words and who he was referring to?"

Larry thought, studied the priest and said, "I'm sorry Father, I have no idea who spoke those words."

"Well son, it may be a surprise to you that these words are attributed to a Mexican governor at the time and he was referring to Americans who were coming into his territory." The priest took a puff of his cigarette and continued, "My point is, that man has always had some prejudices against any newcomer, no matter who they are. That's one of the biggest sins that seem to almost be inborn into man. It's one of those things that we must continue to guard against. That was Jesus' main message and concern when he said, Love your God and love your neighbor."

Larry smiled, "It's ironic isn't it that now we are saying the same thing about Mexicans who want to come to this country."

"It's not just Mexicans. In the 1830 the mayor of New York said, *All Europe is coming across the ocean…they increase our taxes, eat our bread, encumber our streets, and not one in twenty is competent to keep himself…*"

The priest continued as he seemed to be enjoying himself, "The humorous thing about these comments is that they're rather complimentary when compared with what was said about eastern Europeans. And you don't even want to hear what was said about the poor Chinese and other Asians. It's what I call the *school yard syndrome*. That is, any new kid in the school yard is viewed with suspicion and fair game to be harassed."

"I think I can understand that, but what does the Church specifically say about immigration?"

"Well, first let me say the Church itself has a mottled and shameful past when it comes to people who are different. You can start with the Crusades, the Inquisition and the many religious wars. We have a past that's very uncomfortable, but if I could reduce the Church's position in one word; that word would be **dignity…human dignity**! That is, we should treat everyone with dignity. It's an easy concept, but hell to put into practice and so easy to forget!"

Larry was quiet for a long time and then smiled sheepishly, "Life isn't easy is it? Father, we're leaving for several days working our way north; eventually we'll wind up in Seattle, can you recommend some reading material? I'll have lots of time by myself and I thought I could do some reading to pass the time and to learn something about the Church and its teachings. I would especially like to read about immigration."

The priest stood up, went to a small bookshelf and removed a slim volume. The gold title was almost illegible from usage. "This is a book I traveled with many, many miles. It contains just the New Testament and all 150 psalms. Our beliefs are mostly contained in this little book. It's tough reading, even contradictory in some cases, but it has the answers. Read it carefully; repeat it, read it at different times and under different circumstances. Get comfortable with the words and more importantly get comfortable with how it might apply to the situation that you have in front of you." He handed the book to his young guest and then said, "Tell me Lorenzo, what is the main feature of the legislation you folks are seeking. I mean, what's so unique about your effort? Tell me in simple terms."

"Well, as I understand it, most of the enforcement efforts in the past have been directed against the people coming into the country. Either with fences, fines and jail time for breaking the immigration law in effect. Our effort simply focuses on the job and particularly on the person who gives the job, to the undocumented person. It's the owner or employer who gets the fine or the jail time."

The priest took another puff from his cigarette and started to laugh, "I must admit your approach is unique and it will certainly solve the problem. I assume there must be an alternative to bring workers in legally otherwise, we'll all starve."

"There is a guest worker provision in the proposed law that will allow workers to come to work under appropriate supervision. I'm not too familiar with the details of how that would work, but I do know that the onus of the law would now be on the job giver not the job seeker." Larry ruffled the pages of the New Testament as he spoke. He noticed that there were many underlined phases and some passages were highlighted. There were also several cards and pieces of paper throughout the book. "He asked, "I notice there's many notations in the book, I hope I don't lose it or damage it."

"Don't worry. First I'm giving you the book; it's a gift. Write in it. Study it carefully. Ask questions. Question the book itself. Question the ideas. Apply the concepts to the work you're doing and come to your own conclusions. The book is to be used. To squeeze the knowledge out of it, just like you would squeeze juice from an orange." The priest took the last puff from the cigarette and ground it out in the ashtray and said,

"Listen Lorenzo, it was a pleasure to meet you. I wish you luck in your efforts. When you return from your trip up north, come back and share your thoughts with me. I'll be very curious how this campaign evolves. And may God bless you for all your efforts," the priest said almost as an afterthought.

"Thank you Father, for your time and for the book. I must tell you that my knowledge of the Church and scripture is limited at best. So I'll give it a good try. And you can be assured that I will check in with you often."

"What do you mean you spent the whole morning with a priest? Are you sick or what have you done? Asked Cipri when he called her that evening.

Astonished, Larry answered, "What do you mean, you were the one who told me that grandmother wanted me to check in with a priest and so I did. That's all. Father Sean has spent lots of time at the border and knows the issue from the perspective of the people. I liked him; he was down to earth and not much on BS. He also gave me one of his old books on the subject."

"What book did he give you?"

Larry had the book in his hand and opened it as he spoke to her, "*The New Testament and the Psalms*. From the looks of the book, it's had much travel and usage. It's all marked up and has many of his notes in the margins. In fact, some of the stuff marked are some of the same questions I have."

Chapter 21

TOM AND ALICIA WERE LEAVING the Los Angeles airport working their way back to the 405 freeway to return home to Santa Paula, when Licha said, "Larry looked sad and lonely as he got on the plane. I almost felt like going with him." Alicia had been pensive all day as she helped her son prepare for his trip to Seattle. He was going to be gone for five days and she had helped him pack. Her main emphasis was on his underclothes. The outer clothes were Goodwill clothes purchased over the last few weeks. The clothes were old, worn, but would be warm and comfortable for the northern climate. He was making the trip alone. Lucinda was to meet him at one of the motels by the airport. That evening he was scheduled for a radio interview. He was told to be prepared because this time he was going into the lion's den. The Seattle station was specifically chosen because it had one of the most anti migrant radio personalities and because it had a very limited audience. If it went well, it would reassure every one of Larry's preparation and abilities. If it went badly, the poor performance would be geographically limited—so it was thought. It was, in a sense, an off-Broadway performance, before going on to the big time. En route, Larry read and reread the Gospel of John about the Samaritan woman at the well. He pondered the significance of the suspicion and distrust of that encounter. He wrote it down as a question for Father Sean.

Lucinda parked her rented car in the radio station's lot. She turned off the lights and said, "Now Larry, let's just make sure you're alert with this guy. Charles Oliver is a real charmer. He's the type of guy you'd enjoy having a couple of beers with. He's bright and articulate except when it comes to immigration issues. In fact, when it comes to immigration, he makes the Nazi party look passive. He doesn't even like people who look like him and he turns into a nasty piece of work with other nationalities, especially Hispanics and Asians. So just state your opinion and try not to get sucked into his hate."

Larry took a deep breath as they walked into the radio station. The place reeked of cigarette smoke. Oliver was of medium build, sandy hair and had freckles all over his face. He had a big smile as he introduced himself, "Hi, I'm Charlie Oliver. Thanks for coming to share your story with us. Have a seat and we'll be with you in a few minutes. This program we'll be doing live so we have a few buttons to push and then we'll be ready. Larry had just settled in the chair in front of a microphone when Charles Oliver began, "Good evening friends. Welcome to our chat about immigration and the blight it creates over our God loving country. This evening we have a young guest who crossed our borders illegally as a two day old baby. On top of that he has been apprehended by authorities multiple times and has served time at our expense in one of our prisons. Yet he comes to us this evening as an example of the type of people who want to overrun our country." He actually smiled at Larry and continued, "Well, tell me Larry, what right do you have to complain about our country and the treatment of all these undesirable felons that come to our country?"

Larry was stunned momentarily, he ran his hand over his long hair, smoothed his growing mustache, took two long, deep breaths, smiled and answered, "First Mr. Oliver, let me thank you for your kind hospitality in inviting me to be on your program. Many people who have similar views like you just expressed, wouldn't have the guts to have someone with a different viewpoint on the air. They hate so much that logic is not even in their lexicon. Let me make a couple of points on your introduction if I may. You're correct I was apprehended by the Border Patrol and actually spent a couple of days in one of their faculties. What you failed to mentioned that these same authorities released me, apologized both verbally and in writing. I have a copy of that letter which I'll leave with you. In addition they actually apologized monetarily to preclude any legal action if you know what I mean."

Larry again smiled at Oliver and continued, "I'm also very glad Mr. Oliver, that you are apparently diligent about following our laws and regulations. I fully agree with you that workers should not break our laws to come here to work. Then I'm sure you would agree that it should be against the law to employ these same workers. So I ask you if an employer breaks the law, shouldn't they also face similar consequences?"

"Well Larry, it's different for Americans, they don't know who's here legally or illegally."

"Let me ask you another question Mr. Oliver. Washington grows lots of apples and those apples get harvested mostly by people who speak Spanish. Don't you think it might occur to the farmer that some of those workers might just be here illegally? Our proposed legislation is simple, let's have laws and have people, all people, follow them and let there be legal consequence equally if they're not observed. What can be fairer than that, I ask you? Simply, if it's illegal to get a job then it should be illegal to give the job. Both actions need to be treated equally with similar consequences, don't you think?"

"Then who would harvest the apples, if a farmer has to adhere to employing...only legal persons?" Oliver was no longer smiling.

"There's a simple remedy in the law that provides for a guest worker program to provide these seasonal workers. This is not a new concept. During World War II much of farm work was done by seasonal, contracted foreign labor. And we were very grateful for them. It was all above board. Basically that's what this new law will do. It would be fair; it would provide workers when needed, but it would put the employer on the same plane when it comes to responsibilities of insuring a legal workforce."

"What about the 10 to 12 million people that are already here? What do we do with them? That many people are a drain on our country's assets and largesse. I mean, we can't just let in all those people south of the border. A country has the right to control its borders, doesn't it?"

"That last question is easy. Of course every country has the right, and should, control its border. And we should do what's necessary to do so, but all the best information we have is that the majority of people want to come here to work. So if we can control the employment process the border issue solves itself. Now the first question is more difficult. We do have many people already here working in the shadows. Studies show us that in general, these people are not a drain on our society; that in fact, they are a net contributor to our economy. We need to recognize that and not demonize them. Not only that, but some of these people have an entrepreneurial spirit that we very much need. And somehow we need to incorporate them into our societies like we have the waves of immigrants that have come to our shores over the last 200 years. Now it will not be easy. It may take a couple of generations, but we will be a better country for doing the right thing."

Oliver had a blank face, he was actually shuffling some three by five cards and finally looked up and said, "I'd like to thank Larry Franco for coming to our station and sharing his thoughts with us, but you folks, my listeners, should continue to monitor this debate on immigration as it will eventually affect all of us. With that this is Charlie Oliver bidding you all a good evening." With that he removed the headphones and came over to Larry and shook his hand and said, "Larry thank you for your time, I wish you luck in the work you're doing."

Again Larry was surprised as he had been in the beginning of meeting the man. It seemed that Oliver could turn his thoughts and feelings on and off almost at will. Whereas, Larry's anger and frustration reacted quickly, and it took a long time for him to calm down. In his own mind the rhetoric of the situation continued like a whirlwind. He tried to settle down as he gathered his thoughts and walked out to the lobby where Lucinda was waiting.

Lucinda smiled, but as soon as they left the building she stopped and gave him a hug and kissed him on both cheeks. Larry was still trying to compose himself, but then again his emotions roiled. At this rate he was a candidate for ulcers he thought. That night before going to bed he opened the Bible given to him by the Jesuit priest and he found a folded piece of paper with these words written in a small script: *"Give me your tired, your poor, your huddled masses yearning to breathe free, the wretched refuse of your teeming shore. Send these, the homeless, tempest lost to me. I left my lamp beside the golden door?"* He noticed that the words, *yearning to breathe free*, were underlined twice.

Chapter 22

THE NEXT MORNING they had breakfast at the airport hotel. Lucinda was waiting for him; she already had several cups of coffee. She looked up from the book she was writing in and said, "I was just writing a few notes of my day. It's a habit I picked up in college. In fact, I suggest it might be a good idea for you to keep a record of your days; especially about what you're doing for us. The problem is that soon the days will run together and you'll begin to wonder what day this is, or what city you're in, or who you spoke to, or even what you said for that matter."

Larry looked at her book, "Who else reads your notes?"

"That's just it, they're my notes. No one else reads them. It's kind of a reminder system and it's simple. About the only thing I'm consistent in is that I write the date and then I just write a few paragraphs of what I did. If I did nothing, I might write about the weather or who won the game. Enough of that; except that this morning, I was writing what a great job you did with Oliver last night. I heard from a few friends who listened to the interview and they were impressed. In fact, they want to meet you, but that'll have to wait. We'll be in Phoenix this evening and will do a morning talk show tomorrow, that should be fun. Later in the day we'll be at a local college to see if we can mobilize some of the young desert dwellers."

Larry asked, "Lucinda, as you know, I have some family in Jerome, would it be okay if I asked them to meet me? And I also have another favor, I wonder if you have an extra notebook with you. I tried to buy one, but I couldn't find anything that seems adequate."

Lucinda grinned and said, "I just happen to have an extra one in my room which I'll donate to the cause. I now buy them by the box. I just hope that in your old age, you won't hate me for this habit, or as my mother calls it my *addiction*." She took another drink from her coffee and said, "I'm assuming the family you'd like to touch base with is Cipri. In fact, invite her; she can spend the day with us...or you."

The flight from Seattle left on time and stopped briefly in Las Vegas. Lucinda and Larry didn't even bother to unbuckle their seatbelts as people exited for the bright lights of Las Vegas. Those leaving the gambling Mecca boarded and the plane was up in the air quickly. Before they could finish their cold drink, they were landing in Phoenix. Lucinda asked, "Did you get hold of your folks?"

"Yes, in fact someone is going to meet us at the airport." As they made their way to the luggage area he saw Cipri and Luna Martinez.

"I see Cipri; she seems very happy to see you...However, I don't know the lady with her."

"That's a friend, her name is Luna Martinez and she's a spiritual leader of her tribe near Jerome. She's become a friend and I asked if she could come. Come; I'd like you to meet her. I know you'll like her."

Suddenly Lucinda was on guard, "What do you mean spiritual leader? Is she some kind of a priest?"

"Well, I suppose she's some kind of a priest, or perhaps a *medicine woman* would be a better title. By the way, she has a Ph. D., so don't be fooled. She has her feet in two cultures, but more than anything else, she's a nice person."

Before he could finish speaking, Cipri ran up to him and gave him a big hug and kissed him longingly on the mouth. Then she pulled away embarrassed as she looked at the others. For a few seconds the four just looked at each other, finally Larry said, "Lucinda this is Luna Martinez and of course you've already met Cipri."

Luna said, "It's my pleasure to meet you Lucinda; I've heard of you and your organization. And of course Cipri told me about your work on this immigration issue. In fact, I was looking forward to meeting you. I'm not too sure I know the more subtle points of this legislation, so I look forward to sharing some time with you so I can get more informed on the issue."

Lucinda took Luna by the arm and began to walk away, leaving Larry and Cipri by themselves. "Well Luna, one thing for sure is that this immigration business is a complicated and controversial issue. It gets people on both sides hot under the collar in a hurry. So let me tell you what we're trying to do…"

As they walked away, they left Larry and Cipri alone to follow at a distance. She said, "I'm sorry if I embarrassed you. I was so glad to see you, I just acted without thinking."

Larry grabbed her hand and said, "I'm glad you did. I missed you and I wanted especially for you to be here. I would have died to be in Arizona so close and not be able to see you…and the rest of the family of course."

"Of course, *Abuelita* said she wants to see you if you can spare some time from your schedule."

"We'll see. Lucinda has me on a short leash. That's why I wanted to meet you here. I also wanted to talk to Luna. I sometimes wonder where all this is going. If you had told me a few months ago that I'd be doing this, I would have laughed and said you were nuts."

That evening they all sat in Larry's motel room. He said, "I asked Luna if we could just sit and have a quiet conversation of what we're doing; to try to listen to ourselves. I'm still not too damn sure what I'm doing in all this."

Lucinda appeared anxious and reluctant, "You know, I'm sure that you two young people want to be alone. I have some calls to make and some reports to write."

Luna noticed the woman's reaction and quickly said, "Listen, Larry asked me to bring some of my extra special sage to have a cleansing ceremony. It's not a religious gig; it's just our ancient way of getting right with our surroundings." She removed a large abalone shell from a colorful hemp bag. She also took a bunch of tightly bound sage and raised it to the four corners and then lit one end. She blew gently on the smoldering end until it glowed. She again raised the smoking bundle to the four corners and placed it on the shell. She was quiet for about two minutes and then she began to chant. The soft words were in her native language and were uttered in a low, guttural voice which sounded like humming. The humming prayer was short; followed by a long silence. Finally, she brought everyone back to the present and said, "This little ceremony was an ancient way of reuniting friends and family when they got together after a long absence. It basically asks for forgiveness, understanding and peace. It's meant for each participant to get involved or say anything, pretty much as you please. To get whatever is on your mind at the moment out into the open and into the fresh air as it were. I hope you all didn't mind it."

Lucinda smiled. She was a reluctant observer as she watched the medicine woman work, but when the sweet smell of the sage hit her nose she closed her eyes and let the unique smell of the sage overwhelm her. It was so easy to get uptight in the work she was doing. The immigration debate was especially draining on her. Most of the campaign issues she was involved in were intellectual or just part of the business she was in, but immigration was a personal issue. She was a two month old baby when her parents had come from Argentina with student visas; then came graduate studies and subsequent various jobs. Somehow returning home became a long forgotten journey. Citizenship for Lucinda was never asked for and the issue never came up in the hectic day to day life of a young lady. She grew up watching the Disney Channel and was an American in everything, but birth. The only void was during elections when she discussed the many topics with her friends, but then she stayed home on Election Day. Not being able to vote was a huge cross to bear. She even rationalized her marriage to Ron Nelson to begin her naturalization process. The marriage lasted only a couple of years and yet she would always be grateful to Ron for providing her the road to the legitimacy she longed for in this country and the right to vote. To the present, they remained good friends and occasionally worked together on some campaigns. So citizenship and voting were passionate issues with her. Furthermore, she was astonished, even angry, with all the people she knew who were born in the country, but didn't exercise the privilege. Her mission in life was to make people passionate about voting. She was particularly incensed with Hispanic citizens who didn't bother to vote. Increasing the turnout of this ethnic group was her goal. She and her campaign were making headway, but the effort was also full of disappointments when she encountered the all too present apathy. All these thoughts flashed through her mind as the smell of the sage lingered. "For some reason, the sage reminds me of my parents. They grew up in Argentina and left to attend school in this country and never left. Yet it was things like tastes and smells that would remind them of their homeland. It was strange that sometimes they would stop in the middle of a sentence or what they were doing as their minds flashed back to a former life. A couple of times I noticed tears in Mom's eyes. I almost knew what was going on with her, without asking. It was sad that she never got to see her homeland again."

"Studies have shown that the sense of smell is one of the more powerful stimuli that will generate emotions by the tons. It's well documented that the first things animals do when they encounter a strange thing is to smell it. And we humans still do it to some extent. Some studies even say mothers can smell and identify their babies." Luna carefully cleaned the ashes from the abalone shell, wiped it clean then wrapped it with a white cloth and replaced it in her bag.

Larry was quiet and then said, "It never occurred to me, but one of the things that reminds me of the few days I spent in prison was the smell of the place. Twice recently I've run across similar odors that almost left me in a panic. I mean within seconds I felt a cold sweat forming down my back. It was frightening and it scared the shit out of me." Larry noticed that Cipri moved closer to him, she gently took his hand and smiled at him.

"My Daddy would go nuts when he smelled meat being cooked on an open flame. It reminded him of being with his father and brothers on the pampas and eating a variety of game animals they killed to eat. It was the smell that took him back to his youth, family and homeland...a home he never saw again."

Luna looked at the odd assortment of people gathered in front of her, experiencing a simple almost primitive ceremony that elicited similar primitive feelings. In a sense it was the soul of the individuals that was being stirred by the smoke. She knew, because it stirred her deepest feeling when she performed the sacramental incensing that was rooted deeply with her ancestors. The connection with her people was real and palpable as she shared it with the small group in front of her. "Many people misinterpret this ceremony as some sort of miracle, but it's really more of an opening to the light and to freshness of life. It's that part that precedes the healing process or in other words; it facilitates the healing"

Larry cocked his head, "What do you mean healing? Does that mean that we're sick? I mean, I feel fine."

"I suppose sick and healing might not be adequate words to describe what my ancestors meant. We tend to use sick as a term that means more than some physical aliment of our bodies. My people say sick when things are out of kilter, when harmony is disturbed. Being cured is returning things to a balance. It even means that when we die, as sad as that can be; death brings balance to one's world."

"You mean that death can be a healing? How can that be? It sounds like a stretch to me," asked Larry, in anticipation of a satisfactory answer.

"Think of wheat that gives us nourishment. It's not until the seed germinates, grows, withers and dies that the kernel returns to the soil to be reborn. The birth is in the death; the beginning is in the end. On a family level, death is not only rebirth, but also the start of the healing process as it eliminates pain. And it ends one's life when we no longer can participate or contribute to our community. I know it sounds harsh, but there can be no life unless there is death. In the meantime, this simple action of watching and inhaling smoke gives us the opportunity to make us right in the present so we can be right in our afterlife." Luna finished packing her bag and smiled and said, "Now, how about some refreshments?"

Chapter 23

"MAX, I CAN'T BELIEVE that you're supporting this damn immigration fiasco. We hear from some of our folks in Washington that this legislation has a chance of passing and the president has already indicated that if Congress passes the bill, he will sign it." Roger Garvey looked at his friend and then took a bite of his BLT sandwich. They sat in their usual booth at the Mupu Grill. They met after the lunch crowd had left and they sat in the corner booth alone. It was in this booth that many of the farming problems were discussed and acted on when necessary. The restaurant staff were aware of these frequent meetings and was quiet, efficient and discreet with these powerful members of the community.

Maxwell Martin looked at his friend and acknowledged his concern with a slight smile. Actually, it was his concern as well. Even though he agreed with his wife to support the legislation, he was well aware that in the process of putting together legislation, many extraneous items could creep into the bill at the very last minute. "What are the main concerns of our boys in DC about the legislation?"

"Well the whole damn thing. No one was worried at the beginning because this has been such a hot topic for many years that no one wanted to touch it. And hell, as you know, that worked well for us. There's plenty of labor around, it's cheap and not too demanding. So in my viewpoint, it worked pretty well, even though it was a mess. Now these guys are getting serious and are changing the rules of the ball game. I mean, shit, they now want to put our sorry asses in jail! What kind of crap is that?"

"Well I'm not too keen about that, but it's my understanding that they will provide a guest worker program so we won't have to hire the illegals. That part is still in the proposed bill, isn't it?"

"I think it is, but listen Max, we have about 400 workers on the farm most of the time. About half work for us directly and many have been with us for years. The other half is provided to us by contractors. I mean, we have a tough time vouching for our own people much less for those who work off and on with the contractors." Garvey was getting flustered as he rattled off his concerns.

"Listen Rog, I have similar concerns. Our operation is pretty much like yours. Except a larger percentage work for us directly and on top of that, they live in our housing. Some of the families have lived with us for years. We have no idea about their legal status. Except for some who have applied for residency and have asked us for letters of employment. It seems to me that the big problem will be with the farm labor contractors. Most of these fellows don't have the wherewithal to comply with the present regulations, much less with immigration rules on top of everything else."

"It'll be the biggest mess we've ever seen, I can bet you that." He paused for a minute and said, "You know the boys in DC are concerned about this kid from town who is the face of their campaign. He's apparently very effective and is convincing voters about the need for immigration reform. I understand you know him and his family."

"His grandfather worked for us until he retired. Even his dad worked for us during the summers when he was at Stanford. You know his dad too. He's Tom Franco, the pharmacist, who owns Santa Paula Drug store. You probably get your prescriptions from him."

"Are you kidding me? Tom and I went to school together. Hell, I even gave him many rides to Palo Alto. We got to know each other pretty well. He's a nice guy and a good golfer, but what's he doing with a kid like the one who wants to put us in jail?" Roger had a surprised face as he spoke.

"I agree, Tom is a nice fellow. He's a credit to his family and to our town. Frankly, his son Larry is a nice kid as well. One of these days I'll tell you the story about him."

"Well if this kid is heading the campaign, maybe we can head it off by talking to Tom. He's a reasonable guy. I bet we can put together something that will entice him to pull his kid off this race."

"Roger, I know this family well. They're the type family who want to do the right thing. And by the way, I've already spoken to Tom and told him I was okay with what he was doing. Or rather what his boy Larry was doing."

"I suppose you had no way of knowing how effective the kid would be on the political circuit. Whoever selected and trained him did a hellava job. I don't know why our people can't get effective people like this kid. We always seem to wind up with some overweight farmer type as our spokesman."

"I've been thinking about that. Actually, let's assume the legislation is going to pass and we'll get some kind of a guest worker program. My guess is that the unions will try to use the permitting process to block the acquisition of farm workers or will try to control the process by organizing. The union has been mostly unsuccessful in organizing farm workers in the past and this will give them a new opportunity. Perhaps we should try to educate Larry and his family about our point of view so at least we could have a fair shot at getting our fruit off the trees under this new system."

"So what does this kid do when he's not working on immigration?"

"He's in school. I understand he dropped out for a semester to help out with this project. You know, that might be it. Perhaps we can hire him part time when he returns to school. Maybe even award him one of our scholarships. I mean, our industry can use bright, young people; so it would be a good investment for the future." Max took out a notebook and made some notes.

Roger began to laugh and said, "Max, I thought I was being confrontational, but you are as well, and more devious to boot." He looked at Max making notes, "I just sent a nice check to my buddy at Stanford. I bet we can make arrangements for the kid to get in…assuming he's got the grades."

"I'm not too sure I like the word devious Roger. My family has been farming in this valley for three generations and I'd like to continue the tradition in peace. Putting up with unions and their BS is not my idea of a pleasant business. Not only that, but my employees will not benefit by their machinations. In the long run, we'll all wind up being losers…, but in the meantime, why don't you call your friend and ask him about this kid. His name is Larry Franco."

"Listen Max, with the check I recently sent them, there's no doubt in my mind that we can get the kid in, but what do we ask in return?"

"That's just it Roger, we ask for nothing. We hope he just gets a good education and then perhaps we can lure him to work for us or in the industry. We need good minds and folks who can make a good presentation to the public. You'll have to agree that we farmers have a rotten public image. I know in a few years I'll be looking for someone to run our operation. The girls are not interested and their husbands have their own lives. In a sense, we would be training our own people to be our eventual replacements."

"I tell you what Max. Why don't you arrange a meeting with this kid and perhaps his parents? I'd like to get to know him before I pull any strings at Palo Alto."

Chapter 24

"ACTUALLY, LARRY WILL BE HERE tomorrow for a couple of days. He says he needs to get some clean clothes and some of Licha's cooking before he goes on the road again. We're having some of his friends over. Why don't you and Roger come over and you can talk to him. We can have a couple of beers and Alice will be sure to have some good food for her son." Tom Franco was counting capsules to complete a prescription. He had the phone wedged between his ear and shoulder as he multitasked. Doing two things at the same time was not unusual for the lone pharmacist in his own store. Juggling was the norm for the owner, pharmacist operation in a small town.

"Larry, you know Mr. Martin, and this is Mr. Oliver, a friend of mine. We both went to school together. These two guys heard about the work you're doing and wanted to meet with you, to see what you were up to." Tom took a drink from a beer bottle as he introduced his son.

"Hi, thanks for coming. I would very much like to talk over a couple of things that has come up over the last several days." Then he took Lucinda by the hand and said, "This is Lucinda Llamas, she's the lady who has been my teacher over the past several weeks. Her firm has been retained to coordinate the Immigration Reform Project. And in a way, she's retained me to help in this effort."

"Gentlemen, it's a pleasure to meet you. And frankly it would be an honor to chat with you about our project. I suppose since you're both in agri-business you're very well aware that this legislation will affect your operation." Lucinda was cordial and flashed a warm, friendly smile at the two men.

"Miss Lamas, it's a pleasure to meet you. We've heard many things about you and your organization," said Roger as he shook her hand.

"Please call me Lucinda. I hope what you've heard is positive. Sometimes some of us who work in the legislation arena tend to get an unflattering reputation." She paused and again smiled at the men and continued, "Frankly, Larry and I would very much like to chat about your concerns. The facts are that it's operations like yours that employ many of the people we seek to help. And, if you're not healthy nor viable, neither are the people we purport to help. So you can see that we are not just concerned with the effects on just the workers. We're concerned about the health of the industry as a whole. If the industry thrives, so do the workers. Our whole concept is very simple and straightforward."

"Well Lucinda, it's good to hear that, on this issue, we're on the same page. In a sense, we farmers are in a similar boat to those in your industry. We tend to get painted with a very unflattering broad brush. Sometimes I tell people I'm in the distribution business so I won't have to explain or defend what I do. However, you should know that our families have been farming in this valley for several generations. Similarly, we both have had families work for us for years and are an important part of our community. Without them there would be no agriculture as we know it. Additionally, we also see that these same employees and their families have an opportunity that this country gives them. That is the opportunity to improve themselves beyond what we have to offer them." Roger opened another beer and took a drink.

Tom took another drink from his beer and added, "Listen, let's get some food and we can sit outside and continue this conversation."

Lucinda watched the men eat as she nibbled on a tortilla, "So tell me Roger, what are your main concerns about this immigration legislation?"

Roger looked at Lucinda and Larry, "First is that our operations are very different from those in the Midwest. For example, on my operation I may have 100 workers on my row crop division which consists of a little over 100 acres and the work is of very short durations. However, a farmer in Iowa may have 100 acres of corn and he needs only one or two workers. It's the intensity that is different. Furthermore, some of my acres might produce two or three crops in one year. So our crop's needs vary dramatically by types and months in the year, so does the need for labor."

"So how are your needs different than in the past? Or better yet, what's different now that we need this immigration reform?" asked Lucinda.

Roger looked at Max who answered, "During World War II we had Public Law 78 or what was known as the Bracero program. This allowed us to contract mostly Mexican workers who would come to work on a seasonal basis. They would come without families, live in camps all under the supervision of the Feds. It was a good program and lasted until the mid 60s, when it was terminated and essentially replaced with nothing. There were several years of turmoil, but eventually the Braceros were replaced by the same Mexican people who now crossed the border illegally. For the last three decades this has been the norm. Everyone was well aware of how it worked. The Feds, the States, growers, all were involved in a see-and-say-nothing program. One big difference was that Braceros came as single men and lived in camps. However, since it became more difficult to cross the border frequently, the men would stay longer and longer and eventually they would bring their families over as well. So now we have families in the mix. The irony is that in some cases, it was the same man that worked for us legally under the Bracero program and now illegally with no program."

"Max, you mentioned labor camps, how were they part of the system?" she asked.

"There were different types of camps. The most prevalent was a camp owned by growers who formed a co-op to contract and house workers. These workers were shared by growers and so the work and the workers could be utilized more efficiently. It worked well for the workers and the growers. It was a good system and it worked well for everyone."

"If it was such a good system what happened? Why did it get eliminated? It doesn't make sense." Larry was listening carefully to what was being said as he asked the question.

"Excellent question Larry. I'm not too sure I can articulate a good answer, but it seemed to me that it was a variety of reasons. I suppose one reason is that a war program was no longer part of our thinking as a country. There was unemployment and it was thought that the program was taking jobs away from citizens. Also, unions were trying to get a foothold on the farm and frankly they couldn't and I suppose they thought they would have better luck without the Braceros. And lastly, a few farmers abused the program by using workers in jobs that could be done by citizens. Also some camps were terrible and some workers no doubt were abused in the process. These few bad apples were used as an excuse to get rid of a good program that needed only a few slight adjustments."

Lucinda said, "I've always heard that farmers became addicted to this labor and wouldn't consider any alternatives."

"In a sense you're right Lucinda. The program was so efficient and positive that it was easy to get addicted to it. And when you compare it with what we got in its place; it was miraculous in comparison." Max looked at both Lucinda and Larry as he spoke. He noticed that Larry took out a small book and made some notes.

Lucinda was quiet for a time as she looked at the men the table, finally she said, "Okay, but what about our current situation and what about the legislation that's being proposed?"

Roger reacted quickly, "Well for one thing, I'm not too keen about the idea of going to jail just because I want to harvest my crops. On top of that, we're concerned that someone will add something at the last minute that will make it impossible for us to use it. Then there's the problem of how the law will be administered; that can make all the difference in the world." He paused for a few minutes, "Frankly, our company is looking into some type of partnership in Mexico to grow our product there. Some of our competitors have already made that move and we're considering it. It's really ironic that we'll use the same worker we've employed here, but now we'll employ them in Mexico. Curiously, the worker will have less protection and earn less money in Mexico!"

Again Larry interjected, "What do you mean grow the same product in Mexico? I don't understand?"

Roger answered, "Well just as an example; take green onions. We grow them here, but it's a labor intensive crop to handle. They grow exactly the same onion in the Mexicali area right across the border and ship it every day to the Los Angeles market just like we do. They use the same seed, the same trucks and ironically the same worker as we do. On top of that, they can do it cheaper because they don't have to put up with all our regulations."

"How can we continue to produce the onions here if that's so?" asked Larry.

"Excellent question Larry, and many of our competitors have said they can't. They moved most of their operations to Mexico. However, there still are some hard heads like us that want to work and grow our produce here, so we continue. We do it in the short term, but the long term looks iffy at best. Now, the threat of going to jail on top of that makes the decision to move abroad even easier."

"Another reason I'm told is the earnings in the field are too low, that they ought to be increased," said Larry.

"A good point Larry; I doubt very much that we could get citizens to work in the fields no matter what we pay. We tried; people just won't do it. And the other one is Mexico. They can already produce cheaper than we can that's for damn sure!"

Chapter 25

A FTER THE TWO GROWERS LEFT, Larry, Lucinda and his parents were cleaning up and putting dishes away. Finally Larry said, "Dad what was that all about. Why were Mr. Martin and Mr. Garvey here? I mean, why did they want to talk to us?"

Lucinda took a piece of fruit from a plate and ate it and said, "I'm not too sure, but it was curious that they wanted to talk to us. It tells me a few things. First it appears that our message must be getting through and is effective. Apparently some folks think it might have a chance to pass. Secondly, now they're considering the implications of the law being put into effect and how it might affect them. And thirdly, they were telling us of some of the possible consequences like moving their production off shore."

"Dad, how well do you know these men? I know this is a small town, but how significant are they in the farming community?"

"Your grandfather worked for Mr. Martin for years. Actually, we lived on the Martin Ranch and I worked there as well during the summers while I was in college. Mr. Martin encouraged me to go to college. Roger Garvey is also from an old family and I got to know him while at Palo Alto. He gave me many rides to school. So I've known them for a long time. I consider them friends. Now they're my customers as well."

"One thing that has bothered me Dad, is that some of the people I met recently along the way say that all farmers exploit workers and keep their workers in shackles on the farm. They say they don't give a shit about the workers."

Tom frowned at his son and Lucinda, he said, "I suppose, like in any group, there are a few farmers that might fit that description, but we've been involved with these people all our lives and they're just like the rest of us; no better, no worse."

Lucinda was embarrassed, "It's my fault Larry, as we've gone making our rounds we met mostly anti-farmer groups and people. They never have anything good to say about farming companies. Your Dad is correct. Farmers are no different than anyone else. Most are honest, hardworking people, but then there are a few assholes, just like in any other profession, including those of us who purport to help people."

"One interesting thing is that some folks are quick to bitch about farmers, but don't give them any credit for the great variety and quantity that comes from their fields. On top of that, they do this at very reasonable prices compared with other countries. All you have to do is look at our dinner tables and waistlines," added his father.

Larry smiled and asked, "Which group do we belong to Lucinda?"

Chapter 26

"WELL, ROG WHAT DID YOU THINK of the kid?" Max was driving back to his office where Roger had left his car.

"I was impressed. Not only with the kid, but even with Lucinda. I think we should have someone like her and her group work for us; to promote our issues, but perhaps even to promote our product. There are a good number of people of a liberal persuasion that avoid our products. Not only that, but they tend to be a more affluent part of our society. I gave her my card and suggested we talk after the election. She sounded interested."

"What about Larry?"

"Nice kid. Seems sharp enough; I know when I was his age doing something like what he's doing would never have occurred to me. I would have no problem opening a few doors for him at Stanford. I think it would be good for him, good for Stanford and good for our industry if we were ever to get him to work for us somehow."

"I agree. We need to think about this. Perhaps I could somehow get his parents involved in a suggestion. I know Tom would be more than willing to go along with any idea that would make that happen."

"Max, a while back you said you would tell me about the kid and his family. You sounded a bit mysterious. What did you mean?"

"Actually, Larry is not Tom's son. Tom is, in fact, his uncle. The kid is actually the son of Robert Franco, Tom's younger brother. Larry's parents were killed in an auto accident in Arizona a few days after he was born. A day after the accident, Tom and Alice picked up the boy and brought him home as their son; which in fact he is. Curiously enough, a few months ago the Border Patrol picked him up as an illegal immigrant and actually put him in prison for a few days; which is how the kid got involved with Lucinda and her people. Then on top of that, he was picked up again and I suppose that led him to work for Lucinda."

"Wow; that must have been a real blow to the kid, to be tossed in detention," said Roger.

"I'm sure it was. I know it was a terrible blow to Tom and Alice, but in a way, as I understand it, at least the kid learned about his real parents and eventually about his adoption. Then on top of that he became acquainted with his birth mother's family who live in Arizona. They have connections there with some of the old Mexican families and some Indian relatives in that part of the country."

"Wow, that's quite a combination of DNA. It seems to have built in some resilience in him. If he's just got hit with two blows like that, he seems to function pretty well and still have his head on straight. Well Max, what's next?"

"Roger, I think we should make our next move with Lucinda. Let's see if we have a little job she could do for us that would give us a chance to judge what she can do."

His friend thought about it and said, "What do you have in mind."

"Think about this as an idea. For the last several years we have been developing an interesting lemon. The interior is different; it has a pink flesh and the skin has some interesting, green stripes or striations. It looks different, it's pretty. So we think people would be willing to pay a premium for it if we promote it to the right people; the more affluent folks if you will."

"Since you're the only one that has any significant production, maybe you can make a special deal with her; a trial run proposal. She knows you and this could determine if she's interested in broadening her promotional skills. It's worth a try."

"Well, let's see how this campaign develops in the next couple of weeks. That will give us time to mull this notion over and then we can approach her and check out her reaction."

Chapter 27

Lucinda noted that Larry was unusually quiet as they drove to the Los Angeles Airport. "So young man, you've been awfully quiet, what's going on?"

"I don't know how you do it Lucinda. Running from place to place, living out of a suitcase. Dealing with strangers all the time, in many cases, people you don't even like. It must get kind of lonely."

Not taking her eyes off the crowded Ventura Freeway, "I must confess that every once in awhile it does get me down, but with this campaign, I know the end is just around the corner and it'll be over. What's the matter, are you running out of steam? I just assumed that a young man like you would like this hectic life."

"Don't get me wrong, it is interesting. It's an experience I never would have dreamed of just a few months ago, but I do miss my family and..."

"Let me guess, you miss your girlfriend? What's her name Ginny? She seemed like a nice girl."

"She's not really my girlfriend, but we've been friends since grade school. I like her, but she's not my girlfriend."

"Ahh, Cipri...it is Cipri isn't it? Your long lost cousin. Now I understand. And frankly, I don't blame you, she's a nice girl and very pretty. On top of that, she seems like someone who stands on her own two feet and doesn't put up with BS." She drove quietly for a couple of miles after they merged onto the 405 to the airport. "I tell you what, I've got a couple of extra bucks on this contract and we're getting to the most interesting, but hectic time. Why don't we call her and ask her if she wants to work for me as an intern. I can't pay her much, but it will include all the expenses while we're on the road."

Larry's face brightened and his voice took another tone, "but what would she do?"

"You've been with me long enough to know there's lots to do. And I can tell you things will even get more hectic here in the next few weeks. There's plenty to do just to keep our schedule. And of course, it'll keep my ace from becoming moody."

Somewhat embarrassed by Lucinda's comments he replied, "Sounds like a good idea."

"Good, let's wait till we get to the airport and we'll give her a call. Do you think her parents will agree?"

"I wonder, but I think the first person she'll talk to is our great grand-mother, her namesake, Cipriana. Then she'll check in with Luna. If those two give their blessing, she'll take the job."

"Let me talk to Larry please." Lucinda handed Larry the phone. "Larry, how are you? How do you feel about Lucinda's intern idea? I mean, I don't want to be a distraction to your work. I mean, it really sounds interesting…" Cipri's voice was a combination of hesitancy mixed with anticipation.

Larry could note a certain amount of hesitation. She seemed to be reaching out to him for an extra nudge. "I'm not too sure how this business works, but I've noticed that things are getting more intense as we're getting close to the end. There's a lot to do and some things are not getting done. Apparently, Lucinda has enough in her budget to make sure everything gets done…and…and I personally would very much like you to join us."

"Oh, Larry it all sounds exciting, but let me check with the folks. I'll let you know later today. Where will you be?

"We're flying to Denver and will be there this evening. We'll be there for a couple of days making the college circuit. You can join us there."

Larry was speaking to the college students when he noticed that Cipri walked in. She stood for a second, silhouetted in the doorway of the auditorium. She had a backpack and a small suitcase that she put in the corner and sat down. After his comments, there were numerous questions that seemed to go on and on. The questions were now predictable and his answers well rehearsed. Yet he made sure he sounded enthusiastic with his answers. Both Cipri and Lucinda watched as Larry worked the crowd and marveled at the confidence, good humor and respect that he treated the crowd. He seemed to enjoy the interchange with the audience and more importantly the crowd seemed to be drawn to him. After the program, he spoke patiently with several students who wanted to ask more questions. Finally, he worked his way to the back where Lucinda and Cipri were waiting.

Lucinda quickly gave him a hug. "That was excellent, outstanding, we couldn't have planned it any better. Let me talk to the organizers and we'll be ready to get something to eat." She left the two young people alone.

They stood for a moment and then Larry said, "I'm so glad you could come. This is interesting work, but it's damn lonely. The hotel and the food are pretty much the same, it gets old. Two weeks ago we spent a Sunday morning in Dallas. We stayed near a Catholic church and I actually went to Mass just to get away from the motel. I don't know why they call it the Holiday Inn."

Cipri said nothing, but she gave him a big hug and then kissed him lightly. She stepped back and looked at him curiously and then laughed. "You mean you actually went to church by yourself! This speaking business must have a strange effect on people. No wonder you wanted me to join you."

Later at the hotel they bought a soft drink and sat in the lounge. Larry said, "Has anyone said anything to you about us? I mean, is there a problem that we're related? I guess what I'm trying to say is that I'm unsure. What's going to happen if we get serious...which I think I already am?"

"Oh Larry, I've been concerned about the same thing. And when you asked me to join you I talked a long time with our *Abuelita*. She didn't seem too concerned. She said if we had met in college just a few months ago, the same thing would have happened. She also said in the old days when people lived in small, remote villages, marriage between cousins and distant relatives was not unusual. She said the important thing is not so much blood as is love, dignity and respect for each other. Those are the important things in a relationship, she said."

Larry began to laugh, "You know, for a long time I was angry...no, I was pissed off for being arrested and thrown in jail. It was the worst experience in my life. Then to top that off, I find out that my parents are not really my parents and that my real parents had died in an accident. Yet, but for my arrest, I would not have known about a whole new part of my life and of my new family. And I wouldn't have known about you. It's mind boggling. And now, also as a result of that arrest, I find myself in politics for God's sake."

"Luna talks about the mysteries of life. And you even attended Mass all by yourself. Frankly, I don't understand Luna much of the time, but then she says if we understand them, they wouldn't be mysteries. *Abuelita* also tells me the same thing when I ask her about the Church and its mysteries. Some of these things we have to take on faith; even though that's hard to do at times."

Chapter 28

Lucinda was still in Denver when she called Max Martin. The phone was answered by his secretary who said, "If you give me your number Miss Llamas, I'll have Mr. Martin return your call as soon as he comes in."

Max looked at Roger who was getting a Coke from a small refrigerator that Max kept in his office; he said "Did you hear what happened to our buddy Jim? I went to see him in the hospital a couple of days ago."

"How's the old guy? I heard about the heart attack."

"Well, he's doing okay. His wife told me he's going to be fine; that is, if he can control his blood pressure and keep his mouth shut."

Max focused his attention on his friend and asked, "What happened; what did the old grump do this time?"

"The cardiac technician came in to check his equipment and connections when Jim yelled at his wife, 'These damn Mexicans are everywhere now. They don't want to pick my oranges anymore, but now they think they can connect me to these fancy machines. And that god damn slant-eyed surgeon; I can hardly understand him. What the hell's happening to our country?' His wife told me that the technician was standing right there and heard him rant on."

Max laughed, "It's a wonder the guy didn't pull the plug on poor old Jim right then and there."

"She told me later she followed the tech guy out into the hall and apologized. The technician said that he occasionally gets a similar reaction and has to hold his tongue. He added that the heart surgeon came from China during the Vietnam conflict and that people confuse him with the cleaning staff. He's insulted often and yet Doctor Fong continues to take care of the people. Jim's wife said that the surgeon is considered one of the best on the West Coast."

"Good Lord, it's no wonder that we farmers have such a terrible reputation. It's a wonder they don't pull the plug on him!" At that moment the phone rang and he was connected with Lucinda.

"Good morning Lucinda, how's it going? I was wondering if you had time to consider our effort to market our new Pink Lemons. In a way, it's a small venture, but if it works it could be a winner for us and for you as well."

Lucinda's voice was upbeat, "Max, as you know, we're a relatively small PR firm and our focus has been in the public sector, but this would give us an opportunity to spread our wings and broaden our scope. We'll be in the Denver area for several days, then we'll be home, perhaps I can put together a proposal that we can discuss early next week."

"Excellent, I look forward to the meeting. By the way, how is the campaign going? Is Larry still doing okay?"

"Max, the kid is really good. In a couple of years he'll be running his own company or running for political office. Although he's only in his early twenties, he operates at a much higher age level. I kind of wonder how you guys on the farm raise these fellows in your backyard and then let them get out of your grasp. Of course, we're not much better at recognizing the latent capability in these folks."

"You're right Lucinda, there's lots of talent all around us. All we have to do is cultivate them and put them to work at all levels of our operations; not just in the fields, but in the corporate office as well."

After the call he said to Roger, "She's interested and wants to come by early next week to talk. We'll see what she comes up with. By the way, she said Larry is really shining in this effort. I think we need to get serious of how we can get him leaning our way."

"Actually, I already checked with my buddy up north and he said he's all set. Apparently, they touched base with our local college and Larry has good grades and it would only take him a couple years at Palo Alto to finish. Depending on his major, he said, they might even give him a few credits for the work he's doing with Lucinda. I mean, that's the kind of stuff the guys in academia look for. So I suggest when they get here next week, we also try this idea on Larry as well."

The confidence and ease that Larry felt, and his performance in Denver, was remarkable. Even on two occasions when he was confronted with some angry students, he was able to make his points without getting ruffled. In fact, he seemed to enjoy the sparring with antagonists. The fact that he was able to discuss the issues, without denigrating a hostile audience, seemed to give him an upper hand. Cipri looked at the young man with new found respect. However, in a way, it did make her feel inadequate in comparison. The flight back to Los Angles was quiet and uneventful. At the airport they parted company. Lucinda said she had to go to her office to work on the proposal for Mr. Martin. The young couple took a rented car and drove home on scenic Highway 1. They stopped for lunch on the coast and took their time driving home. Cipri said, "I'm glad we're going to stay put for a couple of days. I need to wash come clothes. In fact, I need to stop at a mall or some place just to get a few extra things; if you don't mind."

Chapter 29

"So tell me Max, what's so special about these Pink Lemons? Does it have special properties; will it make the blind see, the deaf hear and the dumb speak?" Lucinda looked at the men around her in the board room. On the middle of the large Board of Director's table were several baskets of fruit. Each basket had a different mix of fruits. In the middle was a simple, plain basket with the company's new product. The fruit was shining and seemed to gleam under the light. Then the office secretary brought in a tray of lemonade. The goblets were beaded with condensation and topped with a slice of the multicolored lemon. The secretary again entered the room and brought in several silver trays of hors d'oeuvre with cheeses and other delectables. One tray had caviar with dark crackers. Each tray had sliced lemons and wedges for decoration which made the presentation distinctive and elegant. Max took a glass and handed it to Lucinda without saying a word. He then passed out a glass to everyone in the room. Larry and Cipri looked curiously at the cold drink and then at each other.

Max announced, "Friends, let me introduce you to our new product. Now some will say this is just an ordinary lemon and ordinary lemonade. And in a way that's true. On the other hand, a vintage Cabernet is also just a wine, but the distinction, the taste, its very nature is beyond comparison. For example, I usually have a glass of plain Burgundy with dinner at home. It comes in a large jug and it's very nice and quite adequate. However, when we have company and want to celebrate a special occasion, we go to our wine cellar and bring out a unique wine. These Pink Lemons are the equivalent of that fine wine. It's indeed a unique and distinctive fruit; worthy of a special market niche."

Roger raised his glass and added, "And of course, it comes with a distinctive price. Added Value, I think they call it."

Max smiled at Roger's comment and said, "Price or value is directly related to quantity or lack thereof. This is what makes an item unique; rare jewels are valuable because they are indeed rare. This fruit is rare. It doesn't just grow on trees like other lemons, it requires special breeding, cultivation and attention; which of course, is more expensive. Today we bring together this special drink and food to contemplate perhaps a unique way to introduce this product to the public—special in a way that is beyond how food products are usually introduced. That's why I've asked Lucinda and her group to look at this item differently from the market-ing *concepts* and *people* that she normally works with."

Lucinda first held up the glass and viewed it carefully as she swirled the crystal around to view it in a different light. Then she carefully took a sip of the liquid. Then she made a slight bow toward Max and said, "Salud!" She took another drink and then said, "For years we have been a small, ideological operation and we have done very well. Recently we've considered expanding our efforts. This recent foray in the immigration thicket has brought us into contact with the farming community. And frankly, we've had an education or eye opener as they say. Like many of the folks we deal with, we assumed that farmers were exploiters of not only our natural resources, but of the people who work for them. The reality is that farmers come in all kinds of stripes like any other segment of society; no worse or no better. I must confess; that surprised me. It also surprised my staff when I asked them to brainstorm promoting something beyond our normal clientele. And on top of that a *lemon*! Not just any lemon, but a pink lemon! My partner thought the altitude in Denver had affected my thinking, but I think not only is the product unique, but our thoughts on promoting it are also unique and that's what I'd like to discuss with you.

After Lucinda's presentation, they all got refills and were sampling the food. Roger walked up to Cipri, introduced himself and then asked. "What do you think of Max's spread of food and drink?"

Cipri smiled at the man and answered, "I have to confess, I've never tasted caviar before, it has an interesting taste. A little salty, but something I could get used to. And the entire setting is so luxurious. I can see how we could easily consider this lemon in a similar vein."

"I understand you're doing an internship with Lucinda on this immigration campaign. What's your impression of their work?"

She looked directly at Roger, smiled, and said, "Well, I had no idea how much planning and work it is to put together an effective campaign, but the key is their spokesman. I haven't known Larry for a long time. My first impression of him was not especially notable, but on the stage and with a microphone, he's able to transform himself and more importantly, he's able to transform his audience. It's amazing to see him in action, it really is."

"Do you think he can sell lemons?"

"I think if he's sincerely convinced of the issue or the product, he can sell or promote anything."

"What about you Cipri? How are you at selling or helping him to sell?"

"Well I don't think I would be very effective on stage, but I think I have a better sense of what's right and what isn't." She paused for a second and continued, "Choosing what's important and what isn't may be just as important as being *quick of tongue;* to use a phrase that my people use."

"I can't argue with that. I understand you're still in school. What are your plans for later on?"

"Well, I just finished two years in our local community college and I've already been accepted at the university. It's where my dad attended." Cipri spoke easily to Roger as the others talked about the idea of promoting the unique Pink Lemon.

"What about Larry? What are his plans?"

"I'm not too sure. I know he wants to finish college and get his degree, but recently he seems to be wavering where to attend. He found out that his birth father was going to the University of Arizona on a basketball scholarship. I know he's talked to my dad about going there, but all this recent upheaval in his life, and even this job with Lucinda, has put a wrinkle in his thinking."

"What about the schools in California? You know we have some excellent schools in this state."

"I know, he told me his dad went to Stanford, but he said it was very expensive and wasn't too sure he wanted to saddle his parents with the expense of going there."

Roger took a drink from his lemonade and said almost as an afterthought, "Wow, wouldn't it be great if both of you could go to the same school, at the same time."

Cipri lowered her eyes and shuffled her feet, "It would be great. That's why Larry's attending an Arizona school would be nice."

"If you could attend a California school, say, like Stanford, you would still be together and attending one of the top schools in the country."

"That's true, but my family could never afford the tuition at a place like Stanford. My dad works for the state and we live comfortably, but I know that he could never afford that school. It would only be a dream."

"Ah, but dreams can come true. It happens all the time. In fact, Larry's dad went to Stanford on a dream and many scholarships. I'm sure he's still paying some loans off, but he attended and he graduated. And look at him. He's a professional and now owns his own business." He smiled at the young lady in front of him, "You know the strength of this country is that someone like Tom, who came from a poor family of farm workers with his education, was able to surpass his own father's expectations. Now the trick is for Larry, and you, to do even better than your parents. That's the great secret of this country."

"But Stanford...?"

Chapter 30

"LARRY, I'M GLAD YOU HAVE A DAY OFF. I have to visit a friend of mine who had a heart attack recently and is now recuperating at home. He's an old time farmer and a good friend of my father and he's interested in this immigration bill you've been talking about and wants to meet you.' Max's voice trailed off; then he continued, "I need to warn you, he's a real old timer, but he can be a real son of bitch to be frank. So no telling what he'll say, but I can almost assure you it will be insulting. I understand he even chided his cardiologist who happens to be Chinese for being just that, Chinese. He did that even after the doctor saved his life. He's not too keen about people who step out of their place—at least from the place he thinks they should be. I think you know what I mean."

"Wow, he sounds like a real winner. I ran into many of that type recently, and although they're unpleasant, they don't bother me anymore. So why does he want to see me? I could very well upset him and affect his health and that would really bother me."

"Well, beyond the fact that he's hard headed, he's also a great supporter of our industry. He's one of the most successful farmers in the county because he's always willing to try new crops or techniques which we've all have learned and benefited from."

Jim Johnson was a very tall, unbending, slim man with a head full of white hair. He was pruning some roses in his garden when Max and Larry walked into his garden. At his side was a large French poodle with a distinctive red coloring. The dog growled at the two men approaching, "Red, quiet; they're friends." The old man put away the pruning shears and walked confidently up to meet them. "Max, it's good to see you.

Glad you haven't forgotten your old friends…Now let me guess, I suppose this is the young man who wants to put my old, skinny ass in jail!"

Larry walked right up to the old man offered his hand and said, "Yes sir, my name is Larry Franco. Recently I spent a couple of days in jail and I wouldn't wish that on anyone, skinny ass or not."

The old man took the young man's hand and held it for awhile as he looked Larry over carefully, "Well young man, I've heard much about you. Frankly I don't like your name. Larry is not a name fitting for a man who wants to put my skinny ass in jail. Your name wouldn't be Lorenzo, would it?"

"Yes sir, it actually is, but only my mom calls me Lorenzo; when she's pissed at me."

"Well Lorenzo, I'm pissed at you for wanting to put me in jail. From now on your name is Lorenzo. Lorenzo has dignity to it and I don't like to mess with people who have no dignity. Lorenzo, I want you to meet Red. He's my best friend and if you even get close to putting me in jail he will tear your balls off." The old man was smiling and he put his arms around Lorenzo and led him to a table on the veranda overlooking his garden. Max and the red dog followed the two. No sooner had they sat down at the table than a young lady brought out some iced tea, lemonade and snacks. "Lorenzo, this is not the fancy product that Max is trying to foist on to the gullible public, but it's just an honest home grown product. Now tell me why this new immigration bull shit is good for me."

"Well Mr. Johnson, this bill makes an effort to…"

"Sorry to interrupt you Lorenzo, but I am not Mr. Johnson; my good friends call me Jim and I wish you would do that. Now continue."

Lorenzo swallowed hesitantly and continued, "First let's just agree that the present immigration system is a mess. We have over ten million people working and living in this country illegally in the shadows as it were. In agriculture, the situation is even more dire. Because farming is an entry work level it has the highest employment of these workers. I don't know your workforce, but I would guess that 60, 70 or perhaps 80 percent have no valid documents. That means you could lose all your workers overnight. I wasn't around in the mid 60s, but that's exactly what happened and as I understand, it was chaos until it settled down. The problem is that we went from a fairly good program under PL 78 or the

Bracero program to what we have now…a damn mess. Now this new legislation is complex and not perfect, but it would address several principal areas. First it would deal with the millions that are already here. Secondly it would secure the borders to prevent a repeat of the last several decades. And thirdly it would resurrect a seasonal labor program that would allow workers to be contracted to come to help with the seasonal work that requires many workers for short periods of time. Now as in any legislation there's going to be some compromises and some things you might not like and be a pain, but on the whole I can assure you that it would be less of a pain than what you have now."

"Okay Lorenzo where does my jail time come in?"

"Jim, it's now illegal to hire illegals, but the usual consequence is that it's the workers who get apprehended, punished, jailed and then deported so they can try to sneak in again the following day. Nothing happens to the employer who has also committed a crime. The boss just hires another illegal and perpetuates the problem. So it's a revolving door, one without end. The new law would give plenty of warning to employers to clean up their act. Even more importantly it would give them the opportunity to obtain workers legally via the new legislation. So with this law if you choose not to participate in the legal program and you were fully informed and aware of the jail consequence and then still hire illegals, then it's jail time plus a fine."

"Lorenzo I have a good size operation and have very skilled managers and if I told them to comply, I have no doubt we would comply. Max I think would also have no problems, but what about some of the smaller operations or someone who is just starting, how could they get aboard?"

"It's my understanding that during WWII, Public Law 78 worked fine. I understand grower associations got farmers to band together to make sure they complied. In fact, I heard you were president of one of the largest labor associations in the country during that period. So you probably know better than anyone how that would work."

"You know Lorenzo, we farmers get all the blame. Now granted, we do employ many of these folks, but what pisses me off is all that righteous Beverly Hill crowd; they all have gardeners and maids who are also illegal. What about them? What will happen to them?"

The section on fines and jail time applies to everyone. There'll be a period of notices; warnings and an educational process, but after all that, if some gal from Beverly Hills gets caught with an illegal pool cleaner it's off to the slammer with her."

Johnson started to laugh, "Damn Lorenzo, I just might support your efforts to see that happen. It would be worth the price of admission. Damn if I wouldn't!"

The conversation lasted for a while longer. The old man wanted to know more about Larry, his family and Max's new venture in these exotic varieties of Pink Lemons.

As Max started the car and drove away, he said, "Well Lorenzo, that beats the shit out of me. I've known that old man all my life and I never knew his friends called him Jim. He's never put his arms around me. That near death experience made a real transformation in him. It's a bloody miracle that's for damn sure."

The young man giggled and said, "You know Max, I like the name Lorenzo!"

Chapter 31

THE CAMPAIGN WAS ENTERING the critical phase. Yet in a way the last part was almost anticlimactic. All the work of promoting the Re form Immigration Bill, or the RIB as it was now called; was almost done. The polls indicated that although it was expected to be close, it was projected to win. The main opposition from farmers in California did not materialize, and to the great surprise of many, several prominent growers in the southern part of the state actually supported it. The biggest caveat they had was to make sure they got a practical, reliable supplementary worker program. Lucinda and Larry made sure it became an important part of their pitch. So much was this stressed, that the factions that would have opposed any assistance to farmers were either convinced on the merits of the idea or were so overwhelmed with the general support that they gave in to insure the passage of the total bill.

Larry and Cipri found themselves in another Holiday Inn. It was now a routine. After a presentation, they had a late snack and if the place they were in was safe, they took a walk and checked out the sights. Also part of the routine was attending Mass on Sundays. They had gone to the University of San Diego to give their last talk. The Catholic University Chapel was crowded and the couple felt welcomed. They joined the many students for coffee and donuts. They sat on a bench by themselves. Lorenzo said, "The other night Mr. Martin called me to his office and wanted to talk about the campaign. From what they told me, they pretty much are convinced that it's going to pass and become law. Now, actually, they are looking at the consequences and the actual implementation of the law. They want to make sure that it does what we said it would do.

For them it would be to make sure that the supplemental farm labor provision of the law gets implemented and efficiently managed. They implied that since Lucinda and I were the principal spokesman for the law, that they expect us to make sure that farmers get a fair deal. Also they want us to be involved in the promotion campaign for Mr. Martin's new exotic Pink Lemons."

"I'm not too sure what that means. Once the law is passed and goes into effect, isn't it the government's responsibility to administer it?" Cipri took a sip of her hot tea.

"That's true, but they want someone to keep their eyes on the bureaucrats to make sure it's implemented fairly." Larry paused for a long time as he watched the young church goers mingle..."And Lucinda and Mr. Martin made me an interesting proposal. Actually if I understood them correctly, they made the proposal to both of us."

"Okay Larry, or should I call you Lorenzo, what the hell are you talking about? What kind of a proposal and what does it have to do with me?"

"As I understand it, they want us to continue working for Lucinda, but my main chore would be to keep an eye on the legislation and its implementation."

"But Larry, what about school? I thought you...I mean we...we're committed to finishing school."

"That's just it Cipri, school is part of the deal. They want us to finish school. While in school we would be active; especially during vacations and even during school if needed."

"Damnit Larry, I don't understand. What are you talking about? Now tell me specifically, what did they propose?"

"Well if I understand them, they want us to enroll at Stanford; they'll pay all expenses plus some additional spending money. For that I would be on call to help out when needed. I would have to keep well informed of the law and its workings. Frankly there are several things I need to consider and clear up, but that's essentially it."

"What about me?"

"As I understand it, you're part of the deal. The offer is for both of us."

Cipri's eyes glistened, finally she said, "Are you serious?"

"Yes, I spoke to Lucinda and that's the essence of the proposal, but we need to talk to her again and Mr. Martin, to make sure we understand each other. And we need to talk to our parents. And we need to do all that soon and be ready for the next semester. So what do you think?"

"Well Lorenzo, you're right, we have lots to think about and we need to talk to our folks, but right now I wonder if we can go back to the chapel, I think we need to talk to Him and get His thoughts and His blessings."

The two young people drove back to Santa Paula. Both were quiet and puzzled. They were thinking of the extraordinary offer that had been made to them. The first hurdle was to convince themselves that it was real and legitimate, just that by itself was a significant hurdle. Believing it was a prank or a cruel joke was easy to imagine. Again they drove north leisurely on Highway 1. They stopped to eat and twice just to enjoy the view of the ocean. Normally it would have been a pleasant trip, with much talking, listening to music and joking, but the concern of the offer made to them and the implications it would have on their lives was overwhelming. Also weighing heavily was the way the offer was made; there was some suspicion of this seemingly altruistic offer. They wanted to see it as deserving, but they felt there must be something else; something perhaps, not quite apparent to them at the moment.

"We have an appointment with Lucinda tomorrow at noon. I understand she will explain more fully the significance of this offer and the details. She also said we should think about it carefully and ask any questions we might have. She said we should talk to our parents. So tonight we're having dinner at our house to talk to Mom and Dad. Then you can call your parents."

Tom and Alicia listened carefully as Larry explained the offer that Lucinda relayed to them. They said nothing while they finished dinner. Finally Tom said, "I ran into Roger Garvey the other day. We had some coffee and he told me about the offer. Let me see if I can fill in some gaps. First let me tell you that Lucinda, her group and the local farmers were very impressed with your work to get the law passed. They were impressed with both of you, but I think they saw you guys as a team. They see passing the law as only the first half of the game. It's the implementation, the nuts and bolts if you will, that they're concerned with. They know that how the rules and regulations are developed and applied will make the law a viable tool for them or the bane of their existence. They see the continued involvement of Lucinda and her group as part of their insurance that they won't be screwed. They're doing this in a couple of ways. First she's getting some business from Max and his new Pink Lemons. If she sees farmers as potential clients she's more likely not to be bashing farmers all the time."

Cipri asked, "I can see that, farmers are in a sense protecting their investment. It makes good sense, but what does all that have to do with us?"

"Well they see you as part of the reason that Lucinda was successful and they want to make sure she stays on their side or perhaps even neutral in the implementation of the law. So you're part of the investment to make sure that Lucinda isn't lured away by some anti-farmer effort. And here's the final pitch that Roger made and this he made confidentially; they see you Lorenzo in some part of their business in the next few years. And they want to make sure you get the best education you can get, so that, if they can lure you into the business, they will be sure they have someone who's well qualified."

"Wow Dad this sounds like some Machiavellian plot. I mean, it never occurred to me that I might be working for farmers, it's probably the last thing on my mind. There's got to be something else behind this."

"There may be something else, but I don't think so. Look at it this way. Farming on the scale of Martin, Garvey and your friend Jim is big business. I mean, these enterprises are huge. Granted, much of their operations are based on production, but many are also huge land owners and even developers. So they need the best talent they can get just like any other part of the economy. So they're making a small investment in the short term to insure their continued viability in the long term."

"But the tuition money, books and no telling what else is huge; how can they afford it?" asked Cipri.

"That's just it Cipri, from their perspective, it's an investment and a small one at that. If it doesn't work, they just misspent a few bucks that will be a tax deduction, but if it works they'll be getting dividends for many years into the future. It's all relative. To both of you it's a very large and generous offer, but to their bottom line it's probably of little consequence."

As they put away the dishes Larry said to Cipri, "You should call your parents."

"I thought about it, but I think I'll wait until we meet with Lucinda. I just want to get all the parts of this strange puzzle. That way I can give them a complete picture of what we're talking about. And frankly, it'll give me time to think if I want to be in the picture. And finely I think I'd first like to call Luna."

Cipri spent the first ten minutes explaining her recent work with Lucinda and Larry. Then she tried to summarize the offer made to her and to Larry. As she outlined the proposal, it didn't make any sense to herself even as she tried to explain it to her friend. Luna listened carefully, but said nothing. She even waited several seconds after Cipri stopped talking before asking her first question. Finally she said, "Oh Baby, have you prayed to our Lord about this?"

"I have! It just happened that we were at the University of San Diego after Sunday Mass when Larry or Lorenzo, as he now wants to be called, told me what little he knew. My first thought was to return to the Chapel where we spent some time in a quiet corner talking and listening to the Lord."

"Good; that was an excellent move. Now you need to make sure that you continue that conversation with God in church or even when you're going about your normal day. Tell me, do you know the people who are behind the offer?"

"Mostly I just know them superficially. Lorenzo knows them a bit more since they're farmers in the area. His dad knows them better and seems to have a good relationship with them. In fact, Larry's grandfather worked for one of them. They seem to be nice guys."

"Do you have any reason to doubt the authenticity of their offer? What makes you think that there's something unseemly about it?"

"I really don't have any basis to doubt the sincerity of the offer, other than I'm suspicious of anyone who wants to give me something for nothing."

"That's just it Cipri it isn't something for nothing. It sounds like they're doing this as a reward for the work you all did for them and to keep watch or guard their interest as this law is implemented. When you think just about the latter concern, they're probably not paying enough. And that's not counting the dividends they may recover if Larry or Lorenzo ever goes to work for them."

"I know, I just have a suspicious nature. I want to talk to *mi Abuelita*, I wonder what she'll say?"

"Call her; tell her what you told me. Then after you talk to your parents and pray about this, then just follow your heart. Follow your heart just as you are with regards to Lorenzo. At the beginning, you had no idea about this young man, yet you went to work with him on this journey and look where you are. You're facing choices and opportunities and that's what life is all about. Sometimes these choices are not easy, but that doesn't mean they can't be good opportunities."

John and Linda Mendez listened to Cipri's explanation of her dilemma, they were on a speaker phone, but everyone listened carefully. Her mother finally said, "*Mija*, that sounds like a wonderful opportunity for you and for Lorenzo even though you'll be far away from your home. But in the end, this is a decision only you can make. Whatever you decide, we'll support you both."

"Listen Cipri, I know it sounds too good to be true, but sometimes generosity is just that—generosity. There's no reason that Stanford can't' be just that, someone's effort to do a good deed." John Mendez's voice was quiet and seemed to echo all those at home listening to the phone. "Listen Honey, think about it, pray and then call us back and let us know what you guys decide."

The following day the two young people met with Lucinda and one of the company's attorneys. Lucinda started, "First let me tell you both how grateful I am for the work you did for our clients and for our firm. To be honest, some folks in my group thought I was being foolish by putting much of our effort on two young and inexperienced people. I was glad to be vindicated. Now as to this offer, it may sound complicated and perhaps somehow strange, but a group of growers who, based on our word, agreed not to oppose this measure, now want to make sure that it's implemented in a fair and appropriate manner. And they asked us to perform that oversight. On top of that they think, and I agree, that you were the reason for our success so that's why they want you to be in the picture. They're also aware of your need to complete your studies and so they are willing to subsidize the costs of your stay at Stanford for the next two years."

The attorney handed each a copy of an employment contract and added, "You'll also note that part of the duties may require you to assist, if and when you can, to help the Martins bring their new product to market. The clients understand that the main thrust of this agreement is for you to complete your studies in the next two years. The additional duties that Lucinda mentioned are just that, additional duties to be performed as your studies permit."

Chapter 32

THE THREE FARMER FRIENDS sat for lunch after the annual meeting of the San Cayetano Mutual Water Company. Jim Johnson asked, "What do you hear from the two young people at Palo Alto. It's been a while since I got a note from Lorenzo. He seemed to be doing okay. I wish you two had let me in on your scheme. I could have gotten him in at SC."

"Oh Jim, you just can't help but support that football factory you went to. Actually SC would have been fine or Cal Poly who already had accepted Larry, but since Roger had connections with Stanford, that's where we made the deal."

"What about the young lady, how's she doing?" asked the old man.

"My friend and Lucinda both tell me they're doing well and should easily complete their degrees as planned. One thing we need to think about is what to do with them this summer. They could attend a couple of summer classes and ensure their graduation. Or we can put them to work to see if they're for real."

Max stirred his iced tea, "It's good for us to talk about their activities, but I think we ought to give them some space and see what they would like to do."

"It goes without saying, but it doesn't hurt for some old guys like us to push them in the general direction of what we would like them to do." Jim smiled as he drank some of his tea.

"Well I understand they'll be here for spring break. That might be the time to have a nice chat with them. That will give us a notion of what to do next." Roger continued, "You know I'm involved in getting some farmers together to form a labor co-op to contract the workers and to operate a common labor camp and all the other issues that will come up. We also need to touch base with the folks in Mexico. I'm flying down to Hermosillo to check things out. I think it would be a good idea to take these two with me so they can see what's going on."

"That's a great idea, it would only take a few days and then they can have a few days to spend with their families or at the beach." Jim was in good spirits. Since he had his heart attack, he seemed to have mellowed considerably. His brief meeting with Lorenzo also appeared to stir up his interest in the young couple.

Larry and Cipri drove to Santa Paula for the spring break. Larry said, "Roger and Max have a small project that they want us to look at. We're to meet them for breakfast tomorrow at the Mupu Grill."

"What do they have in mind; did they say?"

"Actually, Roger has to go to Hermosillo, Mexico to check out the new contracting center and wants us to go with him."

"Wow, are you kidding. It sounds like it could be interesting. I can't wait to hear what he has in mind." Cipri paused and said, "You know, since we're going to be in that part of the world, maybe we can stop to see my folks?"

The two growers were already drinking coffee when the two students walked in. They quickly ordered breakfast and chatted briefly about school. Then Roger explained, "I'm flying to Hermosillo tomorrow to check out the new contracting center for our local group. And we thought it would be a good idea for you guys to check it out with me. We need to keep tabs on that organization since they will be key in the selection process that workers will have to go through. The better they do their jobs, the better workers we'll get. We'll be gone two maybe three days."

The young students hungrily ate their breakfast as they listened. Finally Cipri asked, "What are the chances of us staying in Arizona for a couple of days to visit my folks?"

"That shouldn't be a problem; I'll just have our pilot add a stop at the nearest place next to Jerome. So pack lightly and we'll see you at the airport at 8:00 am."

"What airport?" asked Larry.

"Our airport...here in town. I thought you knew we're going in our company plane. That will give us more flexibility in case we need to make a change. And I'll check with Tommy our pilot to check out the airport nearest to Jerome so we can drop you off on the way back."

The young couple was excited about flying in a private corporate plane. They landed in El Paso to cross into Mexico and within a couple of hours were deplaning in Hermosillo. They went directly to the recruiting center. The complex was one of complete, but orderly chaos. The applicants were in the hundreds and yet they were subdued and obeying the directions by the wall signs and by those directing traffic. A U.S. representative gave them a quick tour and explained the procedures. Then they were taken to a conference room and were provided refreshments. The representative gave them a two-page report of the center's activities and asked for questions. After reviewing the information Cipri asked simply, "Where are the women?"

There was silence for a while and the Representative asked, "What do mean women? Our center only contracts men. That's what the orders are for; no one said anything about women. We're not prepared to process women." The man's face was one of astonishment indicating the impertinent question.

"Let me see if I got this right. We worked hard to get legal replacement for farm workers. Strawberries and other similar crops are our main crop in our county and they are intensive labor users with a large percentage of the workers being women. So it would seem that if women are doing the work at present, shouldn't women be included in this seasonal program? Or am I missing something?"

"In a way Miss, it would be an inconvenience. To process, to transport and especially to house women would be a nightmare. So it was decided administratively to process only males. In a way, we were following the guidelines of PL 78 or the old Bracero Program."

"I appreciate that it was done because it is easier this way. Discrimination of convenience is still discrimination, but I'm looking at this program for the long run. When the public, and by that I mean my liberal sisters, hear about this discrimination, they'll raise hell. It's dumb decisions like this that killed the old program and will destroy this one. As it is, there's a large group of people who don't like this program and will use any damn excuse to kill it. For Christ sakes, do we have to give them ammunition? Come on guys, I know it can be a pain-in-the-ass, but let's not take our eyes off the ball. The important part is that we got the program; now let's utilize it in a way that will benefit our industry and all the workers that participate in it."

The plane stopped at the border to clear customs and within hours they were landing in a small private airfield just outside Jerome. The plane paused briefly at a small hanger; didn't even turn off its engine and within seconds was off and continued the trip home.

The three growers met at their regular table at the Mupu Grill listening to Roger's report. "You know we've been focusing on Larry in all our recent talks, but I have to tell you, that Cipri is no shrinking violet. That is one sharp young lady. She immediately focused on one of the weak parts of this program that we all fought to get. Basically she said that by bypassing women, it will give activists all the ammunition they need to begin tearing down the new law. Those of us who were just trying to get workers the easiest way, with the least complications, just overlooked the obvious. The discrimination of women is a public relations nightmare. We will piss off one half of the people with just that one action. I called Lucinda and talked to her about Cipri's concern and she damn near had a heart attack and apologized that she didn't think about it. However, she recovered quickly and reminded me that Larry and Cipri are on retainer with her firm to keep us informed on this program and such problems."

Jim said, "Now what do we do?"

"Well, the big issue will be to arrange for adequate housing for women and start a program that will integrate women into the program and into our workforce," said Roger.

"It won't be all that easy," said Max. "We're going to have a fair chore just to convince some of our own members of the necessity of incorporating women. Some of our good ol'boys will bitch at the additional cost and inconvenience."

"Well that's what we're paying Lucinda for. What did she say when you talked to her?" asked Max.

"We actually have a meeting later on today. So we'll get her take on what to do. In the meantime, we need to make sure that we talk to our own group and provide as much information as we can; so we can all march to the same tune." Roger signed the tab for the breakfast.

Chapter 33

IPRIANA WALKED WITH HER TWO great grandchildren to morning Mass. She hung on to them; one on each side of her. Not that she needed assistance, but she wanted to be close to the young people. In a strange way she wanted to be close enough so that she could smell them. She even tasted them when she kissed them. She inhaled deeply, it was an instinctive reaction. There was comfort in their closeness. "I invited Luna; she said she'd meet us at the church. Then we're going home for some chocolate and some conversation. I want to know everything you two have been doing."

At the breakfast table the conversation flowed just like the hot chocolate and coffee. The kitchen was overrun with friends and neighbors going in and out. There were hugs, kisses and lots of chatter. Everyone was happy to see the young people. There was a general understanding that they were a couple. There was no pronouncement or proclamation, but it was just understood. Even Cipri and Lorenzo understood and accepted the reality.

During one part of the morning, Larry was the only man in the kitchen and he took a cup of chocolate and went outside to join John Mendez, Cipri's father. Larry said, "There's too many females in the kitchen, it's overwhelming."

"I know that's why at times I enjoy my coffee out here in the cool of the morning. I'm really glad you two had the chance to drop by. To be honest, deep down I was hoping you would choose the U of A, but if it had to be another school, I can't argue with Stanford. So how are the studies going?"

"We're doing well. On top of all the help we're getting from our work; the school gave us credit for the work we did during the election. As I understand it, we'll get some additional credit for this work, but we have to write and submit a paper. Writing is easy in a sense since we have to write a report for Lucinda and then it's not too difficult to make a few changes to make it a school report. So if everything continues like this, we'll both finish next year as planned."

"And then what?' asked John.

Larry laughed, "It's kind of funny, but our effort in this immigration business has opened some doors in farming in our county; something that would never have occurred to me. There's especially one old man who is considered a real SOB by everyone. He recently had a heart attack and is recuperating. For some reason he's taken a liking to me. He's written to me several times; he says 'just to keep in touch', but in almost every note he hints that he wants me to join his organization."

"Hmm, now tell me about your trip to Hermosillo. How do you see that operation going? Do you think it will be viable program?"

"The premise is correct; it's the right thing to do, not only for the farmers, but for the workers as well. The trick will be to have it administered correctly so everyone feels comfortable with it. And in particular, we don't need to make any stupid mistakes like the one Cipri saw immediately. So as a result of our trip and her insight, a program for female workers will be considered. So the industry must just remain vigilant and ready to adapt to changes quickly when needed."

"Do you think that's possible? You know in some quarters, farmers are known for being hard headed, prehistoric in their thinking some would say. I know some of the ol' boys around here are scary at times," he joked.

"I know I don't have that much experience with them, but the ones I've met recently seem to be good, hard working business guys who just want to stay in business and make a few bucks. I know there must be a few nuts. In fact, I understand Jim Johnson, the man I told you about is among that group, but he seems to have changed and I can't say anything but good things. And, as I said, he seems to be interested in me. He's also the one who calls me Lorenzo; he said it was a name with more dignity than Larry."

John took his coffee cup in both hands, inhaled deeply of the liquid and after taking a drink said, "I hear the women talk about you and Cipri. They talk like I can't see what's going on, but I think it's time that you and I talk, so that both of us know what's going on between you two and more importantly, what to expect in the future."

The question was not unexpected, "You know John, my life has been tumultuous in the last year. So many things happened I would have never dreamed about. The most astonishing thing that has occurred was Cipri and all of you. Cipri has affected me beyond anything else. Recently we talked about it. We discussed our family relationship. We talked with some people we respect and we came to the conclusion that the feelings we have for each are real. We decided not to formalize it until we finish school. That's our first priority, but if we can wait, it will be the first thing I want to do. I know it's kind of awkward for me to be asking here, but I hope you agree and would give us your blessings."

"Well Lorenzo...by the way, I like Lorenzo better too. Of course you know that around here, people will soon be calling you *Lencho*. Beyond what people call you, it's character that I'm concerned with. I think character is partly inherent in people, but it's also developed in everyone by our surroundings and our values. And I must tell you that with the things you've gone through, you have handled it remarkably well. In the end it's not what I think, it's what Cipri thinks, and from what she tells me, she thinks it's a good idea. That's a long ways around to tell you, I have no objection, but only my blessings for you both." Cipri's father took another drink and then said, "Okay, *Lencho* let's go see what the girls are up to."

Later in the afternoon the two young people met with Luna who was preparing to return home. "I'm so glad Cipriana asked me to join the family to visit with you both. After the few recent bumps in your lives, things appear to be going well. Perhaps the best thing of adversities is that you can be assured that there will be plenty more to come. That's how life is. The trick is not to be so traumatized by an incident that you become incapable of living your life. In the military they call this PTSD or Post Traumatic Stress Disorder. We know it will occur, so we steel ourselves to cope and to learn from our adversities. We do this by having a positive moral compass and a strong spiritual life." Luna smiled at the two and continued, "You'll also find out that ironically, even good things can have negative impacts. Things like joy, excitement, like winning the lottery, can cause a stroke or heart attack. Again the trick is to be able to cope with these incidents, regardless if they're positive or negative ones."

On the short plane flight to the Burbank airport, Cipri asked, "What did you and Daddy talk about while you guys were outside alone?"

Larry was hesitant and then said, "He wanted to know how we were doing in school. Then he was wondering what our plans were for after we graduate. Then...then he wanted to know what my intentions were regarding you and me."

"What did you tell him?"

"Well, I told him that school was going fine and that we should graduate in two years as planned. I also mentioned that Mr. Johnson had hinted at a job in his company and that even though working in agriculture never had occurred to me before, that I was becoming interested in the idea. I told him there were some real possibilities in that industry."

"And?"

"And, what?"

"Lorenzo, what did you tell him about your intentions regarding you and me?"

"I told him that after we graduate I wanted to be with you and I asked him for his blessings."

"And?"

"He said he had no objection, as long as you thought it was a good idea and he gave me ...he gave us his blessings."

"And?"

"What do you mean, And?"

"Aren't you going to ask me?"

"Ask you what?"

"To marry me. A girl wants to be asked."

Larry took a deep breath and stammered, "Cipriana Agundez Mendez will you marry me?"

"Yes silly, of course I will; you know I will!"

Chapter 34

L UCINDA MET WITH A SMALL COMMITTEE of well known growers in the back room of the Mupu Grill. The waitress brought the individual orders without asking. The consultant made a mental note that she was the only one who looked at a menu and ordered from it. Roger was the apparent leader of the group. "A few days ago we took a quick trip to see the operations in Hermosillo. Some of you might have seen a similar operation in the past. It was a hectic place, but it seemed to be an efficient operation, except for one thing. They were only processing men."

"What's wrong with that, we can all use men. In fact, the old Bracero program was all men I think," said one of the men.

"I believe that's true, but let me turn this over to Lucinda, who will put this in perspective."

"As you all know, to get this supplemental labor program in the immigration law was no easy chore. We campaigned hard and it was passed because we didn't make any dumb mistakes. One of my staff members, who helped in passing the law, went to Hermosillo and saw the process and the first question she asked was; where were the women? Here's her point, especially for you berry growers and other similar crops; everyone knows just by looking at your workers that the majority of these workers are women; right now I can go out to your fields and see the women. Now my gal's reaction was that there are many people who were against the law and still are. And we can be sure that they are waiting for some fatal mistake so they can jump on it. So here we are with this program just starting, and we're about to piss off fifty percent of our population."

"But if we bring in women, it will be difficult to house them," said one of the men.

"Where do the women working for you live now?"

There was quiet in the room finally one said, "Hell if I know."

"Well my friend, that's my point. You damn well better know. Under the old Bracero program, a labor camp or some type of housing was provided. You are scrambling right now to find adequate housing for the men; I suggest you do the same for the women."

"But that'll cost a fortune, even if we can get the local government bureaucrats to approve such lodging."

"I have bad news for you; either you make an effort to treat everyone equally, or I can assure you the supplemental program will just be a dream in a year or so."

"How can you be so sure that will happen?" she was asked.

Lucinda's laugh was somewhat muffled, "Perhaps you all are not aware of who we are. My firm accepted this challenge of working for farmers, but our main efforts in the past, and still is, is to accept what you would all call liberal or far left projects. If a group came to us and asked us to start a campaign against this program, I can have a group of well financed, committed people in the streets practically overnight. And if my firm can do it so can many others; and most of them are friends of mine."

"Yeah, but if we bring in girls, the next thing that will happen is that they'll get married and we'll have to bring in more," said one of the quiet men in the group."

Lucinda said, "That may very well be true, and I'm sure it will happen, but that's no reason to discriminate and jeopardize the program. And if it goes down, it'll be the whole program and you'll be back where you were before."

"What do you suggest Lucinda, in a sense, you brought us to this point, where do we go from here?" asked Roger.

"I just said you don't want to piss off 50 percent of the people, so you need to make an effort to show that you at least did consider the fairer sex. Now you still might be criticized about the numbers, but you'll have something to show. And as far as housing, it'll be a problem no doubt, but how difficult will it be to rent a couple of houses. Or you could put them up in one the houses you own now. I think you just need to show an effort. I mean; a sincere effort."

"Do you have any suggestions how to do that?" asked one of the men.

"Well one of my associates, the one who started this conversation said she did some quick research and in Florida, one grower bought ten mobile homes and put them on his ranch. He put four people in each home and voila, he had places for forty people. On top of that, each house had a kitchen so the people took care of their own food needs. With women, this would be perfect."

"Yeah, but we have so many regulations and bases to touch that it will be a pain in the ass," said one of the men.

"I have no doubt about that; then it's even more important that you get moving on the idea as soon as you can." Lucinda looked at her watch and said to Roger, "I have to leave, and it looks like your group has more to chew on than just their breakfast."

Chapter 35

"WHERE ARE WE GOING"? Cipri asked Lucinda.
"I want to show you two what can be done with the right idea and a little encouragement. One of the largest berry growers got wind of some government trailers used for disasters. He has a ranch right across from a grammar school. It just happened that he donated the land for the school. With a little prompting, he got the neighbors to support the project and so he applied and got a conditional permit to build a mini mobile home park. While he was getting the permits, he got the homes completely remodeled and brought here from the desert. The place still looks a little undone because the landscaping and some of the other amenities are still being worked on." Lucinda parked the car next to the house.

Cipri and Larry were quiet as they drove to the camp. Larry was especially interested in the fields and the activities as they drove. Directly across from the school were six single wide mobile homes. They were placed three facing the other three with a common patio and a small basketball court that could be used for other activities in the middle. Each home still had a government look even though they had been painted in different colors. It was Sunday and several women were sitting and talking around the BBQ area. Next to the mobile homes was a neat, small wooden house where the caretaker and his wife lived. The man was a retired employee of the berry grower. The man and his wife lived there rent free and for that they took care of the landscaping and small repairs. "We made arrangements to look at a couple of the homes and talk to the residents," said Lucinda.

"Wow, this was all done in six months, that's quick work," said Larry.

"Well, I can tell you it wasn't easy. We chose this place because the owner is well respected and well liked and it didn't hurt that he had given the land for the school. On top of that, many of the people who live around here work for the man. In fact, I think you know him Larry, his name is Jim Johnson. I understand he was quite an old grouch, but recently he's become the darling of the community."

"Well it's not too late for people to get their lives in order," commented Larry with a grin. "What's the capacity of the camp?"

Each trailer has a bedroom at each end with two beds and a kitchen, living room and bath room in the middle. They're completely furnished. So each house has four beds times the six homes, so the place will house twenty four women. Right now I understand there are only about twenty workers. Curiously, I hear four are not part of the supplemental program, but are workers born in the U.S. Let's take a look and talk to the women."

Larry and Cipri had driven down from Palo Alto and had been met by Lucinda who was waiting for them at the Franco home. They had enough time to unpack and Lucinda indicated their work for the summer. "If we can get this experiment to work for the women, it can set the tone for the foreign workers in the county and perhaps become a model for the rest of the country. I have to tell you, getting the necessary permits for these homes was a real pain in the ass. Your chore for the next several weeks will be to document everything about this project beginning with your trip to Hermosillo. It needs to be well documented and fact-based so if we have to replicate it, it will become a template for others. To be frank, if it's done well and we set the tone, it could bring us clients that we never even considered in the past. It'll be good for business."

The women were all relatively young and it was easily determined that most of them were from the same village, were good friends and several were related. "In fact, these were selected to come as a group, that is either friends or relatives so none would be alone and get homesick. We'll see how this work's and then perhaps we can branch out beyond this experiment." said Lucinda.

Cipri became the lead person as they walked around. She immediately established a connection with the residents. Soon she was joking and sharing girl talk like old friends. They talked about their homes and families. Larry chimed in a couple of times asking about the work. As they were leaving, Cipri asked if they needed anything.

"One of the older women shyly said, "One thing some of us would like is some way we could go to church on Sundays if we don't work. Some of the other workers told us there were a couple of churches nearby, we just need transportation."

Larry smiled and said, "We'll see what we can do for next Sunday."

"Well that was an interesting visit. It seems like the program is working well. Is this the only one or are others giving it a go?" Cipri asked Lucida.

"Actually, to my surprise, even though this was a pain to complete, a couple of other growers are making a similar effort. One about the same size should be completed in a couple of months. I tell you, if this works like we think, it will pretty much eliminate women in the field as a potential problem. They will be a real asset. So your chore this summer will be to keep your eye on this program and give us a report before you return to school this fall. You might also keep alert for any other problems. One other thing, Max Martin wants to talk to both of us about our thoughts on how to promote their new Pink Lemon variety. We'll give him a call and see what he has in mind."

"It sounds like we'll be busy most of the summer, but we need to have a few days later on to visit our folks in Arizona. We need to make some plans with them before we return to school this fall." said Larry.

"That should be no problem, take as much time as you need to get a good idea of what needs to be done this summer, see Martin, and then plan some time in Jerome. Just let me know when you're ready. By the way this work you'll be doing will be important to the program and to our firm. So be careful. And if you need any help let me know."

The following Sunday Larry and Cipri showed up at Campo de Las Rosas. One woman had planted some roses and the name of the little camp was born. There were eight ladies waiting for them. They were all dressed in work clothes, but they were neat and clean. Two of the younger ones still had wet hair when they got into the van. The driver drove them to Our Lady of Guadalupe in Oxnard. The people were gathering for the 10:00 AM Mass. Once the girls, the driver, Larry and Cipri joined the crowd, they melted into the congregation and no one paid any particular attention to them. The Mass was a familiar celebration to them and they blended right in. After the Mass, they joined the others in the parish hall for coffee and *pan dulce*. Mostly, they sat together, but there were several contacts with other parishioners. Many of the other people worked in the same fields and came from similar little towns in Mexico. The only difference was that eight were contracted under the new Seasonal Agriculture Program. When they got into the van, Cipri asked them, "Is there anything else you want to do before we return?"

One of the girls sitting way in the back of the van said, "One of the workers in the field told us that we were close to the ocean. I've never seen the ocean; what are the chances of going by before we go home?"

Larry nodded to the driver and within 20 minutes they were driving by the ocean. The women appeared to be astonished. He pointed the driver to a parking space and the van stopped. Next to the sidewalk, a peddler was selling ice cream. Larry bought an ice cream for each lady. Then they walked on the beach and to the very edge of the surf. There was much talking and laughing as they walked on the sand. After a half hour, they drove the women back to the camp. They said goodbye and Lorenzo assured the women that the van would be back the following Sunday to take them to Mass.

As they drove home Larry asked, "What were you girls giggling about?"

"One of the girls said you were cute. They asked if we were married, answered Cipri."

"What did you tell her?"

"I told them the truth; that we were happily married...and that she better not get any ideas!"

Chapter 36

J IM JOHNSON HAD HIS PERIODIC appointment with his cardiologist in Santa Barbara. The old man, for the first time in his life, felt...old. Not only was his physical vigor greatly diminished, but his interest in the challenge of running his operation had almost ceased to exist. This disinterest was worrisome. Johnson Farms was one of the largest, most diverse operations in the county. Its holdings consisting of land and buildings were significant. Up to this point, it was operated as a one-man show. He had many skilled and loyal supervisors who had worked themselves up though the ranks, but he had no one to augment and carry out his vision. He had two daughters, who were very bright and well educated, but they had married educators and lived in other states. There was no family member who was even remotely interested in the operations of the farm. Additionally, he was well aware of his poor reputation in the community as a terse, hard-headed operator. He had mellowed considerably after his attack, but his adverse standing in the county was based in the past and was well deserved. He was aware of this poor reputation, but he suffered fools and those who didn't agree with him poorly. Yet it was his business skill and tenacity that made him successful and disliked at the same time.

The drive up the coast to Santa Barbara made him reflective about his time left in the world and the operations of Johnson Farms. Somehow this personal reflection brought Lorenzo Franco to the forefront of his thinking. He liked the young man. He also liked his story of his birth. He could relate to the young man's beginning. He knew that no one was still alive that knew of his similar birth. He was born to a young, unmarried mother. His father was the son of a well established family who refused to recognize him. Before the father could establish any relationship, he joined the Air Force and was subsequently killed in an air raid over Germany during the Second World War. His grandparents refused to acknowledge him, but did provide all the necessary money to complete his education and a small plot of land. With a small financial beginning and hard, diligent work, he became a successful farmer. He never acknowledged his father's family and used his mother's name Johnson throughout his life.

"So how are you doing Mr. Johnson?" asked the cardiologist.

The old man thought about the question and said, "Funny, but physically I feel pretty good. My problem seems more about my state of mind. My days used to be filled with running my business; it was fun. Now the day to day stuff is more of a chore. I get no satisfaction. Everything just seems futile."

The doctor sat on the exam table and looked down at his patient. "Mr. Johnson, your feelings are not unusual. It seems that when we have a serious incident like the one you just had, we tend to reflect on our life. We reflect on what we have done and what needs to be done. We tend to focus on the worth of what we've accomplished and wonder about what we'll do and the significance of those years to anyone including oneself. From a medical viewpoint, you seem to be doing well. However, you might want to take a look at this phase of your life. Some folks look at the mental side of our lives and some folks look at one's spiritual side. I suggest you think about this for the next several weeks. You might want to talk to someone from your church or just someone you feel close to."

For the next several days Jim drove around his farm mostly just to get away from the phone and ponder the rest of his life. That evening he called Lorenzo and invited him to lunch. "He said, "Would it be okay if we met in Piru? I have to check out one of my ranches out there. Make sure you bring Cipri, I'd like to see her."

The two rode east to the little town of Piru saying little. "Why does he want to meet us in Piru for goodness sake? I've never been there, but from what I understand, it's not much of anything," she said.

"He really didn't say except he said he just wanted to talk and he has some property out there. Besides, he's part of the folks that we're working for so I thought we should see what he has in mind."

The old man smiled when he saw the young couple enter the small coffee shop. The place was empty except for two men at the counter. "Thanks for coming out here. Actually this is one of my favorite places. It gives me a chance to be alone with my thoughts and to mull things over. It's a great place. Although most folks would think I'm nuts; I like it. Maggie will be over in a couple of minutes. I've ordered my favorite; a chorizo and egg burrito. I recommend it."

Cipri looked at Larry and then at the young woman, "Sounds good, we'll have two of the same."

Johnson smiled to himself as he noted that the young woman took the initiative to place the order. "I come here often. Marta, the girl's mom, makes her own chorizo. So I have it every time I come here. You just can't go wrong."

It was obvious to the young couple that the man was just making conversation. They ate the burrito and the old man was correct; it was delicious. "They really are good," said Larry, he looked at his fiancé and said, "I have to thank Mr. Johnson for my name. Actually he's responsible for discovering my given name, Lorenzo."

"Well, I'm glad he did. I like Lorenzo better than Larry."

"Well I disliked the name Larry especially when Lorenzo is just a fine name. And I dislike it as much as I dislike Mr. Johnson. I wish you two would just call me Jim." He hesitated then asked, "I understand you're both graduating after this term. So what are the plans after you finish?"

Lorenzo looked at Cipri, "Well, we're not too sure, except that we're going to be married soon. We haven't set a date, but right close to our graduation. So we have to select a date pretty soon."

"How about after graduation and marriage, what's your next step?"

"We're not too sure. Just a few months ago I thought I knew. Dad's a pharmacist, he's successful and that seemed like a good thing to do, but to be frank, many things have happened recently that kind of makes me wonder. I know that Lucinda Llamas has hinted at continuing our work for her. In an odd way, even Mr. Martin has indicated some interest in what we're going to do. To be honest, farming has never been of interest to me, but our recent activities with farm workers and immigration has given me a new interest in this industry. And after all, it's still one of the most important businesses in the county."

Johnson smiled as he said, "You know I was in a similar position. I graduated from USC with a liberal arts degree. Farming was the last thing on my mind, but I was left a small legacy, a plot of land. Then over the years my liberal education developed what is now Johnson Farms. So in many ways, life is accidental, the trick is to be prepared and take advantage of it as it's presented to us."

"In a way, fate has already prepared us. In the last year or so things have happened to me that could have been a catastrophe. And they were terrible at the time and in retrospect they still are. However, the events led me to other arenas and to other people which have changed my orientation and in some ways my entire life. So I guess one has to be open when these things occur and make the best of them." Lorenzo finished his burrito and took a drink of water.

"And what about you young lady?"

"I agree with Lorenzo. Just a short time ago, I was living in a small ghost town in Arizona and within a few months I'll be graduating from THE FARM. Just think; a Stanford graduate and of course a new bride and a complete new and unknown life ahead. Curiously enough, Luna, my friend on the reservation, even hinted at these changes, but I couldn't have imagined this. And in a way I cannot imagine what's in the future. I just hope I'm wise enough to recognize any adversities as well as my opportunities."

Johnson looked at the young couple for some time. The plan that was fuzzy in his mind was beginning to come into focus. In a way it didn't make sense and the risk seemed inappropriate, but he said, "I have a proposal for you two. After graduation and your marriage, I'd like you to come to work for Johnson Farms. I'd like to work with you over the next couple of years and then I'd like to take my grandkids, whom I seldom see, around the world. Maybe spend a year or so just checking out life, if you will."

Lorenzo looked directly into the eyes of the old man and said, "Wow, I don't know what to say Jim." He then looked at Cipri who returned his gaze and then they both looked at Johnson.

"I understand that I have just piled your plate high with many courses, but what I really want is for you to both consider this offer over the next several months. And in the meantime, when you're in town, we'll continue our chats. Then let's say by next spring or sooner you give me an answer."

The drive back to Santa Paula was quiet. Lorenzo drove slowly. He turned off the main road in Fillmore and returned by the old South Mountain Road as if to prolong the trip. Instead of returning home, he stopped at St. Sebastian's Church. They walked in and just sat in the quiet, empty church. Finally Lorenzo said, "Man, I was stunned. I actually wondered why he wanted to meet with us, but his offer just blew me away. What did you think?"

"I'm not too sure what to think. What is really weird is that Luna hinted that something unlikely like this would happen, but never in a million years would I have guessed this. What's your reaction?"

"Wow...talk about mysteries. In a way, my only thought was to come to church and just sit here for awhile. That's the only thing that makes sense to me right now. The reality is that we have lots to talk about. And I think we should consider his suggestion. It's curious that Jim is not well liked. He has a terrible personal reputation, but he's well regarded as a shrewd business man. For some reason I like him and for some strange reason he seems to like me. I think that we should talk to our families. I especially want to talk to Dad."

Lorenzo tried to explain Johnson's sketchy offer. It didn't make sense as it was still unclear in his own mind. Yet even though many details were missing, he tried to communicate the sincerity of the offer. Tom Franco listened to his son. At first he hadn't paid attention to his son until he heard the name Jim Johnson Farms. His first reaction was to say nothing, but to stop eating and look directly at Larry and then to Cipri who was also listening carefully. "To be honest, having lunch with Jim in Piru of all places and to be given a job offer was enough to knock me off stride. So much that the first thing we did was go to church and just sit there. Although church has not been a big part of my life, it was the first thing that occurred to me. I'm not too sure what sitting there accomplished other than just thinking about the implications for us."

Tom looked at Cipri and then again at his son. "You two had lunch with Jim Johnson and then spent some time in church by yourselves...in a way it rather makes sense." Tom's comments had a tinge of humor and he was smiling. He continued, "I'm well aware of his reputation in the community. He's considered a hardnosed SOB, that's for sure, but you know, I've never heard any of his employees say one derogative word about him. In fact, most of his workers live on his ranches and have been with him for decades. In fact, I went to school with a couple of kids of families who worked for him. It was my understanding that he made it possible with encouragement and financial help. I tell you in the quarters that count he's well respected and even idolized." He then looked at Cipri, without asking her, directly questioned her.

"Just going to Piru was an experience for me. Of course we have many such small towns in Arizona. I was surprised and frankly I thought it was some kind of a joke, but then I noted a sense of sadness in the man's demeanor; of someone questioning his very being. In a way, there seemed to be a spiritual connection to what he was telling us and perhaps what he was telling himself. That's why when Lorenzo suggested stopping at the church for a while; it made sense."

"And you Lorenzo, what do you think? And perhaps more importantly, what are you going to do?" asked his father as he continued to eat.

"Well, it was my thought that we'd spend our last year in Palo Alto and enjoy life, but now it seems like we have to make some decisions. I know that Lucinda has some ideas about a place for us in her organization. And I haven't even considered anything else; haven't given it much thought to be honest. Graduation and marriage are first. Then we'll see."

"Although I come from a rural area, farming has never been part of my vocabulary or way of thinking. Yet Mr. Johnson, who I really don't know, made his offer in a very interesting and dramatic fashion. It seems that if one wants to be in the essence of American life, farming is the industry to investigate. The fact is, this is where we find the entry level of work to give us the best diet in the world to date. In fact, it may be even too good, judging from our collective waistlines. Thus one of the lowest segments of society makes sure we all eat well. So I can see the next few months as an interesting exercise in personal decision making." She paused, then said, "I know that sounded a bit preachy and perhaps incoherent, but the meeting with Mr. Johnson was interesting to say the least."

"You mean you don't see it as a major family decision?" asked Licha.

"Of course it's a major decision and we should consider it carefully, but at the same time, I'm very grateful that we have the luxury of having the time and the family support to take our time to review our options." She paused for a second, "At the same time, it makes me wonder about Mr. Johnson. Who's apparently willing to put, from what I understand, a very large business in the hands of young, inexperienced persons."

Tom answered, "I suppose many folks would make that assumption, but Johnson has always been underestimated and underrated by his peers. He's been very successful. His success has been, in my opinion, his focus on the important issues and people. His reputation as a curmudgeon is that he doesn't suffer fools well and lets them know. And he doesn't give a damn what people think of him. Sometimes, some of us spend so much time and effort playing to the crowd, that we lose sight of important matters. He doesn't. Having said that, my only advice to you both is to be as straight forward with him as you can."

Chapter 37

The year seemed to fly by. The sequence of events made the weeks seem like a blur. There were classes of course, but these appeared to be just like tying a ribbon on a present. The main goal of graduation was essentially achieved; it was now a matter of ensuring that the finish line was reached. A couple of classes were worrisome, but with both of them studying together, success was a foregone conclusion. The two other issues of the impending marriage and job offers were more complicated and caused increased tension. On several occasions, they almost went to the local college chaplain for a quick ceremony. The thought of an elaborate wedding made them both shudder. Finally, they agreed that the wedding would take place in Jerome. In a way, it was to honor his parents, her namesake Cipriana and a way to keep the wedding small. When told, Tom and Alicia quickly agreed and the arrangements were set for a September wedding. Getting that out of the way, eased tensions considerably. Yet the job consideration was still undecided. Twice during the year they had met with Johnson and he reiterated his offer. In fact, one long weekend he spent almost two days touring several of the properties, his office and even introduced Lorenzo to some of his workers in a small, informal BBQ he had for his employees. Johnson even hinted that his medical condition and his wanting to spend some time with his family made the decision more important to him. On one occasion, his feelings were more than just a hint, he actually said that the accumulation of assets would have been futile if he did not have the opportunity to share it, and himself, with his family and others.

During the meeting, it was agreed that a decision would be made during quarter break. Even though it was, in a sense, not the decision itself that set the clock in motion. It was during this time that Luna Martinez was going to attend a spiritual conference in Carmel. When she contacted the couple; it was quickly agreed to meet. The two drove to the beach side community as Luna's meeting concluded. After the usual greeting and gathering antidotes they settled in Luna's room. Cipri had already told her that the couple wanted to talk about the upcoming wedding, but especially about the employment situation.

"So tell me about this Mr. Johnson, he sounds like an interesting man."

"He is interesting, perhaps even fascinating," said Lorenzo. "He's also a walking contradiction. That is, he's not well liked by many in his community, but he's very successful in his farming operation. Yet from talking to his workers, he's respected and very well liked by them. Some of his older workers seem to have an almost fraternal relationship with him. He has two daughters as his only family and of course his wife. The daughters and their families seem to be well off living elsewhere and apparently not interested in the farming operations. Recently he's had some medical problems that have made him reconsider his life. He said to me that he'd like to spend more time with his grandchildren, even to do some traveling with them."

"Curiously, added Cipri, when I first met him he scared the heck out of me. He seemed kind of gruff and in a way he was and still is, but he knows of his reputation and I think he rather enjoys it. I think this medical situation has made him rethink his life and relationships. The most interesting thing is his interest in Lorenzo. I mean, I know why he's of interest to me, but I wonder what he sees in him. It really makes little sense, especially when we found out how extensive his operation is. Johnson Farms is one of the largest operations in the county with significant land holdings. And up to now it has basically been a one man operation."

"Mortality, reputation and assets have been the bane of mankind since the very beginning," said Luna. "Curiously, the most important of the three, mortality, is a foregone conclusion, a guarantee if you will. This becomes a private issue with each one of us and our relationship with our Supreme Being. Sooner or later we find out that we can't take it with us so assets are of little use. So in some ways, man attempts to make and leave a legacy. That can be done with assets and monuments. We see the latter all over the world. Think of the pyramids and the Easter Island statutes, for example. This may be our way of reluctantly departing from this world by hoping to leave a trace of our presence here."

"I'm not too sure how my being in the mix makes his legacy a better picture. I've been thinking seriously of what my position would be with him if I took the job. I see it as somehow working with the land, the employees and the community to make a better and more prosperous operation for the benefit of all these individual and collective segments."

Luna smiled, "Perhaps it's his way of leaving a sort of a pyramid of his legacy."

Lorenzo laughed, "Me a pyramid builder!"

"Why not? The reality is that we're all builders to some extent. We all want to have an impact. The real concern is how significant that impact will be and how concerned we are about that impact. I get the sense that Mr. Johnson doesn't want to leave a monument to himself, but would like to leave a legacy to his family and to his community. I mean, apparently he's been careful about building something and to let it crumble would be wrong. Somehow, he sees you Lorenzo, as the continuation of his efforts. In a way, it's one way to extend one's immortality. I know this may sound odd to a young couple, but the older one gets, the more concern we have for others."

Cipri shook her head a bit confused, "I'm not too sure I understand what you're talking about Luna. Our main concern is what to do about his job offer? I mean, we're fortunate to have several options. We know friends at school who have no such options. And here we are wondering what to do. What would you do Luna?"

She laughed, "The first thing I would do is go back to the Res and walk out to my favorite mountain and sit there for as long as it takes to get some insight. Now you don't have a reservation, but I take it you have such a place. I heard the last time Mr. Johnson made the original suggestion you wound up in the back of your church. The church may be your mountain. Check it out. It may not be too conclusive, but it will give you time to contemplate and eventually lead you to a decision."

"On a more practical matter, Mr. Johnson has talked about his interest in me, but only in general terms. We have not talked about specifics like responsibilities, authority and...and compensation," said Lorenzo.

"Well, I understand that, said Luna. Then you need to tell him you're serious and would like to discuss these issues specifically. My guess is he would be disappointed if you didn't make an effort to get a clear understanding of a mutual agreement. It would indicate to him the manner in which you would deal with the assets of Johnson Farms. From what I understand, those assets are substantial, so in a way he would be reassured."

Chapter 38

"You would be the Assistant General Manager of Johnson Farms for the time being. The only suggestion I have for you for the next several months is that you divide yourself in thirds. One third of your waking day I'd like you to spend it with Antonio Martinez. He's in charge of all the farm operations. He's one of the best farmers in the county. My success has really been his success with the land. Just ride around with him and listen to him; maybe even take notes. The next third I want you to spend in the office. There Lori Tyler, my office manager, will clue you in on what happens in the office. Lori has been with me for close to 30 years. She knows everything about our operations and even our personal family accounts. The other third will be more difficult. You'll spend it with me. Unfortunately, I have to spend much of my time on industry matters. We belong to several co-ops and eventually you'll replace me on these boards. I have to tell you these are a pain in the ass, but some matters have to be attended. The main one I want you to focus on is the Pacific Labor Association. This is the local arm that is contracting for our foreign labor."

"But that's throwing me into the deep end, don't you think?"

"Perhaps, but the reality is that you'll be a big asset for the group. I mean, you were in on this from the inception of the idea. We're going to need someone on that board who can see the big picture. I know some of the boys on the board. Most of them are good fellows, but they need someone to set the pace. My hunch is that'll be you."

"But will they accept me? I mean, here I am just out of college. What makes you think they'll listen to me?"

"They'll listen to you because you represent Johnson Farms, but mostly because you'll be making sense. Remember most of them were not around or active when we had the Bracero Program. So from that perspective you have a head start on all of them."

Larry's smile faded as he paid close attention to Jim. He was making mental notes. He said, "I guess it will be hectic by graduation. You know we're getting married right after we graduate. Then we'll take a few days off and then I'll be here punching the clock."

The old man's face turned serious and said, "Actually, I expect you to accomplish all those things, but I want you to start working for Johnson Farms today; right now. So when you get here, you'll hit the ground running. By that I mean, every chance you get you'll come in and check things out. Also, I want to make an official announcement to our employees, to my colleagues and to the community in general that Johnson Farms will continue to be an important factor in the county. And of course, we'll provide the appropriate compensation."

Somewhat embarrassed Lorenzo asked, "Jim, we haven't discussed my compensation."

The old man pulled out an envelope from his desk and gave it to Lorenzo, "I had my attorney draw this up; I hope it meets with your approval."

Larry opened and read the one page letter, his face reddened and said, "It's quite satisfactory Mr. Johnson."

Larry showed the letter to Cipri who said, "Wow, are you serious?"

The months seemed to be crammed together. The graduation ceremony for the two was almost anticlimactic. The focus really was on the wedding two weekends later. Although it was a small wedding, the ceremony had a large impact on the little Arizona town. Guests from all around made sure San Yldefonso Catholic Church was full and the flowers were overwhelming. Jim Johnson and his wife hitched a ride on Roger's plane. He said he wanted to make sure that the future of Johnson Farms was secured. Yet Lorenzo was overwhelmed by something other than all the activities of the wedding. He was contemplating all that had happened during the last few years to lead him to this little town. The trauma of the arrest was ameliorated by all the positive things that eventually led to Jerome. Yet the scar of the arrest was like an itch that needed to be occasionally scratched. All the hectic activities of the wedding paled in his continuing infatuation with his new bride. Her radiant beauty outshone everything else at the church and reception. Lorenzo was pleased, but surprised to see Johnson and all the people from Santa Paula. The old man said, "I understand you two are taking a little tour of Mexico."

"Neither of us has really spent any time in another country, so first we'll take a look at our next door neighbor before we venture anywhere else."

"Any place specifically?"

Lorenzo seemed embarrassed, "I spoke to our foreman Antonio and he mentioned that his cousin runs a small resort hotel in Uruapan, so we're going to spend a few days there.

"You know that area is one of the largest avocado growing areas in the world, don't you?"

"Antonio mentioned it. He also made arrangements for us to see some of their growing areas and a couple of packing houses. I thought since we were there it didn't make any sense not to take advantage of the opportunity," replied Lorenzo."

"Tell me, how did your new bride react when you mentioned that you were mixing in some business on your honeymoon?"

"Actually, she was there when Antonio suggested it and she was excited. She's never been in that part of Mexico so it will be all new and interesting."

The old man smiled to himself and as he and his party boarded the plane for the return flight. His wife asked him, "What were you and Larry talking about that made you smile John?"

Still smiling, he said, "It appears we may be spending more time with our grandkids sooner than I thought."

$\bigcirc$

Chapter 39

LORENZO WAS SITTING as a representative of the Pacific Labor Association. They were listening to a report from Dolan Smith, the Department of Labor official, in charge of approving the Seasonal Agricultural Program. He was saying, "As you know, the regulations state as long as there is domestic labor available, it must first be recruited and after it is exhausted, we will then fill in with foreign workers."

Fidel Corona, the Association Manager said, "I thought we met that requirement. We went to the Los Angeles Metro area at your request and tried to find some folks. We got two and they lasted three days and left. We also went to San Francisco and we couldn't find anyone willing to work."

The government agent said, "We appreciate your efforts, but our DC office informs us that they have lots of folks and we need to touch that base first."

"Where are these workers?" asked Corona.

I understand that there are about 100 men in Selma who are interested in the jobs."

"Where the hell is Selma?" asked the manager.

"In Alabama…Selma, Alabama!"

"Alabama! Are you kidding…You mean you have lemon pickers in Alabama? Come on, that doesn't even make sense!" Corona's face was turning red as he looked at the government man with rage.

Larry could see things were getting out of hand so in a quiet voice, he said, "Sir, it was my understanding that our recruitment area was to be within our adjacent growing area. If that's so, you have to admit that Alabama is a bit outside of our area, don't you think?"

"The regulations aren't real specific regarding the geographical area, but my supervisor in DC said if you're going to Mexico to get workers, that's further than Selma. In addition, there's a 27 percent unemployment rate in that state, and in Selma I understand it's closer to 40 percent. The rule states that citizens must be given preference to any job opportunities."

"Do you know if these folks in the South are capable of harvesting lemons and willing to?"

"Of course, I haven't seen them, but our offices tell me they're willing to come to California to work."

"Of course they're willing to come to California to work, but are they willing to pick lemons? That is what we're talking about. I'm not too sure who's pulling the strings in Washington, but must be a string that he has up his ass!" Corona was visibly upset.

Larry smiled at the man, "Our application is for 800 men when we get to the peak. Are you saying that if we get the men from Selma you'll approve our application for 700 men?"

The man was somewhat hesitant, but answered, "We're prepared to sign off on the balance of your request, of course."

Then Larry continued in a calm manner and said, "I suppose you would agree if the men from Selma don't work out then we can fill in with men through the program?"

"Yes…I suppose so," answered the agent as he left.

There was silence in the room for a long time. Some members of the Association got up to get coffee; others went to the bathroom. Finally one of the men said, "Well, what kind of crap was that all about? They know damn well there are no lemon pickers in Alabama. They're just screwing with us. It's just a bunch of shit."

Larry took a deep breath and said, "Ralph you're absolutely right. It is a bunch of shit, but we have to remember that this guy isn't the fellow making the rules; he's just doing what some guy up the chain tells him. We also shouldn't forget that we just got approval for 700 men. And it's my guess that within a couple of weeks the Selma boys will be gone and we'll be authorized for the balance of the men."

"What about the expense of recruiting these guys, bringing them in, and trying to put them to work? What about all that crap?"

"I'm afraid that's going to be part of the cost of doing business from now on. Furthermore, we'll have to do more than go through the motions. We have to make a real effort to make this work. My guess is that this is some kind of a test."

"Okay, we're getting these guys from Alabama; who's going to wind up with them? I can see nothing, but problems with them. I mean, I don't want them," said one of the growers.

"My guess is that this will be a short term affair. I suggest we make this a group effort; that we run the costs under a general account so no one gets stuck with the entire bill." Larry was doodling on a piece of paper, "We have a block of young trees that we can try the men out on; we'll see how it works out."

The following meeting Corona reported, "I know you are all anxious to find out the results of our crew from Alabama. Of the hundred they told us about only forty-two got on the charter bus. Apparently four got off in Phoenix and never got back on the bus. Eight got off in Los Angeles and only thirty arrived here last Monday. Two men left the same day after breakfast. The balance went through the orientation and only twenty showed up at the orchard the following day. By Friday they were all gone. They quit. Most of them said they weren't cut out to do that kind of work and a few said they only wanted a ride out to California. Several of the young men were honest about it. They said it would be a lark to get a free trip to get out of their state. Several complained about having to eat Mexican food at the camp mess hall. They didn't like beans and tortillas for breakfast."

Larry said, "Fidel, did you document all of what you just told us? Did you mention this to the boys from the Fed?"

"As you suggested Lorenzo, we had the folks from the Labor Department here every day and made sure they interviewed the men before we paid them. We sat in on the interviews and that's pretty much what happened. We were also notified by Dolan Smith that we are approved for the additional hundred men anytime we need them. We made arrangement to get them for early March when we expect to be at our peak."

One of the older directors said, "What kind of an operation are we running here? I mean, the government doesn't appear to know what they're doing and we seem to be following their dumb ass moves."

"I don't agree, Oscar. I think they knew exactly what they were doing. In a sense they were testing us, to see if we would cooperate. Additionally, I'm sure they were doing this to answer some upper bureaucrats that they exhausted all the avenues so that they could answer the folks who are against this program and will use any excuse to kill it. I think it was also a test for our organization; to see if we were able to cope with this kind of nonsense and still keep our wits. It cost some additional expense, but when we spread it out among all our growers it will all be worthwhile. I think the best part is that we established some rapport with Smith and I hope from now on, he will deal with us on a more practical and realistic level."

Corona smiled, "Lorenzo is right. Already Smith has become more responsive and cooperative. The other day he found a couple of defects in our community shower and instead of writing us up for the defect, he just mentioned it to me and we repaired it that same day. He seemed satisfied with our rapid reaction. On top of that, the other day he brought one of his supervisors during the morning breakfast. The two actually got in line, were served and ate with the men. They seemed to enjoy the food and talking to the men. He also told me privately that his supervisor wants to bring some camp operators from other areas so they can see our operation. Apparently, we're some kind of a prototype for other areas."

"What do you mean we're a prototype for others; for God's sake, are we going to be running a school for the government?" Oscar was still steamed up for having to deal with any government representative.

"Oscar, I understand your frustration. All this is a real pain in the ass, but I can almost assure you that Smith can really be a pain if he wants to and if we cross him. There's no reason we can't be cooperative with him. If we make his job easier, I think he can make life easier for all of us." He looked at Fidel and said, "Fidel, I think the trick will be for you to assist him in any way you can. If he needs a tour guide, be quick to put on your tour guide hat. Let him know we appreciate him...that we genuinely appreciate him."

"Thanks Lorenzo, I think I understand the rules of the game."

Chapter 40

A NTOÑIO MARTINEZ was now comfortable picking up his young boss and showing him the operation of Johnson Farm. He first worked for Mr. Johnson, as he called him, as a Bracero in the 60s. With the help of Johnson, he obtained immigration papers for himself and his family. He still lived on the ranch in a house provided by the company, but he and his wife also saw the need for their own home. Over time they bought a home in town and in the meantime had it rented to one of his nephews. Then he actually bought a duplex which he fixed up and rented out. He also had a lot with four apartments in escrow. One of his sons looked after these investments. He also had a small investment in Mexico with his brother in an avocado orchard. His first reaction to Lorenzo was astonishment. He was aware of Mr. Johnson's bout with health issues. First, he thought that the heart attack also affected his mind. Over the several months that he spent with Lorenzo, he realized what Johnson saw in the young man. "Trees are very much like people, Lorenzo. If they are treated fairly and with respect, they will provide a comparable return, but when the yields are no longer adequate, we quickly remove them. That's one of the big differences with Mr. Johnson, he's not afraid to remove a whole block of trees even though they may have a few years of production left in them. Some growers don't want to go to the expense of the removal or incur the lack of income while the trees are young. The results are that a grower winds up with nothing, but old trees. We, on the other hand, always have new young trees growing and coming into production."

"That's a good principle for almost any endeavor," answered Larry. Over the last several months he got to know the foreman very well. He was an impressive man. His formal education was limited to a school in Mexico. Yet he was an educated man in all sense of the word. He read widely and he could do math accurately in his head. He needed no calculator, but above all, he faced circumstances with calm deliberateness. He was well respected by all the workers and by his neighbors. So Larry paid close attention to his mentor. "Toñio, we're going through our capital expense needs for next year. Is there anything we need on the farm that needs to be replaced to improve our operation?"

"Lencho, I have a list back at the office. However, in general we're in pretty good shape this year. The main item we'll need is a new water pump for the Piru ranch. The other stuff is small or can wait until next year. However, I would like to recommend a wage increase for our employees. Last year we did nothing, but this was a good year, everyone worked hard. This year I recommend that we give the people a three percent increase in wages plus an additional three percent as a cash bonus."

"Lori, I had a long talk with Antoñio and he says the main expense we're looking at this year is a pump for Piru. He also is recommending a wage increase and a bonus for the workers. I wonder if you can cost that out so I can discuss it with Jim. And I'd like to know what you think of his recommendation."

She answered, "Well I have to admit to you that for the first three years or so I was very skeptical of Tony and his style, but I now have every confidence in his way of thinking. His formal education may be a bit lacking, but anyone who underestimates him will be sorry in the end. I should have the numbers for you by the end of the week."

Larry met with his boss in his house. Johnson still came into the office, but it was with less frequency. Additionally, he now met Larry in shorts and sandals and was usually watering his roses. In fact, his flower garden was now luxurious from his attention. "Well Lorenzo, how are things going on the farm?"

"Things are going well Jim, we could use some rain, but other than that it looks like we're having a good year. I did have a talk with Toñio and Lori and we all agree that this last year was a good one and we're recommending a wage increase for everyone with an additional cash bonus of three percent. Here are the numbers that Lori worked up." He handed his boss a one page summary of the costs.

Johnson looked at the paper, then looked at Larry and motioned to borrow the young man's pen. He wrote quickly at the bottom of the paper: *Approved JJ. (Applies to all employees)*. "So tell me Lorenzo, how's the labor program going. I heard of the recruitment from Alabama. Have we had any similar occurrence or other problems?"

"It's been pretty quiet except for a guy in Wheeler Canyon who was caught with two illegal workers. The owner of the small ranch spent a couple of days in jail. It looks like the fine and jail time will actually be put into play. The immigration folks appear to be serious. I also heard of some gal in Topanga whose gardener was caught with no papers. It looks like she'll be doing a few days in jail. I understand the immigrant supporters are up in arms. Of course, they thought the law and the jail time would only apply to farmers not to their kind who live in the city."

"How are we doing Lorenzo, with our workers?"

"Toñio and I met with all our employees and discovered that two of the men who have been with us three and five years respectively have false papers. We talked to them and agreed that they would turn themselves in, but in the meantime, we had our attorney take their case on to try to help them. One fellow is married to a citizen and the other one will be more difficult, but we'll do all we can to help them."

"Listen Lorenzo, do everything we can to help them. Remember, it's me that goes to jail, and I'd rather not. So I'm relying on you to keep me out of the slammer." The old man laughed, but there was a serious note in the laugh.

"I'll do my best. Jim, I'd like to make an additional recommendation. Antoñio has been a large factor in our success this year. To be honest, he's been a big part of any success I've had. I couldn't have asked for a better role model, I'd like to recommend him for an additional bonus beyond the three percent everyone else is getting."

"What do you have I mind?"

"I think an additional three percent would not be out of order."

"Let me see that paper again…" Johnson borrowed the pen and again, put an asterisk on Antonio's name with the following footnote: *An additional 3% for Antonio Martinez for excellent work*. "Now, anything else?"

"Nothing really, except I don't know if you heard the rumors about some folks wanting to put an end to the guest worker program. They say some farmers in Arizona have been misusing and mistreating workers and they're accusing the whole system of being corrupt. There have been some ugly reports in the news so it appears we'll have to be extra careful in the short term."

Jim shook his head, "I wouldn't be surprised. There's always someone who tries to take advantage of the system. That's why it's so important for us to run a clean operation. This means we damn sure need to keep our association clean as a whistle. I suggest that you meet with Fidel Corona our camp manager, to make sure he and all our members are toeing the line."

"Actually, Corona has already taken charge of this issue. He's well aware of what a PR disaster this could be. So he's called a special director's meeting to make sure everyone's on the same page."

Fidel Corona began his report by saying that the balance of the workers needed would be arriving over the next ten days. "The new men will be sprinkled among the various active crews so in a sense they will not even be noticed and production will not be affected." He paused for a couple of seconds as he shuffled some notes. "The main reason for this meeting, however, is to make sure we're all following the rules to the letter. We've heard that a grower association very much like us was caught with illegal workers and on top of that the Feds cited them for various camp violations; the camp was shut down and the workers removed. That's not bad enough however. The local union has now filed a complaint against the growers and wants to represent the workers. From what our attorneys tell us, they might have a good chance that, if they get the workers back, they'll belong to the union."

"That's all we need; for the damn union to get into the picture. It seems we can't get a break," noted Oscar.

Lorenzo answered in a quiet voice, "Let's not fool ourselves, the union has always been in the picture. More importantly, if they get their foot in the door, it will be our own fault. That is, somebody will make a mistake and they'll come down on us. Worse than that, we will have deserved it because we allowed them in. That's why this meeting is so important; that we make sure we're doing everything by the book. Based on this, Fidel has a proposal for us to consider."

"The fact is that we probably have many people working for us that are illegal. Some have been here for years. They have families, own homes, have kids in school, but they came here illegally and are still illegal. If they get caught, they're screwed, but we too will be tarnished so somehow we need to help them and ourselves as well."

"How can we help, what can we do?" asked Oscar.

I've had several conversations with one of our members who happens to be an attorney and they have a paralegal who works in their office who knows all the ins and out of the immigration process. He said he's willing to take on this chore. That is, he says if we announce this service to our workers and their families, we could help clear up this potential problem over time."

"How much will this cost us?" asked Oscar.

"That's one of two questions we have to answer today. First, do we want to do this as a Labor Association and how do we cover the cost?"

"I think it's important that we get ahead of this situation. We announce to every employee of this opportunity and then make this attorney available to them on a confidential basis. If what I hear is correct, we have a certain percentage of our workers who have false documents. Let's see if we can help them and help ourselves at the same time." As Oscar made this statement, several of the directors looked at him, he smiled, "I know I've been critical of this law and our part in it, but the fact is that these are the cards that we were dealt and this is the hand we have to play. I think we should offer this service to the members of our association. I also suggest that we have a nominal charge for the worker. My hunch is that the individual growers might want to pick up this expense at their discretion, but let's leave that up to them."

"How was your day?" asked Cipri as Larry walked in the door.

"Hectic. You know, at one time I thought this farming business would be boring and uninteresting, but there's a lot going on all the time and the situations and problems that arise are different and so we have to be on our toes all the time. And every day I'm learning more and more. So even though I was somewhat reluctant to join Johnson Farms, I think it's been a good decision. How about you, how was your day?"

"Okay, but I had a little chat with Lucinda. I told her that I would only work for her another three months. So she agreed to let me work on one of her short term projects."

Lorenzo was about to open a bottle of beer when he stopped in mid sentence. He looked at his wife who had a slight smile on her face. "What do you mean you'll only work three more months? What's happened?"

"You haven't noticed have you?"

"Noticed what?" he answered.

"That I've gained some weight."

Finally it dawned on Lorenzo where the conversation was leading. He opened the beer and drank half the bottle in two swallows. "Oh my God, are you serious? How did this happen? Have you been to the doctor?"

Cipri chuckled and said, "Well Lorenzo Franco, if you don't know how this happened, I'm going to be very disappointed with you. Actually, I have an appointment next week, but in the meantime, I've talked to Luna and Cipriana and they both concurred that I'm pregnant."

"You did all this on the phone? I mean, how can they tell without even seeing you?" Lorenzo's voice was almost cracking.

"Well grandma has been doing this for years. She tells me she can tell just by a woman's voice and furthermore she's never wrong, she said. As for Luna, she said she just had a feeling." Cipri had a big smile on her face, she continued, "You're not disappointed are you? I know we haven't discussed a family, but in my mind, it was always part of what I wanted."

"Of course I'm not disappointed; it's just that I've never given it much thought. So much has happened to me, to us; that it was not on my radar…Oh my God, you haven't told mom have you? She'll go nuts."

Cipri went over to her husband and gave him a hug and said, "Let's wait until we get a confirmation from the doctor next week."

"What kind of a name is *Avaleine*? I never heard of it," asked Lorenzo. "Is it a girl's name?"

"Grandmother tells me it's a very old family name used by our tribe. It means *Hopeful dawn*." Cipri smiled as she mentioned the name to her still stunned husband. "The doctor said the test results indicate it's a girl and the tests are 99% accurate."

"We're having dinner with my parents tonight, I think it will be a night to remember," he said.

Chapter 41

Lucinda continued to work on a proposal, but was also pondering a meeting later in the afternoon. Several of her Westside colleagues asked to meet with her. When she heard the names of who asked to be at the meeting, she had the feeling it was about her work on the recent immigration legislation. Frieda Glasser was the first one to arrive in the office. She and Glasser were good friends and had worked on many campaigns and were usually supporting the same issues. They both had graduated from UCLA where they became friends and social activists. "I wanted to come by early to prepare you for an onslaught by our friends," said Frieda.

"What do you mean onslaught? What have I done to them?" Lucinda smiled; deep down inside she had a notion of what the subject was.

The four friends arrived just a few minutes later. They went directly to the kitchen and served themselves coffee. One of the older women started, "Lucy, what the hell is happening to this immigration crap. I thought you told us it would put farmers in jail for using wetbacks."

"That's correct and from what I've heard, several of them have spent time in jail already, so apparently the law is working."

"It's also working in the city. Why the other day my neighbor was picked up and she spent the night in jail. What is the Border Patrol doing here in the city, they should be out on the farms where they're supposed to be."

Lucinda took a drink of coffee and said, "The law applies to anyone who hires undocumented workers, not just farmers."

"Yeah, but it was never our intention that the law should apply to us, here in the cities. The farms; that's where the problem is and that's where the Border Patrol should focus their attention!"

"Now wait a minute ladies, we all knew that when we supported this law, the unique part of it was that it would apply to the employer not the workers; that this would be the quickest way to stop the process in its tracks."

"But we didn't mean it to apply to us, here in the city. It was supposed to apply to all those damn growers and their farm workers. That's where they're supposed to be, not here with us."

"But that's the problem. The fact is that many, if not most, of the illegal people are in the cities. Studies show that most of them work around here cutting our lawns, cleaning our homes or taking care of our kids."

"But my Nena has been working for us for thirteen years; I mean, she's almost part of our family. I mean, our kids think of her as their mother almost. We even converted part of our three car garage as living space for her."

In a quiet voice Lucinda asked, "Tell me when was the last time Nena saw her family? How much do you pay her...for example, how much does she have in the bank?"

"Well she doesn't need much; we practically give her free room and board. She tells me that her family doesn't like her, so we're doing her a favor by keeping her here. I mean, she's like family."

"Like family who sleeps in the garage? Listen to yourself. It's the same story we hear from farmers, except they're more open. They know they've hired illegal workers because they're hard workers and make little fuss. They make no bones about it. Yet here we are, thinking we're better because we live in Beverly Hills, but the fact is, as long as we get our lawns cut and our homes cleaned cheap we're okay. Then we can criticize our farmers for doing the same thing.

"But it's not the same...it's not the same...we're different..."

"Lucy, don't you think you were a bit hard on our friend. It sounded like you almost enjoyed tormenting her." Frieda chuckled as she spoke to her friend.

"The worst thing about it is that I spouted that same crap all the time. In my little dealing with these farm boys I found out they're pretty much like all of us. On top of that, they're in a very competitive business. As a society we spend the least amount of our income on food and when food prices go up everyone gets up in arms. Farmers and farm workers always get the last, as they like to say."

"Boy, you've really changed, haven't you?"

"I don't know if I've changed that much, but I hope I have become more realistic. Farmers are like everyone else, there are some idiots, but most of them try to be good farmers and try to do the right thing. So we need to give them an honest break."

"Besides they're now clients of yours!"

"Ah, paying clients if you will…nothing will change one's perspective like paying clients. They're also very appreciative clients."

Chapter 42

TOM WAS POURING A GLASS OF WINE for Alicia and himself when the young couple walked in, "Just in time," he said as he removed two more glasses from the cupboard. "It's a special bottle one of my customers gave me. I suggested an ointment for a rash; it worked and he repaid me with a couple of bottles of wine from one of his operations up north."

Larry took a sip. "It's excellent."

Cipri smiled at her father-in-law and shyly said, "I wonder if I can have a glass of juice."

"Are you sure? This is really very good, you'll like it. And it'll go perfect with the chile verde Licha made for dinner."

"I'm sure it is, but juice or a glass of water would be fine, thank you."

Finally, Larry couldn't stand it anymore and said, "Mom, Dad we have a surprise for you. Have you ever heard the name, *Avaleine*? It means *Hopeful Dawn* in the ancient language of the hill tribes of Jerome."

"But what does…"

Before Tom could finish the sentence, Alicia came over and hugged her daughter-in-law and said, "Oh what fantastic news! Are you sure?"

Tom was still trying to deal with the realization when his wife said, "Tom, for goodness sakes, get this girl a glass of juice, I made some just this morning." Then she added, "When?"

"The doctor said next spring, actually she said March 24 to be exact." Cipri took the glass of juice from Tom who was still tongue tied. "Thank you," she said as she took a drink from the glass.

Tom recovered quickly, he said, "This calls for a celebration. In fact, I'll open another special bottle of wine just for this occasion." He laughed as he hugged the young couple. He then hugged his wife, "All of a sudden I'm starving," he said.

Licha and Tom sat on the couch as they finished the second bottle of wine. The dinner and the news were overwhelming and they just sat quietly, his arm around her. "Oh, Tom, where did the time go?" she asked.

Tom swirled the wine glass and answered, "Hell if I know, but you know, for the first time since we picked up Larry in Arizona many years ago, I was stunned speechless...just stunned speechless."

"Honey, I can't believe it. Our little boy now has a responsible job, a wife and soon will give us a granddaughter. I can hardly wait to tell the girls. You know, I have a feeling we should take a trip to Arizona so we can celebrate our *Hopeful Dawn* with her people. What do you think?"

"I think we need to get away for a few days and Jerome sounds perfect."

San Yldefonso Catholic Church now felt comfortable. Licha sat between Tom and Cipriana. The old lady held her hand during most of the Mass and quietly mumbled prayer after prayer. She stopped long enough to take communion, but when she knelt again she continued to pray. "I'm sorry I was so impolite with my prayers, but I wanted to make sure that He understood what I wanted. I am well aware that in the end, He gets what He wants, but what I want and need is not much. He'll understand."

Licha smiled at the old woman, "I'm sure God will consider your prayers. If you want to, let me know, I will add my petition to yours."

"Please. I would love for you to help me because I think we're both praying for the same thing. My prayer is simple; to live long enough to see my *Hopeful Dawn*. That's not asking for too much, is it?"

"Of course not, and you can be sure that it'll be my prayer as well. Tell me Cipriana, about the name *Avaleine* or *Hopeful Dawn*."

"As a little girl I remember hearing some of our elders talking about an old legend. We, of course, know that we live in a desert, but many, many years ago there was a severe drought that lasted for years and years. It was thought by the elders it was a punishment for our people not respecting our world. One day a little girl was born premature. She was tiny. No one thought she would live she was so small. According to our tradition, she was put out by a dry stream bed on a straw mat. This was the custom; the people knew she would die quickly and be consumed by wild animals, but she didn't die, in fact she cried and cried for a two days. Finally the distraught mother couldn't stand the waling and she picked up the baby and put her to her breast. The little girl not only lived, but she flourished. That same instant the baby started to nurse, it began to rain. A soft, gentle rain that covered the whole country side and the dry creek revived and the surrounding land gave birth to new vegetation and animals. There was prosperity and especially new hope in the land. The little girl grew to be a mighty warrior of her people. She was called the miracle *Avaleine* or the *Hopeful Dawn*."

Licha's eyes misted as she took the old lady's hand, "Just a few years ago, I would have thought this was just another fairly tale, but look at us. We couldn't have any children. Yet because of a tragic circumstance, we not only have a son, but a daughter-in-law and soon we will be blessed with a granddaughter. So your legend is real enough for me."

"Legends may sound farfetched for some people, but I think many of them are based on fact. Some things have happened that changed people and changed the course of history. In my own lifetime, I've seen children who had little chance of living, but have grown and flourished and accomplished great things. So it's important we not overlook the frail because of our own prejudices, but look beyond their weakness and our own weakness to our humanity." The old lady put her arms around Licha as they walked back home.

Chapter 43

T HE ANNUAL MEETING of the Pacific Labor Association was pre-ceded by much talk and conversation by grower competitors that didn't see each other often. Larry banged the gavel on the table and said, "Ladies and gentlemen, let's call this meeting to order. Our chairman was called out of town and he asked me to chair the meeting for him. This is an historic occasion. We've just completed our first sea-son under the new Seasonal Agricultural Program. As with any new pro-gram, many of us were unsure of what to expect. So our meeting today will focus on the program as it evolved. Our manager, Fidel Corona, will review it from his perspective. After him, Dolan Smith with the Depart-ment of Labor, will give us a review from their perspective. More impor-tantly, he will give us his outlook on the program for next season."

Corona dimmed the lights and focused slides on the screen. "First, let me just give you some numbers so we can get a general feeling about what was accomplished this season. The interesting thing about these numbers is that of the 1200 men we processed, almost three quarters of them had either worked for us or had citrus experience. That means that our screening in Mexico was very effective. You'll also note that only 56 men either quit or were fired for a variety of reasons, but the bulk of the men stayed and did a good job. Their earnings indicate that they did well. The average earnings were at least 15 percent higher than the minimum required. Lastly, we did an exit interview with most of the workers, all but a handful said they would be ready to return next season. In conclu-sion, even though we struggled at the start, from my point of view, the year was a success. Now let me turn it over to Dolan Smith who oversaw the program for the Department of Labor and after that we'll answer questions."

Dolan Smith made a strange appearance. He was overweight and looked like he cut his own hair. His clothes didn't seem to fit and were not properly coordinated. His disheveled look made people underestimate him to their eventual regret. He was not the typical government bureaucrat. He began, "Thank you for inviting me to your meeting. I hope that by sharing information we can eliminate any problems and have even a better program next year. In talking with my counterparts in other areas, it is apparent that we had the largest, and one of the most successful, programs. I think one reason for our success is that we were able to meet with Fidel frequently and were able to head off or iron out any issues before they became serious problems. One thing we were not able to solve, and an issue you all need to discuss, is the care of some orchards. We did have complaints from some workers who had to pick some orchards of large, old, unpruned, poorly cared for trees. Not only that, but it seems the same crew had to work in that same place three times. The men felt it was unfair for them to have to wade through that jungle to harvest the fruit. I don't know what the answer is, but it's something I think you should address. The only other thing that came up was what to do with the down time. That is, on weekends and during wet periods, the men just sit around. Frankly they were bored. There must be some activities that can be dreamed up for those times. Again, as I said, overall the season went well, but I suggest you give some thought to these couple of problems."

Lorenzo said, "Thanks much for your report and for your efforts to make sure that our program was a positive one. You can be assured that we will discuss your suggestions. Of course, you don't have to wait for our annual meeting to come to us. Whenever you see anything that needs attention, come see our manger Fidel or give me a call. Thanks again for your efforts."

The room was quiet as Smith made his way out of the room. Some men got up to refill their coffee cups. "Well gentlemen, you heard the reports. Are there any comments or discussion?" Larry too got up to get some coffee.

One of the older members raised his hand. He said, "Mr. Chairman, I have to tell you that I was the biggest doubter of this program, but to my great amazement it seemed to go well. I'm not pleased that our over-all harvest cost increased significantly, but at least we got our fruit harvested. Also, I'd like to comment on the poorly cared for trees. This matter will take care of itself just because of the increase cost I just mentioned. A poorly maintained orchard can be profitable only so far. The owner will soon realize that with this increase in cost, it will no longer be profitable to keep the trees. I can almost assure you that next year there will be strawberries on that land. Problem solved."

One of the other growers also raised his hand, "You know I spent several years in the military including a couple of tours in the South Pacific. There was no doubt that we were scared shitless when we were on patrol or taking fire, but being bored while we were waiting was al-most as bad. I have a suggestion. My son works in the Superintendent of Education office, I wonder if they might help us with some educational programs for the men while they're not working. For example, English lessons would not only keep the men busy, but it would be a real benefit to the men in the future."

"But how can we do that when we don't know when it will be wet? It's not realistic," said a voice from the back.

"Hell, I know it can be difficult, but let's call them in and see what they have to say. They're in the education business, perhaps they can dream something up. The only thing I can say is that boredom can be hell and it can and will lead to trouble."

"What do you mean boredom can lead to trouble?" he was asked by his neighbor.

"Okay let me finish my story. In the Pacific, we had an old first ser-geant from the old school. It was his experience that kept us alive while we were under fire, but when we were in the rest area, he turned into a real SOB. He was hated by everyone. Hell, we were ready to shoot him, but when he put on his helmet, we followed and obeyed him without question."

Larry smiled, "It seems like a reasonable suggestion, let's at least have Fidel get a hold of the Superintendent's office and see what they have to say. What's your son's name?"

Chapter 44

AVALEINE'S ENTRANCE into this world was not without some drama. She was reluctant to leave the warmth and safety of her mother's womb, but at dawn she popped into the world somewhat unhappy with the abruptness of her appearance. Her first reaction was to greet her new world with a lusty cry. Cipri's soft voice and gentle embrace calmed her quickly. A gentle cleaning and warm clothes and the reassurance of soft voices around her lulled her to sleep. The baby stirred as she heard the murmuring of other voices in the room. Again she was reassured and went back to sleep. Larry looked at his daughter in amazement. She was wrapped in a tight bundle and her grandmother Alicia had already placed a bright red ribbon on her head. Larry sat at the edge of the bed and held the baby and silently said a prayer. He surprised himself that he was holding his daughter for the first time and that he had muttered a prayer something he hadn't done for a very long time. He carefully placed the baby in Cipri's arms and said, "I'll be right back, there's something I have to do."

His father met him in the hall of the hospital. "Larry, good to see you; how's the new arrival?"

"She doing fine, Dad. I'm going down the hall; you want to come with me?" Tom followed his son. They entered a small chapel and they both sat. Larry said nothing; he just bowed his head and stayed in that position for several minutes; then stood and walked out. "I'm not used to this praying thing. I hope God understands the inarticulate!"

"I hear God is multilingual and *inarticulate* is one of those languages he knows very well." Tom smiled, "Now let's go. I want to say hello to a young lady."

The following day, Larry had lunch with his boss at the Mupu Grill. Without saying anything, the order for both was the same and served by the same waitress. As soon as she saw them enter, she placed the order in the kitchen. She also brought out two glasses of the requisite iced tea. Johnson said, "Tell me Lorenzo, how's the family. I understand you have a new addition. Congratulations"

"Yes sir; a little girl. She and her mom are doing fine; for that we're thankful."

"That's great. For a selfish reason, I'm glad as well. I discovered that employees with families tend to be better employees. That's something you should keep in mind as you look for good workers for us." He took a drink of his iced tea, "Tell me about the annual meeting of the Pacific Labor Association. I understand you chaired the meeting and were subsequently elected president for the upcoming year. How did that happen?"

"Well I'm not too sure, but before I realized what was happening, I had been elected. In retrospect I think it was because I get along real well with Dolan Smith and with Fidel. To be honest, that's not very hard because both of them are good people and want to do the right thing and as I said, I get along well with them."

"I understand the Seasonal Ag Program went well and will continue next season. So in a sense, our labor is pretty well secured for next year."

"I think so, that is unless we do something dumb in the meantime. Smith did caution us about a couple of things. One was that some growers have some poorly cared for orchards that are difficult to pick and apparently one crew got stuck doing the work there. I think that'll take care of itself. The other is trickier. When we have prolonged wet weather, the men just sit in the camp with nothing to do and they get restless and bored. He suggested we dream up some programs to keep them busy. Maybe some kind of classes and perhaps some sports activities to keep them active. The other thing that Fidel mentioned to me after the meeting, is that he's heard rumors that the Union is thinking that they would have a big advantage with a captive audience during inclement weather."

"Hmm, that's a real concern. I think you'll need to keep close tabs with Fidel, help him in any way you can. He's a good man, but he needs the support of his growers."

"I agree."

"I'm glad things are going well because the wife and I are going to the Midwest to visit our daughters. They tell me this is the best time of the year and we'd like to spend some time with them. It's something we've never done because I always thought I was too busy running things. Curiously, I always thought the farm couldn't operate without me, but now it seems it works very well in my absence, perhaps even better. So, we're going. We'll still be in touch. I gave the office my itinerary and phone numbers in case of any emergency. Feel free to call, but let's just say you at least call me once a week for an update. I think you, Antonio, and Lori can take care of anything that comes up. I expect you all to just use your best judgment. I can't ask more than that."

That afternoon Larry came home early. First he went to the nursery and found the baby asleep. He looked at her for a long time. Then he went to the refrigerator and opened a bottle of beer. He then walked out onto the back patio and found Cipri sunning herself on a lounge chair. She was wearing shorts and no shoes. She said, "Well, this is something. I am now relegated to third place. I heard you come in, you went to check on the baby; then got yourself a beer and finally you came to find me. It's a good thing we don't have a dog. Then I would be in fourth place!"

Larry smiled, "Actually, I was thinking we could get a parrot as well, but I do think getting a dog is a good idea. Avaleine is going to need one to grow up with." He sat down next to his wife and gave her a hug and shared a drink of his beer with her. "So how was your day honey?"

"Well to be honest, I just love her nap time. To me it's like the last two minutes in a football game...hectic. If I plan it right, I can get more done in those two minutes than I can during the whole rest of the day. And occasionally, I get a few minutes to lie out here in the sun to catch a few rays. This brief time has become precious for both of us." She took another drink, "How was your day?"

"I had a good day. It's interesting that when we're in the peak of activities, everyone is busy and fortunately everyone knows what to do. When everyone is wrapped up in their individual responsibilities, they don't have time for me; so I have time to take it easy in a way. By that I mean the day-to-day issues are not as pressing so I have time just to think about the future and at least contemplate some long term plans."

"So tell me, what kinds of long term plans are you contemplating? Does it include two girls who love you desperately?"

"Well for one, I was thinking that Avaleine is growing so fast, that perhaps she should have a brother?"

Cipri sat up quickly in the chair, took his beer and took a long swallow. "What, do you object to me sitting out here in the sun occasionally? My goodness, can't a girl get some rest around here?" She laughed and gave him a big hug, "It's not a bad idea, but what if we just consider a puppy in the meantime."

Chapter 45

THE SPRING RAINS WERE WELCOMED. They provided good clean water that washed the tree leaves of months of debris that had accumulated. The roots also felt refreshed by the pure water. The aquifers were being replenished and the hills were transformed to a verdant hue almost overnight. By the fifth day, the men in the camp were becoming edgy. They couldn't even go out to shoot baskets. They quickly gave up on the TV room with mostly cooking shows in English. Even the days it didn't rain, the ground was too wet to work. In the meantime, other storms followed and the men just sat in their bunks bored, not earning any money and willing to listen to anyone or anything to pass the time.

By the third day of the rains, the county union office had gathered the local staff augmented by several agents from the Central Valley. They listened to a skinny, unimpressive looking young man. "We're in luck, the weather folks are forecasting rains for the next week; more or less. Then there's a break and then they're talking about another round of similar weather. That means with the rains and the soaked fields, the men won't be able to work for perhaps two weeks...that's all the time we need. If we can't get it done this time, we're not worth being called organizers. Now's the time for a full court press. Several of you have contacts in the camp, let's take advantage of it. The big issue now is that they're just sitting around not earning any money. In fact they're losing because they have to pay for room and board. Then there's the issue of having to work in piss poor orchards where the earnings stink. I'm surprised that those trees are still standing, but that's great for us, let's take advantage of the situation. We need to use anything we can throw at them."

One of the workers, a young lady, said "But how can we promise anything, I mean, we can't promise that we'll stop the rain."

The man smiled, "Sure you can. All you have to do is smile at the men. Tell them you feel their pain. Tell them it's the grower's fault for not being prepared. That it's unfair for them to be charged for room and board. And tell them about the poor men who have to pick those terrible trees. The fact is, we don't need to tell them much. They're already thinking about it, all we have to do is just fan the fire. Then when things really get ripe, we need to play the ethnic card. We need to tell them how we Chicanos need to stick together to eliminate the decades and decades of abuse and discrimination."

The young lady with blue eyes and blond hair said, "It's going to be hard for some of us to make that pitch."

He smiled, "In your case honey, all you have to do is bat your pretty blue eyes and show them some cleavage." There was laughter as the meeting broke up.

Jenny was seething as she walked out of the room, "Don't worry Jen, he was just trying to be funny in front of his buddies. The fact is that he's one of the best organizers the Union has. He's really an asshole, but he's still one of the best organizers around."

"Hell, he's no better than the growers. So who are we trying to kid here?" Jennifer White was close to tears. "I thought our efforts to help the poor and downtrodden was more noble than that. How can one be noble and an asshole at the same time? And how can we not be labeled with the same brush? Aren't we being two-faced about all this?"

"Being two-faced is part of being a human being, I think. I mean, we all do it. It's just that this guy is more crass about it. In the meantime, let's hang on and this fall we'll be back in Berkeley before we know it."

Jenny called on one of the workers. She had met Lalo Raya several times. He was one of the young men that had come in the original group. He was an excellent worker and one of the top earners. He was in his third year at the University of Guadalajara. He was working to get enough money to finish his education. The rain and any action that would disrupt his plans was a big concern for him. He had met Jennifer twice and agreed to have a Coke with her. She spoke fair Spanish and he spoke fair

English so they were able to converse well by going back and forth between the two languages. It was an interesting conversation to listen to. "But *eschucha* Lalo if workers can get together, collectively they can demand better working conditions *y mas dinero*. You know very well that one man by himself has no chance. *Pero juntos*, anything can be accomplished."

"I know, *pero* frankly I just need to make as much money as I can this time so I can finish school." I'm not interested in being a lemon picker *toda mi vida*."

"But what about your *compañeros*, some of them will be picking lemons all their lives, don't you want them to have a better life?" Jenny smiled as she spoke to the young man. Then she remembered the comment about showing her cleavage and she turned red with embarrassment.

"*Es de luego*, I want all of us to do well and we are. *Mira*, We all come here and work two or three months, if we work hard, and save our money, we can earn enough for our families to live well all year. *Tal vez*, they can start a business, *pueden comprar una vaca*, or put a down payment on a *parcelita*. They don't have to pick lemons all their lives. Or as the old *dicho* says, they can bloom where they're planted; *florean donde son plantados*."

"*Pero* Lalo, we just want to help you all by using your collective power to make sure you're not being exploited."

"Well, if you people don't want us to get exploited, then go to Mexico or Guatemala, do some of this work there, that's where the real *pobres* are, the down trodden, *los jodidos*. Let's help the people where they are, where they live."

Jenny smiled to herself as she noticed that both of them were going back and forth with the language and even mixing the sentences. It felt almost natural to her. Lalo didn't seem to notice that he was going back and forth. Whatever word in either language seemed to fit the idea that he was trying to convey, that's what he used. The interesting thing was that it sounded natural and seemed to make sense and at times even improve communication.

The board of the Pacific Labor Association met in emergency session on a Saturday in a community room of the local bank. Lorenzo called the meeting to order. "Ladies and gentlemen, thank you for your attendance on such a short order. I think you all know our attorney, Tim

McDonald. As you probably realize, all this rain and down time has drawn the attention of the union and we think they're going to file for an election. I've asked our labor attorney to come down and fill us in on what this means."

The labor attorney was a tall man, with thinning, wavy hair and a thick, bright red mustache. "I appreciate you all coming to this meeting. In this case, quick reaction might help us out of this pickle. As you know better than anyone, this rain has prevented the men from working. Hanging around the camp with nothing to do, boredom sets in and the workers are willing to listen to anyone. Of course the union knows this and has sent their ace organizer to see what they can exploit. Now the first thing we must do is not to underestimate these people. They're good, this is how they make their living, and they know exactly what they're doing. When you see them, you'll likely see some poorly dressed, shaggy guy who looks homeless. If you get taken in by this persona, you'll soon notice you no longer have your own shirt. Right now we have to keep our wits about us and not do anything rash or dumb."

"What do you mean don't do anything rash or dumb?" asked one of the directors.

"One of our clients in the San Diego area kicked all the workers out of his camp and tossed all their belongings out by the road. The press had a field day with that. Another guy shot an organizer's car and that made an even bigger news day."

"I can see that we don't want to shoot anybody, but if the workers are not working, why can't he ask them to leave his camp; that I don't understand," asked the man.

"Legally I suppose an owner can evict someone off of their property, but this is not a legal question. This is a public relations question! Do not get lulled by your rights; it's not about rights, I repeat; it's a public relations issue. You need to remember the press and the TV stations will have this on the 6 o'clock news. And I can assure you that you will not win this fight; I repeat. You will not win this fight. This means we need to do everything to keep the press out of this dispute." McDonald continued, "Just remember, the union wants martyrs, imagined or real, it doesn't matter to them. They know that they will win in the public arena."

"Then what the hell can we do?" he was asked.

"From what Fidel tells me, this is almost the end of the season. I understand you only have a few days at most. In fact, I've already notified the Labor Department representative, a Mr. Smith, that the men's work was about to be completed. He said he was aware of that fact. Apparently Fidel has kept him abreast of this action, which is a good thing. I had a long talk with Smith and he had mostly good things to say about your operation. He had a couple of minor concerns, but nothing of significance. He did tell me that he's had some dealings with this union rep and he said that we should be on our toes."

Chapter 46

L UCINDA PARKED ON MAIN STREET; she had a meeting with some growers at the Mupu Grill. She deliberately parked a block away from the popular restaurant. She wanted to have a few minutes to clear her mind before she went in. She didn't turn off the key completely since she was listening to one of her favorite songs. She waited for it to finish, then she turned off the ignition. She gathered her purse and her briefcase. The growers hadn't told her specifically what they had in mind, but she brought the association's file just in case. The file had grown over time and in that period, Pacific Labor Association had become a significant client. Not only that, but because of her work with them, and the beginning promotions for the special pink lemons for the Martin Group, she had garnered the interest of other agriculture operations. In fact, she had convinced Cipri to return to the firm when the baby was older. She had agreed to let her bring the baby to the office or in most cases she could work from home. Cipri added her skeptical, but practical viewpoint to her operation. Additionally, she was more sensitive to the outlook of farmers which made a valuable addition to her team. Being the wife of an upcoming farm executive also helped generate interest in her firm.

She quickly walked to the back of the restaurant and noticed that the four men had already finished breakfast and were drinking coffee. Apparently, they had been there for some time. "Good morning. I hope I'm not late, but there was a bit of traffic on the freeway."

Max Martin stood up and said, "Not to worry, we were just catching up with a few things we needed to do. You know everyone, but I don't know if you've met Jim Johnson of Johnson Farm. He's Lorenzo's boss."

Lucinda stood in front of the old man, "I don't believe we've met Mr. Johnson."

"I don't think so, but I understand you know my manager Lorenzo here. He takes care of most of the day to day business of our operation. I understand he's an alumnus of your business. I thank you for the excellent training you gave him."

Lucinda smiled at the older man and said, "Ah, so you're the fellow that swept him away. Well by all that's fair, I should be angry with you, but Cipri continues to work for us and it may be that I got the better deal in the end."

Johnson returned the smile and made a slight bow, "''Let's just agree that we both did very well.''

Larry looked down at the table top somewhat embarrassed about being discussed in his presence. Finally he said, "Thank you Lucinda for coming to see us. Our small group was selected to run a few ideas by you to get your reaction and see what kind of assistance you might provide for us. As you know the first season of working with our new foreign labor program is almost over. In general we feel that the program worked well for us and also for the workers. We had a few snags as with any new program, but we worked closely with our members and especially with the Department of Labor and we were able to address these few problems before they became serious issues. I must confess that we weren't too thrilled with the increase in cost which was significant over past years. Yet we understand the reason and we look forward to a continuation of the program for years to come."

"Let me interrupt, when you say costs increased, what are you talking about?"

"We haven't gotten the final numbers down just yet, but we estimate that costs will be about 18 to 20 percent higher than in previous years," answered Larry.

"Wow, that's a significant increase."

"Yes it is. We think we can live with that, but we have another issue that's come up. With all the recent rains and our employees not being able to work, the Union is making a play to get the workers under a union contract. Our concerns are two-fold. First, we assume that any union connection will again increase costs and after the additional increase I just mentioned, it will make significant impact in the growing of citrus in the county. Secondly, if they can make a big issue of this new immigration program that Congress just passed, after all our pain and effort, that might kill it."

Lucinda took a pitcher of water and poured herself a glass. She did this slowly to quench her thirst, but also to take a few additional moments to consider the dilemma being posed to her. "Well gentlemen, of course I understand your first problem, but added expenses although painful can be managed one way or another, but the union is another issue. As you all know in the circle that I work in, the unions and especially farm workers are the darlings. In fact, I would count myself and most of the people in our firm as part of this group, but tell me what attracted the union to your workers in the first place?"

"For years we've been aware of the interest the union has had in our people. As I've mentioned, the recent rains have kept the workers out of the orchards. Mostly they've just sat in the camp being bored to tears I'm afraid. In the meantime, we understand the union has brought in one of their best organizers and several others to help out. With our workers just sitting around, they have been able to talk to them at length on how poorly they've been treated and how much the union can do for them."

"Say no more", she said with a grin, "I worked in Georgia my last summer in college helping a union in that action. I'm assuming they're using the same drill." She paused for a long time and continued, "I have to let you know that I've actually worked for unions on several occasions and deep down in my soul I have a soft place in my heart for those who toil in the fields."

Johnson was listening and then interrupted, "Well, Lucinda, you might be surprised that most of us here also have a soft place for our workers. We know damn well that without them we have nothing. They are the underpinning of the type of farming we do in this part of the country. However, we don't set the price for our products, so if the public thinks our prices are too high, they'll buy something else or get the product from another state or even another country. So we always operate on the thin edge. Interestingly enough, if we fail, so do our workers; we both go down together; we both lose. So you can see we're closely intertwined. The notion is very simple; either Mexico sends us Mexican workers or sends us Mexican lemons." Johnson realized he had jumped in on the conversation and seemed embarrassed.

Calmly Lorenzo looked at everyone and said, "Jim's insight reflects the feelings of those of us present. And I must admit some surprise when I say that most of the members of Pacific Labor Association feel similarly. Now I'm not naïve enough to pretend to you that all our members go along or are saints. We have some members where I have to watch my wallet, but even those see the value of our non-profit grower association and go along with the policies set by our board and administered by Fidel Corona, our manager."

"Frankly gentlemen, my first reaction was to tell you that it would be better if you retained someone else for this effort because of my obvious concern and support for those at the tail end of society, but after consideration, it occurred to me that by assisting you in this contest, I'm still supporting these same folks. That is, if I can assist in finding some mutual peace where the workers can continue to work and you all stay in business to provide the work, it becomes a win-win situation. Strife just for the sake of strife is of no help to anyone."

Max looked at everyone and said, "That makes a lot of sense Lucinda. So tell us what would you suggest?"

"First, let me take the opportunity to digest the situation and let me check in with you in a couple of days with some concrete ideas. Let me just ask one thing to be sure. The harvest season would naturally end here in the next few days; is that correct?"

"That's essentially correct. There's always some minor work done in the winter, but basically the harvest season is mostly complete here on the coast and then the harvest moves out to the desert," answered Martin.

"When would it begin here again?" she asked.

"By January we're beginning to move again, and by spring we're back to our peak regular harvest. We basically have a spring and summer harvest for our lemons in this county," said Martin.

"Just one more question, what do the men do while they're not working?"

"That's just our problem, there's nothing to do. Mostly the workers just watch TV, shoot baskets, play cards or just shoot the breeze. We've talked to the local school district about some type of educational classes, but nothing's been developed to date," said Lorenzo as he answered Lucinda and looked at his colleagues.

"Boredom is one of the biggest evils in this world. More trouble is caused, I think, by people just sitting around with nothing to do. We all do some really dumb things just to stir things up at one time or another. On top of that, there are people who are experts at taking advantage of such times and if it's the union organizer who I'm thinking about; he's one of the best."

Chapter 47

LORENZO WAS SURPRISED when he saw Lucinda and Alix Raya walk into the Pacific Coastal office. There was another woman with them. Lucinda said, "Alix, you remember Lorenzo and this is Fidel Corona, the manager of the Association. And I'd like to introduce Matty Logan, Alix's new disciple."

Alix went around the room and shook everyone's hand, but when she got to Larry she gave him a big hug and kissed him on both cheeks. She had a different look. Her hair was short and she wore a snug T-shirt. She also wore tight jeans which accentuated her well developed figure, but more than anything, it was her radiant smile and personality which seemed to overwhelm the room. "Lorenzo, eh; wasn't it Larry at one time?" She looked at him critically and continued, "I like Lorenzo better. So how've you been? Lucy tells me that you and Cipri have added to our population. I hope we have time to get together later on. I'd love to meet the baby."

Larry was still trying to hide his surprise and said, "I'd like to introduce you to her. I'll check with Cipri and we can get together later."

Alix moved on to Fidel, "I understand you have a bunch of bored men hanging around with nothing to do. Don't you know that's playing with fire? There's nothing worse than a bunch of guys just sitting around with nothing to do. Hell, wars have started under such circumstances. Tell me, how long has this been going on?"

"Well this year we've had some early rains. More importantly they've been scattered over several weeks so we haven't been able to get into the orchards. Also, we're getting towards the end of the harvest season so things were slowing down in any event. We probably only have a couple weeks till we get down to just a few men to pick some young trees that need attention. We will only keep 20 to 30 men during the winter. The combination of unseasonable rains and the end of the season has made the situation worse."

"Tell us, how long have these men been working for you?" asked Matty Logan. Logan was not a young woman. She was in her mid forties, but dressed and looked much younger. She wore jeans and a tight sweat shirt that made her look very attractive and considerably younger than she actually was. "And can anyone tell me in simple words what the union has been offering the worker?"

Corona answered, "Most of the men have been here since spring and a couple of crews, about eighty, since mid-summer…curiously enough, many have worked for us before under the previous system and most of them under different names. We actually recruited them because they had experience picking lemons and seemed willing to work for us. Many of them told us they knew what to expect and knew that they could make good money with us. In a way, they picked us as much as we selected them." Logan looked at the people in the room waiting for the second part of her question.

"The two issues they are pushing are more money, of course and then the redress of the treaty of Guadalupe-Hidalgo that ceded the southwest from Mexico to the United States. They're playing the ethnic card big time," added Lorenzo.

"Okay, what else; has anyone gotten hurt? Anyone fired recently? Anyone tangle with the law?"

"That's just it Alix, with the exception that this was the first season under the new foreign labor program it was a very unexceptional season. In many cases, as Fidel mentioned, many of the men have worked for us before. We had almost no turnover. The crew's earnings were above average. It was really a good year for them all. It was for us as well even with the increase cost. The biggest problem appears to be the rain and the lack of work opportunity and the just sitting in the camp with nothing to do." Lorenzo looked around the room, "I mean, we have the same problem with our own workers on the ranch."

"Tell me Larry, what did you do? How did you deal with all the rain in your operation?"

"Well first we don't have so many men to deal with, but our foreman, Toñio Martinez has a list of several chores that can be done in bad weather. He also reduces the hours to make sure that everyone gets some time. There's always something to do on the ranch. That however, is not possible when you only harvest lemons."

"Now listen carefully to this question; in general would you want these men to work for you this season? I mean, are these the type of men that you want to work for you all?"

Lorenzo answered quickly, "As you know I have the less experience with the men, but as we said, many of them have been working for us already. In fact, many have worked for us for many seasons under different circumstances. We know them and more importantly they know us, the way we operate and what to expect from us. They have experience and I think they return because they know they can make money with us."

"Okay, I know boredom can be a real bummer. So here's what I suggest; you give Matty and me a few days to talk to the workers, but we want to be able to talk for you, make some commitments if you will."

"What kind of commitments are you talking about?" asked Larry.

"Well let's just assume the men do want to return next season, I want to tell them that we'll keep in touch with them, to let them know how the work is developing and to assure them that they will be the first ones selected next year." Alix looked at Matty to continue.

Matty added, "We were wondering if Pacific Coastal would consider a signing bonus for next year? As I understand, it costs money for you to train a new worker. What would you think of paying them a bonus for this training period for *not having to train them*?"

"How would that work?" asked Fidel.

"Our preliminary thought is that it would work on a percentage basis. For example, let's assume someone earns $5000 this year. When he returns next season he has a check waiting for him for $100 or 2% of his previous earnings. Enough to get him started for the new season. And here's the trick; the best workers would get more money since their earnings would be greater. So in a way it's a method to screen for your better men and encourage your more productive workers to make sure they return."

"But that would increase our already high costs," said Fidel.

"Yep, no doubt about it; but I can assure you that if you get into a contest with the union, it will cost you a helluva lot more…lots more, and more grief than you can bear."

Lorenzo looked at his colleagues and said, "I wonder if you ladies would step outside and have a cup of coffee. We need to have a chat among ourselves."

Lorenzo and Fidel made a quick call to the executive committee and they concurred with the idea. There were inherent risks, but they seemed well worth taking. The two men asked the ladies to return. "Okay ladies, go ahead; see what you can do with these arrangements. Just keep us in touch with what happens over the next few days."

For a good part of a week, the two women met with the men. They met individually, in pairs, in groups and they even took a few of them out to the movies. Occasionally they mentioned the union conflict, but mostly they just had a good time. There was lots of joking and laughing. All the while they collected the names and Mexican addresses of the men. The men were told they would write to them, in essence, the association would keep in touch with the men to keep them informed of the work situation. In an informal poll, it was determined that most of the men indeed liked to pick lemons; they made good money and were willing to return the following spring and thereafter. The men were subtly told that the present arrangement could be disturbed by the presence and influence of any third party, but mostly, the men were entertained, provided with snacks and mostly just kept busy. The rains finally let up and it only took about ten days to finally complete the basic harvest. All the men were laid off except a few who were kept to harvest some young trees. In the meantime the company bought some nice shirts with the name and logo of the association embroidered on the shirt pocket. Every worker was given a nice shirt with the final check and was assured they would be kept informed about the work. Always in the joking, the movies and the boisterous give and take, the welcome back bonus was quietly inferred. It was not an overt offer, but it was there; the men understood and believed it in the quiet way it was presented. The meetings and the offer and especially the two skilled women created a discussion among the men that fortified the message the ladies were giving them. More importantly, they eased the boredom of not working.

Jenny White was driving north on Highway 5 over the Tejon Grade when she said, "What the hell happened?"

"No one seems to know. Everyone felt that this fight was won. Suddenly these two women showed up and blew us away. That was it, they just blew us away! Oh well, back to Berkeley."

Chapter 48

ATHER SEAN FLYNN walked into the restaurant, looking forward to a nice, quiet lunch. In the corner he saw Lorenzo, Cipri and the baby; giving an order to the waitress. He hesitated and then stopped to say hello. "Ah, the young Franco family and the youngest, addition; how nice. How old is the young lady?"

"She'll be a year old next week," answered Cipri as she tied a bib around the baby's neck. "It's good to see you Father, won't you join us? In fact, we were discussing you the other day. We wanted to set up an appointment to ask you a few questions."

"Tell me young lady, why would you be discussing an old, grouchy priest?" the priest sat down across from the young family. "And you Lorenzo, I've been hearing much about you recently. In fact, in some circles your name is spoken in anger. Now tell me why would that be?"

"I'm not too sure Father, but tell me who have you been listening to that would bring up my name?"

"As I understand it, the union has been trying to get their foot in the door in the county for some time, and with the recent rains, they felt they had it in the bag. Then the company retained a couple of well-endowed hired guns and the game was over. I hear the organizers have left town, for better prospects as I understand it. Now tell me why did you want to see me?"

"Avaleine here will be one year old in a few days and we thought it was time she was baptized," answered Cipri.

"Avaleine, that's a different name, I've never heard of it. What does it mean? Is it a family name?"

"It's an old Native American name from my people in the foothills of Arizona; it means Hopeful Dawn. It was a name suggested to us by my great grandmother. She said she saw something in her that gave her hope not only for the baby, but for our people. So Hopeful Dawn, she is. What do we have to do to get her baptized?"

"Well of course this young lady needs to be baptized and it will be my honor to perform this initial, and most important, Sacrament. I do need you to go to our office to give the pertinent information that we need for the documentation and also to select a date. The ladies at the office can take care of all of that. Drop by at your convenience." The priest looked somewhat uncomfortably at Cipri, "I don't know how to say this delicately, but I heard that the men at the Association turned away from the union because the growers let loose two…how can I say this, two loose women among the men?"

Lorenzo almost choked on the hot tea he was drinking, "Good lord," he laughed. "It's true we had a couple of representatives providing basic information to the men. Explaining what was at stake. Once the men understood the real options involved, they just quit listening to the emotional pitch the union was making. It was that simple. Just for your information Father, most of the men will probably be back with us next spring. If the men don't think they're being treated fairly, the union can have another shot at them."

"I understand these were two well endowed females."

"Well, they were woman, that's for sure. I can arrange for you to meet them Father and you can see and ask them yourself what they did. I'm sure they'd be more than willing to explain their methods to you or anyone for that matter. In fact, I can assure you that anyone making even a suggestion that there was something inappropriate going on should be well prepared."

"No, no I don't want to get entangled with this issue. I mean, I have my own problems. I thought you should know what some folks are saying about the grower's effort and even about you. For such a young man who is relatively new to this business, you seem to have made quite an impact in some quarters." The priest chuckled as he spoke to the young family.

"Well I hope the main point of the discussion is that fairness has been part of my effort. By that I mean fairness to all concerned; to the owners and the employees and especially to the latter, because without the workers, we would all be out of work."

Cipri added, "By the way Father, I'm employed by the firm that retained these two ladies and I can assure you that they indeed are professional…and not in the way that's being implied. In fact, I'm offended and could easily get upset with anyone that would make such an accusation."

"Well my dear, I'm sure you're right, but you see, in my line of work I've found that it's wise to put information out in the light so it can be examined carefully. So as long as you're in peace, that's all that matters."

After the priest had left, Cipri was gathering the baby and belongings, "Larry, what the hell was the priest talking about? Was he implying that Alix and Matty were fooling around with the men?"

"I don't think he was implying that. I think what he was saying is that's what the union is spreading around to cover their inability to convince the workers to join their ranks. In fact, they filed a complaint with the Department of Labor claiming such an action. The local Department of Labor official who was around all during this time has dismissed the claim, but the union continues to make the claim to anyone who listens."

"What happens now?" she asked.

"Nothing for the time being, but there's no doubt that we'll hear from them next spring when we crank up again. In fact, Fidel Corona has already touched base with Alix and Matty and they'll be here as we gear up; talking to the workers to make sure we haven't missed anything. So you can bet that people will make a similar claim against them. In fact, Fidel has already told them about it and as I hear it; they're really ticked off. So no telling what excitement we can expect for the next season."

"But what would they do? What can they do that the company can't do for itself?" she asked.

"That's a good question. I think, however, sometimes the supervisors are too close to the men and focus too much on production and not enough on the men themselves. I mean, the men only work eight hours a day and then they have lots of time just sitting around. That's when the ladies can utilize the time to occupy themselves and talk about the realities of work and the company."

"*Ay* Lorenzo, at times I think life is too complicated. Now I know why Luna stays on the Res. It's the simple life she cherishes. I think, perhaps, we should visit her soon so we keep in touch with reality."

"Great idea; things should slow down this winter. Let's plan to get away for a few days. Why don't you give her a call to see if she's going to be around?"

Luna was thrilled when Cipri told her about the visit, but Cipriana was ecstatic. She immediately began to make arrangements. The late fall weather in the high desert is beautiful. The clear, crisp weather and the plants and animals preparing for the winter increased activities. The households were stacking firewood for the cold winter. And the great grandmother was anxious to see her Hopeful Dawn, almost as if she sensed a special importance to the visit. Those around her also caught the spirit as they jumped into action. The little town, with a predominantly older population, soon got word of the impending visit. For a year, the old woman talked to her friends, neighbors and anyone who would listen about her great granddaughter, Hopeful Dawn. Everyone seemed to get into the spirit and began looking for the arrival of the young lady.

When they arrived at the house, there was no one there except Johnny Mendez who was watching a football game on television. He immediately helped the young family into the house and got them situated. Cipri looked around after giving her father a big hug, "Where is everyone?" she asked.

"At the small church; everyone's at the church, waiting for you all, but they're especially waiting for this young lady," He said as he picked up Avaleine and gave her a big hug. The little girl squirmed in the arms of her grandfather. "Hurry, I'm supposed to take you over as soon as you got here."

"Goodness, what has *Abuelita* done? I hope she hasn't gone off the deep end for our visit. We just came over for a few days to get away from our hectic days. I told Lorenzo we needed to get away just to relax and get back to nature."

Johnny chuckled as he hugged his granddaughter, "Well good luck with that. First we're going to the church to see what she's arranged. I know she talked with Hipolito about a goat BBQ this weekend. I think she invited the whole town. We haven't had this much excitement in quite a while."

"Daddy, do you know if she invited Luna?"

"Are you kidding, those two were on the phone for hours planning this visit, so no telling what they've arranged. Luna's already here, she came in this morning and she's at the church now. So we better hurry or there'll be a posse out for us."

They walked to the church. There was no need for the stroller, Johnny insisted on carrying the baby. He also talked to the baby all the way. He pointed out items of interest and gave the baby the historic background of the little town. Avaleine paid close attention to her grandfather. Larry and Cipri walked behind them enjoying the walk, but also intrigued with the grandfather and Hopeful Dawn in his arms.

Johnny led them to the annex next to the church itself. As they walked in, the crowd quieted and began to move apart to allow the old woman to come forward. She walked slowly toward Johnny and the baby, she hugged them both and then she took the little girl into her arms and turned around slowly so everyone could see her. There were tears in Cipriana's eyes. The baby stared at the old woman and then gently reached for the woman's beret that had three small hummingbird feathers attached to it. Then the old woman went to Cipri and gave her a big hug. The people began to applaud and talk all at the same time. Cipriana raised her hand and said, "Friends, before we begin this welcome celebration, we need to give thanks to our Lord for this gift of family and friends. My good friend Luna Martinez and Father Joel will give us a blessing of thanksgiving."

Luna lit a bundle of sage, blew on it gently to make it glow, walking first around Cipriana and the baby. She hummed a soft song as she walked. She then made a larger circle around all those present. The room was soon enveloped with the sweet smell of sage. She then went to the priest; she bowed in front of him and then blessed him with the sage.

The priest made a deep bow to Luna and then looked at the baby, "Heavenly Father, we thank you for giving us your Hopeful Dawn. We ask you to bless her and her parents. We also ask for your blessing for all of us as we gather to celebrate and to welcome everyone to this gathering. All this we ask in the name of the Father and of the Son and of the Holy Spirit." The crowd all said, "Amen."

The following day, Hipolito, an old timer famous for his goat pit BBQ, was removing the bundles of meat from the pit. The guests gathered around him to watch the proceedings. The old man removed the dirt covering over the pit and then the metal lid over the hole. Suddenly the whole area was overwhelmed with the smell of smoke and cooked meat and the party began. All this time Avaleine never touched the ground, she went from arm to arm. However, she kept coming back to Cipriana who was sitting under a tree. The old woman took off her feather beret and put it on the baby. The girl touched it, but made no effort to remove it. The colorful feathers united the two beings that were nine decades apart in age, but joined physically and spiritually for the moment.

Chapter 49

IVE WEEKS LATER as they returned to the little town, Cipri noticed the starkness of the mountains and the dark clouds that threatened rains. The day before, she had received a call from her father that Cipriana had died in her sleep. The old woman had gone to church, had a cup of chocolate and had gone to bed early. She had made several berets from hummingbird feathers, "These are for all my girls," she said as she went to bed. She didn't wake up the following morning.

When Lorenzo, Cipri and the baby drove up, the house was teaming with people. There was a festive feeling with romantic music of the *Trios de Los Panchos* playing in the living room. People were singing or humming to the music. There were many red and swollen eyes as they sang to the music. When Linda Mendez saw her daughter, she rushed to her and grabbed her and the baby in a warm embrace, "Oh, my babies, I'm so glad you're here. For the last several weeks your Nana did nothing, but talk about you and the baby. She was so glad that you came to visit her. Hopeful Dawn was always on her mind and her lips. This baby made her long life complete." Linda took the baby and began to dance with her to *Los Panchos* with tears streaming down her cheeks.

The funeral Mass was solemn yet festive. Many of the women wore colorful berets made with feathers. They fluttered in the breeze as they walked. Avaleine wore a special one made by Cipriana of hummingbird feathers that shimmered in the light. When Cipri walked up to the coffin she had the baby in her arms and the baby became excited when she saw her ancestor. Cipri leaned over and kissed her namesake on the forehead as did the baby. There were tears and sobs throughout the church.

The baby, however, was all smiles as she waved at the woman in the coffin.

At the cemetery the baby walked among the people, she smiled and laughed as she was picked up by everyone she approached. Luna brought several bunches of sage, she lit them and gave them to the family which stood around the grave as she prayed in her native tongue. The festive tears and celebration continued at the house and lasted until midnight. The family sat together after everyone had left and Linda said, "We'll clean things up in the morning, tonight we'll give thanks to our Savior." And they all went to bed. An era had ended.

Chapter 50

The family was preparing to leave the following morning and were gathering their belongings; including a large carton of Cipriana's personal belongings that her namesake was taking home. The value of the keepsakes was personal and of little or no monetary significance. During the morning, Lorenzo received a phone call from Fidel. They talked for several minutes. The conversation from Larry's side amounted to many grunts and other affirmative noises. Finally he said, "Okay, we'll see you in a few days."

"What was that all about?" asked Cipri.

"We're going to take a little side tour. Fidel called me, he said several of our workers were in Yuma picking lemons and were checking in with us about work this spring. Apparently they asked a few questions about any potential troubles and wanted to be reassured. Since we're in the area, I agreed to stop by and chat with them. We're to meet at one of their relative's house on the outskirts of town."

The trip south through the barren Arizona desert matched the starkness of their feelings after the funeral. They drove in silence. Mostly they listened to Spanish radio stations with strong broadcasting signals from Mexico. There was a beauty to the desert and the seemingly barren mountains that was not lost on them. "So tell me again, why are we going to meet with these fellows?"

Lorenzo answered without taking his eyes off the road, "You know this immigration reform law is not perfect. It has several holes in it. It's cumbersome and then there's the chance of going to jail if it's not adhered to. On the other hand, it has mostly worked. Most of the illegal employment has disappeared and workers can come in temporarily to work and then return home under the auspices of both governments. So abuses are reduced significantly, but there's still a small segment of folks that don't like it and want to get rid of it. Apparently, these fellows have heard rumors of potential problems this spring and are wondering if it's worth all the effort to come to work for us."

"So what are you going to do? What will you say to them?"

"That's just it, I'm not too sure; we'll have to play it by ear. All Fidel told me was that the men would meet us outside of town. We'll see what happens."

Lorenzo slowed down at the edge of town and drove into a long driveway bordered by full grown grapefruit trees. The road opened to a large, old house surrounded by several other buildings. There were cars and pickups parked in front of the house. As they drove up chickens scattered and two dogs came out to investigate the new visitors. Several small children also came out of the house followed by a woman holding a baby. "You must be Mr. Franco. The boys went to town to buy some refreshments. They'll be back in a few minutes. Please come in."

The family followed the woman into the house, "This is my wife Cipriana and our daughter Avaleine."

"Please call me Cipri. I wonder if I may use one of your rooms. I think this young lady needs to be changed."

"Of course, this young man is Tonito and he'd be glad to share his room. By the way, my name is Lupe, but everyone calls me Lupita."

At that moment two cars drove up and several young men piled out. There was lots of laughing and joking as the men gathered under a tree. They opened beers and soft drinks and a large bag of *chicharrones*. Lupita showed Lorenzo out to meet the men, she said, "Boys this is Mr. Lorenzo Franco, I understand he's the president of Pacific Growers in Oxnard. I hear you all have a meeting together.

Mr. Franco, my name is Lalo Raya, I and several of my friends worked for you last season. Thank you for coming by. We talked to Fidel Corona and he told us you were in the area. We appreciate you taking your time to visit; especially since you were attending a funeral. We're very sorry for your loss."

At that moment Cipri and the baby came out of the house. "This is my wife Cipri and my daughter Avaleine"

The little girl immediately wanted down and walked over to the men and they gave her one of the pigskins. The men smiled and focused their attention on the little girl. They all watched her as she became acquainted with everyone until she wandered over to where two young puppies were playing. "Well, tell me boys, what seems to be your concern? Perhaps I can help you with some additional information."

Lalo said, "First let me get you a beer."

"Thanks, I'd very much like one, but I'm driving. I will have a Coke."

"Mr. Franco, to be honest, we all liked working for you. We liked the camp, the food and we liked the work. It was hard work, but we were able to save a little money. We've heard, even out here in the desert, that we can expect trouble this spring. That the union and the government will make sure we don't work. They're even saying there will be violence. Frankly, all we want is to work. We don't want to get involved with all this nonsense. We already checked. We can go to another state to work and we will if we have to, but like I said, we already know you and very much like the camp and know what to expect."

Lorenzo opened the soda and took a long drink, "To be honest, we didn't know what to expect with the new immigration law and all the new programs related to it. We knew that if we were to get our fruit picked we had to administer the program as best we could. To make sure that everyone was treated fairly and especially that it was worth your while to work for us. We knew for example, that the additional expense would put some of our farmers in a difficult position. That was too bad, but it was the reality of the program; it had to be done. Overall it worked pretty well and we want to continue. And we want you all to continue with us. Frankly, it's best for us and for you that we have experienced workers. You make more money and we get more production."

"But can you guarantee us that we won't get caught in another labor dispute?" asked Lalo.

Lorenzo looked down and with his boots he leveled off a piece of ground and said, "I wish I could, but in this life there are no sure things. A guarantee from me would be a lie. I just can't lie to you. What I can tell you is that you will be treated fairly, and with God providing good weather, you'll have all the opportunity to work. By the way, we're also working on some additional benefits. Fidel told me that we've made arrangements with the local community college to provide classes in the evening for those who want them. The first class will be one in English. Later on if others want a class in a special subject we will consider it carefully. Now I know that may not sound like a good deal after picking lemons all day, but let me tell you, none of you will pick lemons all your life. You'll need other skills. And one skill that will open more doors than you can imagine is English. English is the key in this country and I would guess that it's also a valuable asset even in Mexico. So it's our effort to provide you the opportunity to earn good, honest money and to improve your own personal lives."

The men listen carefully. They continued to drink and eat the snacks. One of the older men went over to Avaleine and asked permission to pick her up. "I have a little girl about this age at home. I miss her, I miss my wife and I miss all my family, but there's little work. Here I can earn ten times what I earn there if I'm lucky to work. All I want is an opportunity to provide for my family. I want to provide a good education for my kids. Perhaps they can attend college and do better in life than me...all I want to do is work...just the chance to work." The man paused, "What's the baby's name?"

"Avaleine."

The man made a couple of efforts to pronounce the name and he just couldn't get his tongue around it. "It's a pretty name, but what if I call her Avi?" Then he spoke to the baby as he handed her back to Lorenzo, "Avi, I hope I have a chance to see you and to say hello to you in Oxnard."

Larry took the baby back and said, "Well friends, this much I can tell you, we have the work. Lots of work; you'll have the opportunity to make as much money as you can. On top of that, we have a great place to stay and excellent food as you already know. However, there's always someone who wants to raise hell, but we'll do everything we can to prevent that. And remember, all of you who worked last season will receive a little bonus to begin with and then continue to earn one for the following season. We really want you to make money because if you make money, we too make money. It's that's simple. So we're in this together."

Lalo looked around at his friends; they either smiled or nodded, "Great, Mr. Franco, we have a deal. We'll come in the spring. One thing I would ask, however, I'm one of the men who's not married, I wonder if you can make sure that the English teacher is pretty and single." There were lots of hoots and laughter as the men passed around the *chicharrones*. Even Avi reached out and got one of the snacks as the bag came by her.

Chapter 51

THE EXECUTIVE COMMITTEE of the Pacific Labor Association was having a meeting to plan for the upcoming season. Larry had invited Alix and Matty. They all listened to Larry's visit with the men in Yuma. Fidel also gave a quick summary of the work and the tentative schedule for the spring months. "It appears the recent rains and an early spring will bring the harvest sooner and larger up front so we need to get prepared. All the packinghouses are predicting larger crops. We expect a rush and that's why we called this meeting. First, I'd like to ask Dolan Smith with the Department of Labor to give us an overview from his perspective on how the first year went and what to expect for the new season."

"First let me tell you how much I appreciate the cooperation and effort you all made in working with us. Many of us in the department had no idea how the new immigration program would work. There was lots of apprehension to be sure, but thanks to Fidel and his crew, things worked well in this county. From what I heard from other areas, overall the program is getting good reviews. There were a few problems and I understand some growers will not be getting the workers they need and will be working under a different banner, but not withstanding the hiccups with the union, we were very pleased. And I'm glad to tell you that we're getting ready to receive your new batch of workers. In the meantime, if you have any questions, please let me know. I know you have other issues to discuss, so I'll excuse myself and let you continue."

Fidel continued after the representative left, "First let me tell you we were lucky to have Smith, I understand some of the other boys were not as understanding, but let me correct one thing, we are not looking for a new batch of workers. Based on the suggestions of our two ladies present, we have kept in contact with all our workers. I'd like Alix and Matty to give you a quick summary of what we've done to date and what we might expect."

Alix stood and walked to the front of the room, "First, let me thank you for giving us the opportunity to help you out. I was very hesitant to take on this challenge. My perspective of farmers was certainly out of whack with the reality. We found out that you all are no different than any other business. Some of you are better farmers than others and some are better employers than others. Just like anywhere else. So our effort was to stabilize the workforce. We did several things. First we got the names and addresses of all the men that worked here and we sent them a nice Christmas card, thanking them for their work. We sent a second letter with an update of how the crops were coming along and estimated the timeframe of the work. In the last note we again urged them to come and we noted the bonus amount they would get when they got here. This is important because in talking to the men, they told us they make the trip north with almost no money. They try to leave all the funds they can with their families in Mexico. So they basically just have cigarette money, till their first check. So having a couple of dollars here waiting for them is a huge benefit. It makes the link and the motivation to return to the Association much stronger."

Matty spoke from where she was sitting, "In the meantime, we made arrangements with the local college to start up a Conversational English class. One class will accommodate a dozen students. If we have more, we will start up as many classes as we get multiples of twelve."

"Who will pay for the teacher?" asked Max Martin.

"That was the easy part," said Matty, "The Association will reimburse the College for the cost of the teacher and any material used."

"At one time we talked about other classes, is that still on the menu?" asked Max.

"In checking with the men, I think we'll wind up with a couple of English classes. A basic English conversation class and then a more advanced class. There are several men who already are pretty fluent so the idea is that they'll be taught at their level. What's more, the college has agreed to provide the classes for credit. That'll give them more prestige.

If by chance the men ever apply for permanent visas, this can be helpful to them. A few men have inquired about some of the trades like welding and electrical. These we'll have to play by ear."

"Good lord," said one of men present, "Are we going to start our own college at our expense? I mean, where will all this end?"

Matty chuckled, "Welcome to the real world. I'm sure you know that most corporations and businesses of any size have education reimbursement programs. It's the reality of business nowadays. There's no doubt it will add to the cost of business, but we calculated that if we cover the cost based on a per bin basis, we're talking in terms of pennies per bin. It's still money, but it's a different way of looking at this expense."

Larry looked at everyone in the room, "Anything else you have up your sleeves?"

Matty replied, "These are solid programs we're recommending and hopefully you will approve. We also have a couple of other things in our bag of tricks if we need them. For example, just within an hour or two drive, we have all kinds of possibilities to keep the men busy. Just think of all the zoos, the museums and recreation areas we have close by. The possibilities are endless, if we need to be creative."

"Especially with our money," quipped one of the men.

Matty again laughed aloud, "Hey, we're experts when it comes to spending someone else's money, but you also must remember that in the long run, we're really saving you money and perhaps some giant headaches in the future."

Larry addressed the group, "As you all know, the board gave us the authority to approve these programs if we thought them to be beneficial to the organization. What's your pleasure?"

After a short silence, Maxwell Martin said, "I like what I heard. This is a proactive action; it gives us an opportunity to be ahead of the game so I think we should approve these actions. Just one thing Matty, have you discussed any of these ideas with Dolan Smith?"

"Actually, we have. Not in great detail, but he thought the concepts were good. Frankly, he saw it as saving himself a great headache. If everyone is busy earning money or learning English the smoother things will be for him. He also hinted that he ran the ideas by his boss who liked them and apparently he'll be watching to see how it goes."

Larry said, "Well if there's no objection from anyone, we'll go with the plans the ladies presented to us. I'm assuming that you'll keep Fidel and the rest of us informed as things develop." After the meeting he chatted briefly with the two women, "I've had an opportunity to talk to one of the workers from Mexico, he's young and very bright. He's single and seems to be one of the informal leaders. I wonder if it makes sense to focus on him. It seems that if he is a leader, he should be a leader for our Association."

"You wouldn't be talking about Lalo Raya would you?" asked Alix.

Surprised, Lorenzo asked, "How in the world did you know? I mean I just talked to him a few days ago in Yuma."

"It's no surprise to us, we ran across him at the end of the season and it was obvious to us he was a potential leader. It seemed to us then, and it does now, that if he's going to be a leader, he should be a leader for the Association; just as you suggested."

"Yes, I definitely agree."

Chapter 52

MAXWELL MARTIN AND JIM JOHNSON asked Lorenzo to have break fast with them at the Mupu Grill. Lorenzo hadn't heard that his boss, Johnson, was even in town. He spoke frequently with him on the phone and the old man seemed to be having a good time visiting his daughters in the Midwest. The two older men had eaten, and the waitress was clearing their plates, it was obvious the men had been there for some time. "Good morning, Mr. Franco...the usual?" she asked.

Larry nodded, "Good heavens Jim, I just spoke to you and I thought you were with your daughters."

"I was then, but I needed to check in on a few things, but then I have to attend a birthday party for a pretty little girl. I promised I would be back. So we're only here for a couple of days. We can chat about how things are going later on. In the meantime, Max and I would like to share an idea with you."

Maxwell Martin took a drink of his coffee, "Jim and I have been kidding each other for several years about getting on in age. We've also noted that we have no one in the family who is destined to be a farmer in the short term. Yet we have responsibilities to many people and we want to do the right thing for the future."

Lorenzo removed the tea bag from his cup and looked at the two men. He noticed several documents on the table that appeared to be well thumbed through. Max continued, "The Johnsons and the Martins have been farming in the area for several generations and it has been, all in all, a good life, but things are changing; the crops, the people, the cities and the environment continues to change and it's become apparent to Jim and me that we too have to change. What we would like to do at this time is to explore the possibilities of joining our two operations into one. Our notion is quite simple; we think that a large, well managed diversified operation will be more positive to our family members and to all our employees and even to our community. It will, we think, provide stability in the near future as much as anyone can provide."

Lorenzo could feel the blood rushing through his body as he tried to understand what he was being told. Yet he said nothing except pour more hot water into his cup and dip the tea bag several time as he returned his gaze to the two men.

"Now here's the hard thing, Larry. We would like you, on top of your present responsibilities, to take a very, very confidential and hard look at our two operations from top to bottom and to determine if there's a good fit for both groups. We have here several documents from both of us as starting points. We want you to take the time to study the two companies on paper as well as kick some tires, if you will. After you do that, and assuming that you see this as a positive step, then we will bring in the attorneys, the banker, the accountants and the rest of the gang to work on the details. By then it won't be a big secret, but in the meantime we need to keep it under our hats."

Larry looked at the two men, took a deep breath and said, "Wow, you guys can ruin a good cup of tea! He took several more deep breaths, "Curiously, in my recent work with Pacific Labor Association, I've had the opportunity to meet some of our growers and I've seen them struggle with the changes in labor and how that affects their operations. Several of the older folks have talked about just this subject. So it's not a new concept to me. I do have one question, what's the timing of this project? I mean, when do you want this done?"

Jim Johnson answered, "Lorenzo, I know that we've just dumped a big chore on your back, but we need you to have a quick look at the idea. Don't get too bogged down on the details, we'll have the accountants and attorneys do that. We want your best gut instinct of how complementary our two operations are. I mean, get a feel of the land, taste the water, meet the workers, kick the tires as Max said. Perhaps go up on one of the hills and look down on the properties for a different perspective. We want your subjective views on this proposition."

"My goodness Jim, you sound almost spiritual." Larry smiled at his boss.

"In a sense, the spirit is not farfetched, Lorenzo. Think about it, we're talking not only about our own well being, but we're also talking about a legacy for the future, for our families, our community and for you, Cipri and for Avi."

"What's your schedule Jim, you mentioned that you were going back to see your daughters," asked Max.

"Well, the girls want to take a dip in the warm waters of the Caribbean. So I'll be tied up for a month."

Larry said, "Why don't we set a tentative date now; a goal if you will. Let's say we meet here in four weeks. In the meantime, I will keep you informed on what's going on by email and by phone. I'm sure I'll have a couple of questions so I'll be touching base with both of you in any event. In the meantime, if you have further information that needs to be considered, let me know."

"Well Larry, Lorenzo, Lencho, you turned out to be a triple threat man it seems. I'll be around most of the time and I'll be glad to show you around our operation at your convenience. Just let me know. By the way, how is the Association's work going? I understand there's lots of work and things are humming with few, if any, problems."

"I speak to Fidel almost every day and he's very busy. There's plenty of work and the men are making money. He did say that some of the extra curricular stuff, like the English classes are having some problems getting off the ground, but there's more and more interest every day as the word is getting around. To date there seems to be no interest by outsiders to gum things up. He did tell me that Dolan Smith and his Regional Director came by and visited the camp and some of the workers and in fact they sat in on one of the classes. The boss apparently was impressed, according to Smith."

"Great, that's good to hear."

"It is good. It seems this new immigration law is getting its kinks worked out. According to Smith, it's not only here, but all around the country things are working much better."

"Well I'm not surprised Lorenzo; the old system was a travesty. It was no good for anyone. It screwed the workers, it made employers criminals whether they wanted to be or not and the public became cynical about the whole system. I'm sure there'll be problems, but it's one hell of a lot better than it used to be. That's for damn sure," said Max.

The following day Larry met Max at Max's office, "Max, I wonder if I can ask you a question in confidence? I was not completely surprised when Jim suggested that I look at the possible merger from a spiritual sense. I must confess I surely don't know him like many of you do. He has a reputation as an irascible guy, yet our old time workers almost worship him. No one would say anything bad about him in front of them. He seems like he's almost two people. Some others I've dealt with hate him and hate me just because I work for him. How do you see him?"

Max smiled, "To be honest, I've always been a little afraid of him. I've heard those same fellows say terrible things about him. On the other hand, he's always been straight with me. I have to tell you, since his illness, he's a different person. Perhaps a man who faces mortality tends to suffer and reevaluate their lives. Having you aboard has given him some peace of mind it seems, but perhaps more importantly, he's had some time to focus on his girls. You've given him a chance to do that."

When Larry came home he was greeted by Cipri and Avi. Avi gave him a hug and a kiss, Cipri gave him a kiss and a beer. Things were well in his world. These things he needed desperately. For the last ten days he has been nosing around the Martin property. At the same time he was looking at the Johnson operation with a new perspective; like trying to get a feel for a large complex puzzle. His girls were his ground, his home base, a place where he could not only relax, but receive the sustenance he needed. "Guess what? Better yet guess who's coming to visit? I bet you'll never guess?" asked Cipri.

"Luna. I bet Luna is coming to visit," he said.

Cipri looked at her husband in astonishment, "How in the world did you know? Good Lord, have you talked to her?"

"Just a guess on my part, but I have to confess that for the last few days, I've been thinking about her. I just felt there were a couple of things I'd like to run by her. When will she be here?" Suddenly Larry wondered if Luna's presence was no accident. All during his investigation of the merger there was an intangible that he couldn't put his finger on. The hard facts and assets of the merger were relatively easy to discern, but there was that feeling of uncertainty. There were factors which were not easy to measure. For example, the cultures of the two firms were much different. One was very open and even light hearted, and one appeared more insular in nature. The problem was that this observation was just a feeling...his feeling, it was nothing objective. It was not that one company appeared better than the other, but they were just different. The interesting thing was that the employees in general were very similar; many being second generation Hispanics. Yet the cultures of the two entities were different. He wondered if the mystery of culture could be measured and if it was of any significance at all?

Cipri said, "Luna, how nice of you to think about us, I just needed someone from the hills to visit. Don't get me wrong. I love it here, the work is great and it is a nice place, but sometimes I miss my hills."

Luna gave Cipri a big hug and kissed her on both cheeks, "And the hills miss you too. Some folks think they're just barren sentinels, but they're very much alive. We need them and they need us. So tell me, how are things going for the Franco family?"

"Great, you'll see Avi in an hour or so, she's taking a nap...thank God! Larry is up to his ears in work. In fact, he's been really busy and quiet. I know that when he becomes quiet, he's mulling something important. In fact, he somehow knew you were coming to visit and indicated he wanted to run a few ideas by you."

"Curiously, I knew I was coming through and I wanted to take the opportunity to visit, but something kept itching within me that said I should come by. So here I am."

The following morning they were driving to properties on the east side. "I'm glad you brought your jeans because I need to check out some properties and meet some men." Lorenzo hesitated and then said, "I'm really glad you came by. I'm looking at a special project and I could use a different pair of eyes."

"Cipri mentioned you were involved in some project, but wasn't sure what it was all about."

"Really; I wasn't aware that I mentioned it to her. She has a sense about things. Can I confide in you in what I'm doing? This is really important and I need an independent reaction from someone."

Luna looked at the orchard as they drove. She said, "Let's make a deal, why don't you retain me as your consultant. Then we will have an exclusive relationship, and I will report only to you. That way there's less chance of me blabbing."

When Lorenzo looked at her she was smiling, but he could tell that she was serious. "Deal, you just send me an invoice when you go home. Now here's what's up. My boss is up in years and has a few health questions. Johnson Farms owns about 2000 acres and all the equipment, buildings and all the things that go along with a large farm in this area. Martin Farms is a similar operation with 3000 acres. They're very much alike in many ways. A couple of weeks ago they asked me to look into the idea of merging the two operations. Now at this time I'm just looking at the feasibility of such a venture. If I were to recommend that the idea has merit, then we would bring in some experts to work out the details. You can imagine the impact on taxes, valuations and equities for example. To be honest, from this perspective, things look positive, but I'm concerned about the intangibles such as integrating two workforces, cultures and those things that we can't put on a balance sheet. I thought you could spend a couple of days with me just nosing around to get a sense of the people and the idea as a whole." Lorenzo noticed that, as he talked, he unconsciously reached under his shirt with is finger and traced the rough silver cross that Cipriana had given him.

"Sounds interesting; count me in. I can stay away from the Res for a couple of days. Just to be business-like, I usually charge by the hour; so from this moment, I'm on your clock. So, let's see what this is all about." For the next two days Lorenzo and Luna traveled to the various ranches and met workers and suppliers. Luna even attended the weekly Rotary meeting with Larry. Occasionally Larry saw that she would make a note on a 3 by 5 card. On several occasions she would walk up to a worker by herself and talk to him. While in the car she would quiz Larry on various issues. Some related to the farms, but some observations or questions seemed to have no relevance to the merger. The last morning they had breakfast at the house, "Lorenzo, I'll be home by evening, tomorrow I'll have a draft of my report, then I usually take a day to reflect on it and then write a final draft which I'll email to you. That means you'll have my observations by Friday at the latest." The letter arrived as promised:

Luna Martinez, Ph.D
Route 1 Box 151
Jerome, Arizona
Mr. Lorenzo Franco,

Although my observation of the two entities in question was somewhat quick, I feel I was able to get a feel of the two operations. Please note that the following thoughts are very subjective in nature. I made no analysis nor do I imply any input on the financial implications and or economics of the merger of the two firms. As you indicted to me, that determination will be done by legal and financial experts at a subsequent date if the process were to continue.

Looking at the two operations from the bottom up it appears that there is much synergy from the production aspects and from the employee's perspective. On the latter I did get the feeling there was a difference in philosophy in compensation matters. For example, one firm pays workers on an hourly basis; the other on a monthly basis. One keeps time cards and other detailed records and the other is less orderly; almost casual in nature. These need to be reconciled. For example one firm has a quite formal relationship regarding housing with sets rents and signed rental agreements, the other has no such agreement and seems to be based on a 'handshake'.

In fact, the main differences seem to be formal vs. informal. For example Martin has formal annual employee evaluations where as Johnson has an occasional chat with employees. Another example is expense accounts. Martin has monthly submittals with appropriate invoices attached whereas Johnson's folks occasionally go to the office and get reimbursed. Sometimes they have an invoice, but at times it's just a verbal report. In the two days I spent with the workers, I was only able to touch on these examples. My guess would be that there are many other examples of this formal and informal way of doing business. It's not my intention to say one system is right or wrong at this point I would say they're just different. However, in a merger, one system would eventually have to prevail just to keep peace in the family as it were, in short, they have to be reconciled, but there are also some legal reasons that have to be considered. I'm sure you or your attorneys can have a better insight on these issues.

Now the following observation is even less objective and flows into the more subtle world. I tried to get a feel or a sense of the intangible world, or as my people call it, the spiritual world. After lighting some of my prized incense and just trying to focus on the spirits of the two companies, it was my deep feeling that this merger makes lots of sense. I would recommend that it proceed to the next step of having, as you said, the attorneys, accountants and tax folks examine the merger from their perspective. Needless to say, much thought must be given to this huge step. Additionally, I would not overlook the affect of this merger on the community. Although the two firms are mostly family owned, there's bound to be an impact on the local community. For example, the banks, charities and other community organizations that in the past have been favored by the two companies will be affected in one way or another. So consideration should be given to a well thought out public relations program to keep people in general informed about what's going on.

Now, I'm well aware that these thoughts are minor when compared with the financial implications of such a merger and the impact it will make on the employees, but it's at least worthwhile to give some of these matters serious consideration.

Finally Lorenzo, thank you for the opportunity to have some input regarding such a significant and historic decision. Please feel free to call me in the future if you wish any additional services. Also please see my attached invoice for these services. Please make out the payment to the JEROME NATIVE SCHOLARSHIP PROGAM. This is one of my favorite charities as it supports and encourages young people from our tribe to continue their education.

Warm Regards,

Dr. Luna Martinez

Lorenzo drove to Piru with anticipation. Jim had suggested that they meet with Max in the small restaurant at mid morning. He knew there would be few, if any, customers and no one would pay attention to the three men. Jim was already at the corner table when Larry walked in, "Lencho, it's good to see you. Sorry I haven't called, but we just flew in last night and I know you're a busy fellow. How's the family, especially the little one?"

"The family's fine and you're right; things have been a little hectic around here, but on the other hand, I can't complain. There's lots of work, but all of it seems to be getting done. It just would be better if the days were a few hours longer."

Just then Martin came in and ordered a glass of iced tea as he walked by the counter. "Well gentlemen, I'm so glad to see you both. I must admit there was a certain amount of apprehension on my part driving up here. I can't explain it, but it seems that we just might be making history and I hope that it will be seen in retrospect, as a positive action regardless of what we decide today. Now young man, I understand you've had a hectic four weeks. What do you have to tell us?"

Lorenzo opened a three ring binder and removed a one page outline. "I thought about this presentation for quite awhile. Why don't I give you my recommendation up front with a few comments, and then get your reaction and answer any questions you might have. For the last four weeks I have touched base with all the properties. I made an inventory of most of the significant assets so we could have a good idea of what we are talking about. I also included a list of employees, compensation, and other factors related to the men and women that work for both companies. I tried to look at all these factors as objectively as I could. Additionally, I did a lot of thinking and simply, I have come to the conclusion that a merger of these two historic properties makes lots of sense. There are many compatibilities and synergies and the two firms are complimentary. It's my recommendation that we proceed by retaining a team of experts to review the financials, tax consequences and other legal questions that need to be considered. Now I'd be glad to answer questions and then I'd like to add one more element."

Johnson looked at his protégé and asked, "You implied you had some additional information. Perhaps it would be better if you shared that with us as well; before we go any further."

Larry looked at Max who nodded in agreement, "Well as you suggested, I did all this leg work as unobtrusively as I could. However, I'm sure I raised many eyebrows with my nosing around. I told no one what I was doing, but I did confide in one person. As I mentioned in my recommendations, everything seems to fit. The assets, the crops, the people and all the tangibles appear to fall in place, but then I thought of the intangibles; those things that are hard to value. I met Dr. Luna Martinez, a spiritual leader of one the tribes in Arizona sometime ago. I've had the opportunity to deal with her professionally. She dropped by here for a few days to visit. So it occurred to me that she might be one to look at these intangibles, or spiritual elements, as she calls them. Here's her report. Please look at it and then I'll be ready to discuss it with you."

The two men flipped the pages of the brief report. Larry noticed that Jim looked at it quickly, then went back and reviewed it more carefully. He even took a pen, made a couple of notes and underlined some words. Jim looked at his employee carefully and then reread the report. "Well Lorenzo, it was my first instinct that this merger made sense. Apparently you too agree from the points you made a few minutes ago, but I must admit that I also was concerned about those things that can't be quantified, or the intangibles, as you call them. However, I had no way of even being able to ask an intelligent question about this concern. I'm not too sure what Dr. Martinez is talking about, but at least she seems to concur that it's worthwhile to take the next step."

Max laughed, "I think that we need to keep this under our hats. We don't want our bankers, attorneys and others to think we're burning incense or sacrificing babies to make this decision, but I agree with Jim, this seems to reinforce your evaluation." Then he looked at Jim and said, "Jim, I too feel that this merger is worth a more serious look. I suggest that we schedule a meeting of our attorneys, accountants and others to take the next step. What do you say?"

"I agree. I suggest that we get these fellows together say, next week. We're scheduled to make another little trip and I'd like to be here at least for the initial meeting." Then he looked at the report in front of him. "Frankly, I'm curious about Dr. Martinez. I wonder if you can make arrangements for us to meet her. What do you think Max, would you like to meet her; to hear what she has to say?"

"I don't think I would have even considered this notion a few years ago, but this marriage, if you will, is so important to us and too many of our people that we need to look at every aspect of this venture. In the final analysis, it will be people who will make this succeed and we will need every drop of energy, skill, good luck and blessings to make it a go."

"I agree, but also ask her who she wants to meet with just us or with our wives or anyone else?" commented Jim. Then Jim stood, walked around the table, and extended his hand and said, "Maxwell Martin, let's shake hands on what will be one of the most important decisions we will both ever make!"

Max grasped his hand and wasn't satisfied so he put his arms around his friend and gave him a long, firm *abrazo*. Then both men extended their hands to Lorenzo and he too received hearty hugs from them. Jim said, "Lorenzo, I see you have a portfolio full of information. No doubt it's very important and will be a large factor in the respective valuations. My hunch is that by the time we're through, there will be reams and reams of such notebooks full of important information. However, in the meantime, I'm satisfied with your recommendation to proceed with the next step. Let me give it some thought in a few days. I will give you the names of the folks who will represent Johnson Farms. And if Max also gives you his respective names, then you can arrange the first meeting." He looked at Max, "What do you think Max?"

"I agree, it may take a few days to arrange the first meeting and I would suggest a couple of things. First that Larry writes a brief outline of what we propose to do so everyone can start off on the same page. And since it will take a few days to get this scheduled, I wonder if we can get our spiritual Doctor off the reservation so we can meet her. In fact, I'd like to meet with her prior to the business meeting if we can."

"I agree, let's get the young lady out here. Give her a call and fly her in. Tell her there are two old men who need to be cleansed and tell her to bring some of her holy smoke."

Chapter 53

THE THREE MEN WERE EATING breakfast at their usual table in the Mupu Grill when Larry said, "Dr. Martinez will be here later this morning and we have a tentative meeting set for tomorrow afternoon."

Jim said, "Great. Where will we meet?"

"Well, on this she was very specific. When she was out here earlier, we walked around the old Martin headquarters. She was impressed with the old office. One of the rooms seems to be a gathering room with some old chairs and sofas; she wants to meet there if we can."

"That was the original corporate office before we moved it to town. The men use it to gather in the morning, some have their lunch there. I mean it's old, probably dusty, but it's available if that is where she wants to meet."

"Who's going to be at the meeting?" asked Jim.

"Basically, she'd like you two, your wives, plus Cipri and me to begin with. Then she mentioned that she would excuse us so she could talk to the four of you." Then Larry added, "By the way, have you ever been to one of these sessions? I mean it might seem strange." Larry was almost embarrassed by what might appear to be hocus-pocus and on top of that, it was his idea. He just knew his professors at Stanford would think it primitive and weird especially as a consideration of a large and important merger of two of the most significant companies in the county, but it was too late to fret about that, the meeting was set.

Max chuckled and said, "Lorenzo, don't worry that we might think this meeting unconventional; even though it is. Honestly, this decision that Jim and I will be making is of such critical importance to all of us. It's so important that we need all the information, creativity and skills to pull this off. In this case we need to gather and review any and all the information we can get. And if we need to touch on the spiritual, so be it. The experience with Miss Martinez should at least be interesting and it could make the difference in what might happen in the future."

"I mentioned the idea to Rita and she's intrigued with the whole thing. First she was floored when I mentioned the idea of a possible marriage of our two companies, but she seemed fascinated by the idea of getting the input of someone like Dr. Martinez. In fact, Rita did some quick research on Martinez and was very impressed with her professional credentials. Her reputation in the educational field and her work within the tribal nations in her area are well known. So she's *not just another quack*, to use Rita's phrase."

The following afternoon Luna spent a couple of hours arranging the room. By this she did little to change or even clean the room; she liked that it was a functional space. She did rearrange the seven chairs so that they were close and visible to each other. In the middle she put a small, round, marble-top table and on the table she put a large abalone shell. Curious, she went around the room methodically and looked at the photographs, the furniture and books and reading material that was scattered around the room. The photographs were of old scenes of the ranch. She seemed to be getting feelings from these static scenes and groups of men and mules going about their tasks. On one table she found a bowl of lemon drops. She removed the cellophane from one and popped it into her mouth. She was surprised at the sweet and sour taste of the candy. The contrast in the taste, while very pleasant, was also a contradiction. The three couples arrived almost at the same time. "Luna, let me introduce to you Rita and Jim Johnson, Maxwell and Melina Martin and of course you already know Cipri."

Luna went around the group and shook hands with everyone. She actually took the person's hand in both of hers and looked the person directly in the face as she smiled and welcomed them. When she got to Cipri she gave her a big hug and kissed her on both cheeks. "Please be seated," she said. She, however, remained standing, "First, let me thank you for giving me the opportunity to share with you all in this momentous venture you're undertaking. It's not lost on me that you're looking at this merger from a very practical viewpoint, which is the financial aspect as it should be. It's no doubt that this is the foremost factor to be considered. I mean, if this doesn't make sense from a dollars and cents perspective, it makes no sense at all. However, if it makes no sense from, let us say a spiritual sense; then it too makes no sense. So we're here together to explore this latter notion. I would ask you just to relax and open yourselves to that spiritual part of your person and to just allow things to be viewed differently."

Luna went to her leather bag and brought out a tightly bound sage bundle. She continued, "This is a special sage that comes from one of our east facing mountains…where the sun rises. It has been used by my people for centuries to ease the mind, to seek peace and insight into issues of the mind or of the spirit. I'm going to light it, we'll let it burn for a few minutes and just be quiet. You're welcome to close your eyes and let your mind focus or let it wander depending on your feelings. If the idea of the merger comes up, focus on that, if not don't worry about it."

As the sage burned smoke enveloped the entire office; she began to hum softly and then to chant. The words were not understandable yet in a strange way, they were. They spoke of peace, quiet and wisdom and at the same time they spoke of the nebulous and the mysterious. Strangely, the meaning made sense to them even if they couldn't understand the words. After a while she quit humming and slowly they all opened their eyes. "Welcome back," she said. She got up and moved the shell to a small table by the window. She said nothing; she just put her hands on her lap and looked at everyone with a slight smile on her face.

Rita, who had been quiet all afternoon finally said, "I didn't know that sage had such a pleasing and soothing quality to it. It is strangely refreshing. I don't think I will forget this; the first time I experienced it and especially the circumstances of this meeting."

"The indigenous people of our mountains sought many answers of the mysteries of life in these twigs and perhaps even more when they searched for peace of mind. This mattered even more when things were tough and suffering seemed to have no reason or finality to it. That's why when the padres introduced the notion of the crucifixion and the resurrection to our people, they immediately understood the concept and were willing to accept and combine the two cultures and the mysteries of their respective beliefs. Now, why don't we just chat about this notion of a merger?"

"It's funny you mention the resurrection; because my only doubt in this venture is that all the work that the Johnson family put into our operation would cease to exist after the merger. That everything we've worked for so long through good and bad times would be just an entry or a footnote in an attorney's file, but with the idea of a new birth, a new life continues. And that notion of continuation makes me feel somewhat reassured." Jim reached over and held his wife's hand. She felt his hand tremble.

Max responded, "You know, all my life, deep down inside, I've always been suspicious of religious folks. In my mind it seemed ridiculous to believe in the idea of the spirit. I mean, if it wasn't something tangible that I could see, touch, smell or taste it was not real. I'm embarrassed to even let you know what I thought of the notion of the resurrection. Yet the idea of something being turned into nothing also makes no sense. So I now think that if the Martins and the Johnsons were to join up there would be a continuation. I guess some folks could call it a new beginning or a resurrection, but frankly I'm not remotely familiar with the theology of such things and I would just call it a good business decision and let it go at that." Max smiled as he spoke to his companions.

There was a long silence and the others began to look at Larry. "Some time ago you all know I was dragged off the street and thrown into detention. It was only for a few days, but those hours seemed like an eternity. When I got out I was a new person or at least a different one. I was changed, transformed if you will. Then through the effort of you gentleman, Cipri and I wound up at Stanford and again we were trans-formed. Then I went from Larry to Lorenzo…then to a farmer…then to a husband…then to a father…in a sense, a new person or at least a different man at each turn; yet the same person. I mean, every one of these junctures in my life was not deliberate or planned by me. Some-thing or someone else had their finger in the mix. I can't explain it. How-ever, it seems to me that change is just a continuation of life. So the resurrection, while mind blowing as such, is not as far-fetched as it used to be for me." Lorenzo finally looked down as he had been looking out the window at a lemon orchard. He looked at the others with the innocent smile of a little boy.

Luna said, "Many people come to these sessions and are disappointed. They think they're suddenly going to win the lottery; that happiness and good fortune will prevail. So when they discover that life continues; that doubt and despair are still part of their life, they feel cheated. Well I don't change the future; I don't issue winning lottery tickets; at best I try to understand and try to make sense of the things that do happen; be they good or bad." She got up and opened both sides of a large bay window and a fresh, cool breeze came into the room; dissipating the sage. "Think of the merger in this way. Just as opening this window brings us new, fresh air, we're still here. In a sense, we're the same, but some time has elapsed, so we're not exactly the same, yet we are still here. A new atmosphere has enveloped all of us. Whether it's positive or negative depends on you and your decisions."

Luna continued, "You need to remember that my presence here is not some monumental mystery. I'm here really, to verify or justify your thoughts that have already been moving in a certain direction. I can't tell you that once you look more deeply into this merger, that it will actually come off. It may very well be decided not to proceed; and that's fine, but at least you would have considered it and decided one way or another. So I would urge to continue the process. Take the next step. Meet with the experts. Make sure it makes sense from a good, solid business perspective. Just keep in mind that from the mystery perspective, if you want to call it that, it's worth taking a more detailed look at this union at this time."

Now I wonder if we can excuse Cipri and Lorenzo so I can have a few minutes with just you four," looking at the Martins and Johnsons. After the young couple walked out, she said, "I just thought it might be a good idea to spend some time to give you a chance to reflect on this meeting and on the whole idea you're contemplating."

Melina Martin who had been quiet said, "Dr. Martinez, first let me thank you for your presence here. I know that when the attorneys and accountants get here they will be looking at such things as equities and tax implications which, of course, are extremely important, but we also have to look at those things that will affect the rest of us. I'm sure there will be unknown consequences down the road, some good and some bad perhaps, but at least we should have a chance to consider them. And it's those intangibles you have given us the opportunity to mull over. I have no idea what the eventual decision will be, but at least I will know that we made a genuine effort to look at every detail of this momentous decision."

Luna looked carefully and thoughtfully at the two couples in front of them knowing that their lives would be changed dramatically. And she said a prayer for the future.

Nine months later the headline on the local paper read: MERGER: J&M FARMS. The story continued with the first sentence of the story:

Maxwell Martin announced that after a long and deliberate analysis, the two largest family-owned farms of the county have merged and will continue to operate as one entity under the direction of Lorenzo Franco as General Manager. The story continued with more facts and details of the merger.

In the afternoon of the day of the announcement, the employees of both companies met at a small park at the old Martin headquarters. The employees themselves prepared all the food and refreshments for the gathering. Children were running around, people were taking photos and there was a lot of mingling. Many of the workers already knew each other from local sport teams, school and especially from Our Lady of Guadalupe Church. There was some tension as workers from the different divisions and their families mixed, but by the middle of the afternoon, a volleyball game had started and the teams were a blend of people who just wanted to be in the game.

Epilogue

Lorenzo's secretary popped her head into his office and said, "The gal from the Pacific Business Times is here. Do you want to meet with her in here?"

"Yeah, did she say what she wanted?"

"Not really, but she made an appointment while you and the gang were in Arizona for the annual powwow. I'll show her in."

"Hi, I'm June Hill editor for the Pacific Business Times. Thanks for making time to see me. Every year our paper selects executives under forty for our Young Leaders Award and we have selected you as our agribusiness man of the year. Well to be honest, we didn't pick you. It was really your colleagues who selected you. As we went around our news beat we would ask the folks around the area who the most successful young business person was and your name came up almost unanimously. So I'd like to spend some time with you so we can write a little spread for our Special Edition which will be out this spring."

Larry looked at the young reporter and then looked out the window of his office at the lemon grove that extended gradually up the hill. "I don't know what to say. Are you sure that the people you mentioned were speaking of me?"

"I am indeed sure it was you. And it was all sorts of people; I mean bankers, suppliers and folks in education. And just to be sure, we were getting a wide range of opinions. I asked the waitress at the Mupu Grill when I stopped for a cup of coffee. She came up with your name without hesitation. To me she might be the most credible and perceptive person of all the folks we surveyed," June removed a small recorder and placed it on the desk, "I hope you don't mind the recorder, it's that I take terrible notes."

Larry took a deep breath and said, "Well, I'm not too sure I agree with Carlota at the Mupu Grill, but if she feels it's okay, then I'll go along. Tell me June, what would you like to know?"

"Well, let me ask you what we ask all our awardees. What would you say are two of your most important business accomplishments, the two that you're the most proud of?"

"That's easy. One is being given the opportunity to work with two of the most important families in the county and merging their two operations into J&M Farms and making the new venture a continuing success." He then paused for a second, "Secondly, it would be my small effort in getting Immigration Reform passed and the Seasonal Agriculture Program implemented."

The reporter clicked off the recorder. She was surprised at the comment. "I'm not too sure I understand you. What do you mean your work on immigration reform?" She clicked the recorder on.

"A decade ago our immigration policies were a mess for everyone. Employers, workers, educators and the public in general had no idea what the policy was. It was a policy that was no policy; it was a damn mess. It was one that was kept under the table, in the dark if you will. As long as the work got done cheaply, anything was okay. I got involved in immigration by an adverse baptism and before I knew it, I became a spokesman for immigration reform. I went around the country speaking about the issue. In the process we must have been successful because immigration reform passed. The new law was not perfect, but it was one hell of a lot better than what we had. Over the years, some of those imperfect edges have been smoothed out. Now it's still not perfect and the polishing continues, things change and new issues arise, but what we have now is light years better than what we had. A fair Immigration Reform Law Miss Hill, is what I'm most proud of, my small part in…A Fair Immigration Reform Law!"

THE END